'How old are you?'

'I am seventeen,' Bregetta said.

'And respectable,' Sergeant Duncan said, with a touch of mockery. 'I can tell. I've seen enough of the other sort.'

Bregetta eyed him warily. 'I haven't seen you before,' she murmured.

'I'm new to the York Street Barracks. If you were used to Sergeant Davis's ways you'll find mine different. I don't take bribes, and I don't ask favours just because I happen to wear a red coat. How did you come to work in Will Tanner's tavern?'

'His wife is my friend,' she said. 'She helped me.'

He seemed very close and she watched in amazement as he bent forward and gently pressed his lips to hers. A great shudder ran through her, but she did not pull away. His hand slid up her cheek into the gleaming beauty of her hair, and his kiss deepened, his mouth slanting across hers.

Deborah Miles, an Australian, was born in Geelong, Victoria. After much travel, her family settled in New South Wales, and she was educated at Maclean. She began writing seriously after leaving school, with several short stories published in Australian magazines, and two short story prizes to her credit.

After living and working in Queensland, she returned to Victoria, and lives in the old gold rush town of Bendigo, where she shares a home with husband and daughter, and spends her few spare moments writing.

Previous title

A PASSING FANCY

JEALOUS HEARTS

Deborah Miles

First published in Great Britain 1991 by Mills & Boon Limited

© Deborah Miles 1991

Australian copyright 1991 Philippine copyright 1991 This edition 1991

ISBN 0 263 77390 6

Masquerade is a trademark published by Mills & Boon Limited, Eton House, 18–24 Paradise Road, Richmond, Surrey, TW9 1SR.

Set in Times Roman 11 on 11½ pt. 04-9109-68503 C

Made and printed in Great Britain

CHAPTER ONE

BREGETTA bent to the fire and stoked the embers. The heat was barely enough to warm the room, fighting as it was the cold draughts from the gaps in the walls and the mouldy thatching of the roof. Her hands were red and sore from washing in cold water. She was seventeen and she felt like an old woman.

'I need a drink, girl. I thought I told you to get in some drink for me.'

Bregetta sighed and turned. Her mother's pinched face peered up from the straw pallet in the corner, light slanting through broken shutters on to raddled cheeks and sunken sockets. The sight of her brought to Bregetta a wave of despair. And anger.

'You know you're not to drink rum, Ma. And besides, we've no money for it.'

'No money!' her mother squalled angrily, like the demanding child she had become. 'And you workin' at Will Tanner's all hours of the night. No money! What does he pay you, then, but money?'

'There's not enough,' Bregetta retorted stubbornly, and poked the embers savagely.

'Your brother'd get me some drink,' the old woman said slyly, and coughed feebly into her hand. 'He cares for his old mother.'

'If he cares so much why isn't he here?'

The old woman muttered something, subsiding on to the pallet. She was old in life and hardship

rather than years. Bregetta had no expectations
other than to look like her one day. Life for them
was a day-to-day battle to survive; there was nothing
pretty about it.

The room was squalid, though she tried to keep
it clean. Outside she could hear the shouts and
screams and other sounds of riotous humanity.
They lived close to their neighbours, and their lives
were interlaced, like the strands in a fisherman's
net. They were all poor and all hungry, and all
angry. Some were emigrants, come for a better life,
who had drifted into bad times. Some were sailors,
spending their pay, while some were harlots, their
hands held out for money. Some were convicts and
ex-convicts, broken by the system, or seeking
forgetfulness in the taverns and sly grog shops and
brothels which littered that area of Sydney called
the Rocks like pebbles on a beach.

Bregetta's mother had been a convict from the
slums of London. Once in New South Wales she
had married a free man, a draper. Bregetta's father
had made a place for himself in Sydney. He had
worked hard and long, and they had become
respectable. But when he had died her mother had
slipped back into the old ways. They had lost
everything. And now, in this year of 1838, they were
struggling to survive with the other dregs in the
Rocks.

The Rocks occupied a narrow piece of land called
Dawes Point, jutting out into the blue of Sydney
Harbour. It was so called because of the rocky
sandstone ridges and ledges which protruded from
the peninsula. Lanes and alleys in the Rocks had a
tendency to become steps up or tunnels through the
rockface. Houses perched in precarious squalor on

ledges, with roughly cut stairways leading to their doors. Sailors and convicts and harlots congregated here, making use of the numerous taverns and houses of ill-repute. It was said that the noise of the Rocks could be heard a mile out to sea on a still night. Oh, it was a place of gaiety. But it was a place of misery too, and danger, for life was cheap in some of the back rows and taverns, and men and women had been known to disappear without trace.

A pounding on the door interrupted Bregetta's thoughts and she started up, her eyes wide. A hand rattled the shutter, and Bregetta clasped her arms about herself. One never knew, in this place, who might come knocking at the door, and it was best not to take chances. But her mother was made of sterner stuff. She shouted out in her harridan's voice, 'Go on, get out o' it! There's nothin' for you here!'

'Open up!' The voice was loud and harsh, the voice of authority. Bregetta grimaced and hurried to the door, unbarring it and peering out into the cold blustery day.

Redcoats, three of them, and all with guns. The sergeant was tall with dark hair, and as stern as a judge. 'Mrs Smith live here?' he asked, in a rolling Scots accent.

Bregetta nodded her head. 'But she's sick,' she added, her voice husky with fright. 'What do you want her for?'

Redcoats meant trouble. Behind them she could see the neighbours peering from their doors and windows. A mangy dog came up to sniff at one of the men's boots, and he kicked it, sending it off with a yelp. The sergeant stepped forward and pushed wide the door. Bregetta stepped back, angry and resentful, her brown eyes glowering at him beneath dark brows.

Her mother was screeching from her pallet, and the sergeant, after one look around the room, told her to be quiet. Surprisingly, the old woman subsided. 'What do you want?' she asked in a petulant voice, but her eyes were afraid.

'I'm Sergeant Duncan. I'm after your son, Mrs Smith.' But he was looking at Bregetta. His dark eyes were somehow compelling, and the girl could not look away. She knew that she was tall and slim, with hair like muted firelight and skin as pale as milk, speckled here and there with golden sun-kisses. She had been told she was beautiful often enough to believe it might be partially true, but even so the man's stare was rude. Bregetta turned her back.

'What has he done now?' Mrs Smith muttered, drawing her thin blanket about her. 'Been thievin' again, has he?' Her eyes seemed to blur with so many redcoats in so confined an area. 'Just let me get me hands on him.'

'Assault this time,' the sergeant said in a voice as dry as old twigs. 'He's working his way up.'

'Well, I don't know where he is. We haven't seen him in a week or more. That's right, isn't it, Bregetta?'

The girl shrugged one shoulder, and continued to peel the potatoes into the pot at her feet. She heard the man move behind her, but still did not turn. She felt the hair at the back of her neck prickle as though his eyes could bore right through her.

'Is that right . . . Bregetta?'

His voice was soft and deep, reminding her of honey from a big jar, trickling over the lip, warm and golden. Sunlight through the trees.

'As my mother says,' Bregetta retorted, peeling a potato with particular care, 'we haven't seen him in a week or more. We haven't any money, and he only comes back for that. He's in bad company.'

The old woman smacked her lips over her few teeth. 'We're poor,' she said feebly, and now her eyes were sly. 'We've nothin', as you can see. Perhaps you could find it in your heart to be givin' us a few——'

'Ma!' The girl spun around, furious, and her eyes snapped at the group by the door. 'We take no charity from the likes of them!'

The sergeant looked at her for a moment, and then he smiled.

Bregetta had learned to mistrust the military, with cause. Most of them were only seeking to line their own pockets. They cared, she thought, for nothing and no one. The lower ranks were usually recruited from the same class as the convicts and then subjected to the military system's unrelenting viciousness. A private who stole was given as many, if not more lashes than a convict who did the same. Most of them were as brutalised as their prisoners.

Bregetta had seen soldiers in the streets, riding their horses as if they were in a race. They drank and swore and reeled about. They were wicked, most of them. Even the officers, who were supposed to be gentlemen, cared more for racing and gambling than keeping the peace. The only thing worse than a soldier was a policeman—who was probably an ex-soldier or an ex-convict anyway—and Bregetta wanted nothing to do with any of them.

His smile had gone, as though he had read her opinion of him in her eyes. 'Thank you for your assistance,' he said with mockery, and bowed his head, a faint movement only, before turning his back. The door closed on them.

Bregetta hurried to the window and unbarred the shutters, peering out. The redcoats had started back down the lane. The wind blew off the hat of one of the privates and, swearing, he pursued it, while some onlookers jeered or laughed as the fancy took them. That same gust of wind caught the shutter from Bregetta's fingers and slammed it back against the outside wall with a bang like a gunshot. The sergeant spun around and, before Bregetta could duck inside, saw her. That same compelling feeling came over her under the gaze of his dark eyes. And then he smiled as though she amused him, and turned away.

Bregetta closed her eyes. Behind her she heard her mother chuckle. 'Bloody lobsters,' she said, and then made a sound of derision in her throat. 'Think they can come in here an' do as they please. You'd better watch yourself, Bregetta. I seen him lookin' at you, that sergeant. He's got an eye for you.'

Bregetta barred the shutters and turned back to the potatoes, angry with her mother and herself. Why had she gazed after him like that? Didn't she know better? 'I don't know what you mean, Ma.'

But the old woman only laughed again. 'He's a fine figure of a man. But he's got a look about him...dangerous, girl! An' I should know.'

'You're rambling again,' Bregetta retorted.

'Aye, well, I know what I know.'

Bregetta turned suddenly. 'Have you seen Jim?'

'Her mother's eyes shifted, but she said, 'No,' firmly enough, and Bregetta believed her. Her brother Jim had been wild even before her father had died. Her mother said he reminded her of her own brother, and he'd died badly, in a fight in Clerkenwell.

Jim had been running with a bad crowd. At first he had only got into the sort of mischief that could be excused as a boy's high spirits, but lately he had become much worse. Bregetta knew he had been breaking into houses and stealing. And now it seemed he had graduated to beating people up.

Bregetta sighed. The thing of it was, he was such an engaging boy. Sweet of tongue, and kind to his mother—when he thought of her. Which was less and less often, it seemed. But there was a recklessness in him which no amount of talking seemed able to exorcise.

Bregetta cooked their meal, and, after helping her mother to eat, stacked up the few dishes. Then, by the light of the single candle, she brushed her long hair and pulled on her good green gown.

She was a beautiful girl, lovely of face and figure, and with a nature that was both sweet and gentle. She was not particularly vivacious, and mostly kept her own counsel, which was what Will Tanner liked about her. She helped out in his tavern at night, and was not likely to make trouble by fraternising and flirting with the customers, or pocketing the profits.

There was a soft knock on the door, and Bregetta moved to let Molly in. The plump smiling face was welcome. Molly Field sat with her mother until Bregetta came home, and Molly's husband Teddy walked with Bregetta to the tavern. They were old

friends of Bregetta's father, fallen upon hard times
like themselves. These were bad times in Sydney,
times of economic depression and little em-
ployment. Bregetta was grateful for their friendship
and their help, even if her mother did call them
pious bores.

'How is she?' Molly whispered, eyeing the
slumped form in the corner.

'Well enough. Some soldiers were here today.'

Molly glanced away, and Bregetta knew she had
already heard the news. There were no secrets in
the Rocks. 'What did they want?' she asked.

'Jim. He's in more trouble.'

Molly clicked her tongue and shook her head.
The rather untidy bun at her nape almost tumbled
down, the grey-streaked hair framing her round
face. 'It'd be best for both of you if he went away
for good, my dear.'

'Ma would never hear of it.'

The old woman stirred restlessly, peering at them
through the gloom. 'What are you two jabbering
about?' she muttered. 'Can't you see I'm tryin' to
sleep?'

Molly gave Bregetta a speaking look and patted
her arm. 'Teddy's waiting outside. You'd best get
going if you don't want the sharp edge of Will
Tanner's tongue.'

Bregetta smiled, and slipped out into the cold
darkness. It was bitter tonight. The wind from the
harbour whipped up the narrow alleys and lanes,
bringing with it the tang of the sea. Shivering,
Bregetta pulled her shawl tighter about her
shoulders.

Teddy stepped out from the shadows and took
her arm. He was a huge man, over six feet, with

the build of a fighter and dark hair turning to grey. No one would dare to harm Bregetta with Teddy at her side. He had been on the whale boats when he was young, but now he was too old for that life and made do instead with some work in the ship-yards when he could find it. Enough to feed and clothe him and his wife, and keep a roof, such as it was, over their heads.

'Hear the soldiers were here today,' he said, shifting the clay pipe in his mouth.

Bregetta smiled to herself. 'So they were. Ready to break down the door if I refused them entry.'

'After your brother, were they?'

'Yes. Not that they'll get him. He's too sly for them. He knows Sydney as well as he knows the sound of Ma's voice.'

'Perhaps it'd be better if they did. You'd be free of the worry of him.'

It was what Molly had said. They must have been discussing it between them before they came.

'He's my brother,' Bregetta sighed. 'Whatever he does he's still my brother. I can't believe he's bad. Just . . . foolish.'

Teddy said nothing, but she knew he thought her blinded by her love for the boy. Perhaps she was. She remembered him as he had been as a child, not as he had become as a man.

'You met the new sergeant,' he went on after a moment. 'I've heard he's hard, but fair enough if there's injustice done.'

Bregetta sniffed. 'Can they be fair? At least you knew where you stood with Davis. If you had a coin or two to slip him as a sweetener he'd look the other way, and if you didn't you took your chances.'

The lights were muted about them. Sydney was not very well lit, and this part of Sydney was worse than the rest. The narrow alleys were mostly dark and reeking, and drunken men and women swayed in the shadows, already beginning their Friday-night debauch. The Rocks was full of such sights, but Bregetta had learned to ignore them. Will Tanner's tavern was in a relatively better part of Sydney, in lower George Street. He held with no whores and troublemakers in his establishment, and he threw out any who tried to bluff their way in. The soldiers went there, and the merchants, and the more re-spectable emancipists, mingling with labourers and tradesmen and sailors. Will held games of chance in the backrooms, after the doors were closed, and paid off the proper authorities so that there was never any trouble. He received his spirits at cheaper prices than others because he knew who to bribe. And because he knew secrets about people they didn't want known to others.

Bregetta had only come to work for Will through Madeleine. Madeleine was her best friend, really her only friend from childhood. Madeleine had lived with Bregetta's family when her own parents were taken in an influenza epidemic. When she was young Madeleine had always been there. And she was still there, helping out. She had found Bregetta this job with Will. She had married Will a year ago—escaping her work as a presser in a steamy laundry and the poverty which still held Bregetta fast—and wheedled him into letting Bregetta serve at the bar, for an hour at first, and then, when he'd seen her worth, two nights a week, and now it was every night. The money was sufficient, though hardly generous—Will was too mean for that. But

Madeleine helped with food; sometimes there was left-over pie, or some apples, or some eggs... There was always something. Once she had even paid for a doctor to come to Bregetta's mother.

George Street was wide and grand, compared to the place they had just left. Bregetta felt she could breathe deeper here. Will's tavern was of solid stone, of two storeys, with a veranda jutting out halfway down its face. It was squeezed in between two warehouses. Lights shone from the windows, and voices were raised in friendly argument.

'Here we are,' Teddy said, and opened the door for her. The atmosphere inside was warm and smoky, gaudy and gay. Men laughed and shouted and drank. Behind the bar, Will shouted back at them, his little blue eyes swinging over the company greedily, as if assessing the night's profits. He saw Bregetta at once and beckoned her over.

'You're late,' he said. She didn't reply, just hurried to fill glasses, wiping her hands on the apron she hastily tied about her trim waist. The men at the bar eyed her as greedily as Will took their money. But she only smiled at the jests, or ignored the coarse requests, and after a while they left her alone. She was kind and beautiful, and they loved her. But Bregetta had something which set her apart from others in her situation; she was like the ladies in their carriages, beyond their reach.

Teddy sat down in the far corner, crossing his arms over his massive chest and puffing on his pipe. He would wait until Bregetta was finished and then walk with her back to the house and her mother. He had been her father's friend, and he sometimes felt as if he was acting as a proxy in that role for his daughter. No harm would come to Bregetta while he lived—he owed his friend that much.

The girl was lovely. If things had turned out differently perhaps that loveliness would have been enough to snare her a rich merchant, someone to boost her up the social scale. Perhaps her father had had something like that in mind, for he had made certain that the girl and her brother received some education, and made sure that she in particular never ran wild with the other children. He himself had come from humble beginnings, but the draper's shop had done well, and it was not beyond the bounds of possibility that Bregetta and Jim would do better.

Teddy sighed, and knocked out his pipe. But it had not turned out that way after all. Bregetta's father had died still a young man, and she had been thrown back on to the care of her rackety trollop of a mother. The money had soon slipped through *her* careless fingers, and the shop had been lost. Instead of moving up the social scale, Bregetta was sinking down—fast.

Teddy looked across the rapidly filling room at the bar. There was Will Tanner, sly and nasty but the cleverest businessman in Sydney, always staying just the right side of the law. He would be worth a fortune one day, and trust Madeleine to have attached herself to such a one! He had never liked Madeleine. Oh, she was pretty enough, but so sweet that she reminded him of syrup... cloying, sticky syrup. The falseness was in her heart, where Bregetta could not see it. The girl was so enjoying her role as Lady Bountiful that she couldn't let a moment go by without doing something for which Bregetta had to thank her. And Bregetta thought her an angel, and could not see that underneath all Madeleine's friendship there lay a hard core of sour jealousy. For Bregetta had something Madeleine could never acquire—a basic goodness of heart. So thinking, Teddy re-lit his pipe and stared into the smoke-filled room.

'Will?'

Will Tanner, short and stout, turned crimson as his wife slipped in beside him, laying her delicate, white hand on his brown arm. 'Maddy?' he whispered. 'You know I don't like you down here.'

The girl smiled. She was delicately pretty, with long fair hair and blue eyes slanting up, and lips so red it was as though she wore rouge on them. And if one of her legs was shorter than the other, causing her to drag it slightly, that was just part of her fairy-like charm. He loved her, and, though she had told him she loved him as much, he did not believe her. She had wed him for his money and the care he could give her, and that was how it should be.

'I was bored up there, all alone. I'll just talk to Bregetta a minute.'

He would have liked to refuse her, to send her back to the richly furnished quarters he had had made for her above stairs, where she could not be touched by his harsh realities. But she was looking at him with that pleading look, and he knew he could refuse her nothing. One of the customers guffawed, and Will turned with a narrow look. Madeleine slipped past him to Bregetta's side. The two girls exchanged an amused smile.

'How's your ma?' Madeleine whispered, picking up a glass and beginning to wash it in the bucket set aside for that purpose.

'Poorly.'

Madeleine nodded. She did not need to be told
about Mrs Smith. She had known her since she was
five and Bregetta was four, and they had played
together then lived together. They had remained
friends when Mr Smith had died, and Bregetta had
moved to the run-down cottage in the Rocks while
Madeleine had gone to work in the town in her
hated, steamy laundry. And they were still friends,
though Madeleine had moved up into the comfort
of being Will Tanner's wife, and Bregetta had
become his employee.

'And your brother?'

Bregetta stiffened. 'He's not come back, to my
knowledge. Have you seen him?'

Madeleine shook her head. She and Jim had been
sweethearts once. Bregetta had thought Madeleine
might marry him. But then fortunes had turned sour
for the Smiths and Madeleine had drawn away from
Jim, just shut herself off from him as though she'd
been no longer in love with him. Bregetta had felt
sorry for Jim and had pleaded his case to
Madeleine, but the other girl had just laughed and
shrugged and said, 'But, Bregetta, you're asking
me to commit suicide!'

Bregetta knew that Madeleine was much harder
and stronger than her fragile exterior led one to
believe. That she had pursued and caught Will
Tanner was amazing in itself, but it had only been
part of Madeleine's grand plan. When they were
children she had wanted so many things. Bregetta,
who had no ambition, was drawn along in the wake
of those dreams, pleased to be allowed to be a part
of them, however minor.

For her part was always minor. Madeleine would be a royal princess. Bregetta would be her lady-in-waiting; Madeleine would be the squatter's wife, Madeleine would be the governor's wife, and Bregetta would always be two steps behind, the serving-girl. Madeleine would be the one to wear diamonds and pearls in her hair, and Bregetta the one to brush that hair until it shone. But Bregetta knew that Madeleine would never forget her, no matter how high she climbed. She was good and kind, and it hurt when people always seemed to like Bregetta so much better than Madeleine.

'Maddy.' Will was anxiously beckoning his wife. Madeleine gave Bregetta a speaking look.

'I'll have to go. He can't bear me to be down here too long. He wants me to lie on the chaise-longue upstairs, like a lady,' and she smiled a secret smile.

Bregetta wondered what it would be like to be allowed to lie on such a piece of furniture as often as one liked. Then Madeleine touched her arm and turned away. Will whispered something to her as she passed, and her face lightened. She smiled into his round ugly features and deliberately brushed her hip against him as she went by. His colour deepened so much that Bregetta was sure he would have an apoplexy.

It was late when they finally closed. Bregetta smiled tiredly at Teddy, and they went out together. The wind had died, and the air was cold and still, catching her warm breath out of her mouth. She shivered and hugged her shawl closer about her. A woman screeched in one of the alleys, and there was laughter. A riderless horse plunged wildly, careering away towards the foreshore. Bregetta tried not to think of Madeleine with envy, but it was difficult. And she knew she had much for which to be grateful. She did not say anything of her feelings to Teddy—she knew he disliked Madeleine. He did not understand her.

Back at the cottage Molly had been dozing by the fire, and she sat up with a start. Bregetta's mother was asleep, snoring loudly. Bregetta thanked the Fields and closed and barred the door. She sank down on the chair beside the fireplace, warming her hands at the embers, and easing her aching back and feet. Will had given her a couple of coins, and she slipped them into the pocket she had sewn into her petticoat. They would pay for the rent at least, and perhaps some wood for the fire. She closed her eyes and wondered if this was all life had to offer her. Where was *her* Will Tanner? Where was her man, who would love her and worry if she were down among the riff-raff when she should be upstairs, reclining on a chaise-longue?

Strangely, it was the soldier's face she thought of then. The sergeant who had come about her brother and looked at her with his dark, dark eyes and his quiet smile.

CHAPTER TWO

RAIN woke Bregetta, pattering on the roof and dripping through into the corner with a steady, miserable consistency. Bregetta rubbed her eyes and began the business of re-lighting the fire. She set a pot over it at last, searching for the tiny pouch of precious tea Madeleine had given her and adding a little to stew in the water. Apart from rum, her mother's favourite drink was tea. The old woman stirred now, as if aware of Bregetta's movements, and watched her with sleepy eyes.

'Did you see Maddy last night?' she croaked when Bregetta had helped her with her morning ablutions and then straightened her clothing.

'Yes.'

'Fine girl, that Maddy.' The old eyes were sly, seeking to hurt. 'Why couldn't you have married Will Tanner? He had an eye for you at one time, before Maddy came along and dug her hooks into him. You should've hung on to him while you could.'

Bregetta shrugged. It was true that Will had admired her once. But she had thought him coarse and ugly and sly, and could not bring herself to encourage him. Madeleine had had no such scruples, and had gone all out to capture him. And look at her now! Perhaps Bregetta *had* been a fool, as her mother told her so often.

'I'll get us some more wood today,' was all she said.

Her mother muttered. 'That Molly's a bore. Went on and on about your father. What am I supposed to do about it? He's dead and buried, and we've had our share of bad luck since.'

Mostly through her mother's frittering, Bregetta thought, but again said nothing. She put on some of the pease to heat, and broke some of the coarse stale bread. It was dry and hard, but there would be nothing else until next week, unless Madeleine...

Outside the rain continued, soft and constant against the roof. At least it would be washing the alleys clean. The stench of the open drains had made her gag when she had first come here. But she had grown used to them, and hardly noticed them now, except at the very height of summer.

The knocking on the door startled them both, and their eyes met, not, after all, dissimilar. Was it Jim? Bregetta bit her lip. The knock came again, firmer this time, and she knew it was not. She rose and lifted the bar, then opened the door a crack on to the cold miserable morning. Her face lost what colour it had.

'Sorry to trouble you again,' said the sergeant.

The black eyes slid over her untidy, unbrushed hair and down over the green gown she had not yet troubled to change. Her face, pinched and pale with weariness, creased in a frown.

'What do you want?' she asked sharply.

The dark brows rose. 'Can I come in?' he said. The rain was dripping off his hair and his red jacket. The two men behind him stood huddled together under the narrow eaves, looking miserable. She had no choice and stood back ungraciously. He came in, but this time his companions stayed out in the silent lane. She closed the door.

He seemed big in the small space. Bregetta saw him looking in distaste about the damp, crumbling room. It made her even angrier—did he think they lived here by choice?

'What do you want?' she repeated. Her mother was eyeing him from the pallet, her wrinkled face yellowed by the harsh sun and hard living.

Raindrops dripped from his hair. He wiped one off the end of his nose. His eyelashes, absurdly long for a man, were clumped together. 'Your brother,' he retorted. 'The man he assaulted has died.'

Bregetta caught her breath, and she heard her mother moan.

'It's a hanging offence now,' he added softly.

'He's not been here,' her mother said in a breathless voice. 'He'll not come back now. He'll be off into the bush, or on the first ship he can find.'

Sergeant Duncan looked sceptical. Bregetta turned to the fire and stirred the pease, her heart thumping unpleasantly. A hanging offence, he had said. Jim, hanging by the neck. She could not bear it, and jumped with fright when he spoke again, directly behind her.

'I'll need to speak to you again,' he said. 'Do you have an occupation?'

Bregetta looked at him over her shoulder. Her dark eyebrows rose. 'I work for Will Tanner,' she said. 'What did you think I did?' she asked, though it was plain enough what he had thought.

'At the tavern in George Street?' he said with a frown. 'I know it.'

The dark eyes slid over her again, and self-consciously she smoothed her auburn hair back behind her ears. He watched the movement, and she felt the colour come into her cheeks. 'Who,' she began, 'was the man my brother——?'

'Murdered?' he asked deliberately. 'A soldier. Not a very good one, perhaps, but a soldier doing his duty. He had just been paid, too, so he had money on him. It was a callous act.'

Bregetta's eyes slid away from his, unable to believe it.

'That's why I am in charge of the matter, instead of the police. It's military business.'

Bregetta shrugged. It didn't concern her what uniform a man wore. They were all as bad as each other.

'You'll let me know if you see him?' The question was ironic; he knew she wouldn't.

Bregetta nodded without looking at him. The pot was steaming, and she began to pour the tea into the mugs. He watched her quick fingers. 'I would offer you some——' she began in a hard voice, but he cut in.

'That would be very welcome.'

She wondered, for a moment, if she dared to refuse. But she met his eyes again and knew she would not. He could retaliate easily enough. Charges laid against her, lies told. It was easily done. And yet there was something else, too, something in his face that brought that prickling feeling to her nape again. And she knew she did not want to refuse.

Bregetta added tea to a third mug with jerky movements, slopping it. She glanced over to her mother and saw that she had fallen into a doze, lulled by the rain. 'What of your companions?' she asked sarcastically.

The sergeant smiled faintly. 'They can wait. They've nothing else to do. That's one of the benefits of being a sergeant.'

He took the mug, and his fingers brushed hers. She looked at him in the glow of the fire, the lean brown face with its piercing dark eyes and long dark lashes, those thin smiling lips above the strong stubborn jaw and chin. She had never felt so uneasy before with a man. This was not Will Tanner with his coarse, sly wit, nor Teddy, stern and kind like a father. This was someone totally beyond the realm of her experience.

'How old are you?' he asked in a deep, soft voice.

Bregetta looked down at her mug. 'I am seventeen,' she said.

'And respectable,' he said with a touch of mockery. 'I can tell. I've seen enough of the other sort.'

Bregetta eyed him warily. 'I haven't seen you here before,' she murmured.

'I'm new to the York Street Barracks, up from Bathurst. If you were used to Sergeant Davis's ways you'll find mine different. I don't take bribes, and I don't ask favours just because I happen to wear a red coat. And I don't drink on duty, and neither do the men I have in my charge.'

'Apart from tea,' Bregetta muttered.

The thin mouth curved into a smile, and he sipped the hot tea, his hands clasped about the mug. He looked frozen to death, she thought. He was probably soaked from the rain. Before she knew what she meant to do Bregetta had asked him for his jacket. He looked surprised, and then slowly he set down his mug, and slowly began to unbutton his jacket, never once taking his eyes from her.

Bregetta busied herself stoking the fire again, and took the jacket when he handed it to her, laying it over a stool to dry. It was old, but well-kept, with neat darns in places and clean of stains, which was more than could be said for many a soldier's uniform she had seen. The jacket began to steam before the heat of the fire.

Bregetta sat down again, taking up her own mug, and sipping the tea. It was only then that she dared to look up at him. He was looking into the fire, and she let her eyes run over him at will. Broad-shouldered and strong-armed beneath the white shirt, he looked as if he could hold his own in a brawl, which was probably all that was required of a sergeant in this place. How did he enforce not drinking on duty, when every redcoat she had ever known was always drunk or getting there?

'How did you come to work in Will Tanner's tavern?'

Bregetta veiled her brown eyes. Her auburn hair tumbled across her cheek, and she brushed it back impatiently. Again he watched the movement.

'His wife is my friend,' she said. 'She helped me. Otherwise I probably would've been what you thought me the first time you saw me. There is nothing but whoring left for the destitute.'

'It's a pity she could not help you from this hovel,' was all he said.

Bregetta made a movement. 'She can only do so much. I wouldn't ask more of her. Will is not . . . easy.'

She looked up again. He seemed very close. He put down his mug with a deliberate movement. She watched in amazement as he bent forward and gently pressed his lips to hers. A great shudder went through her, but she did not pull away. His hand slid up her cheek into the gleaming beauty of her hair, and his kiss deepened, his mouth slanting across hers.

Bregetta had been kissed before, but never like this—it was as if he drew her soul from her body. And she had never before felt as if she wanted to wrap her arms about a man and let the kiss go on and on and on.

'Bregetta!' The old voice broke on that single word. Bregetta jerked back, her face pale and then red as the blood rushed into it. He was watching her, and then, as if nothing had happened, he stood up and began to pull on his jacket.

'Bregetta!' her mother shouted again. 'Get out, you! Redcoat... bloody lobster! Keep away from me daughter. I'll not have the likes of you makin' up to her!'

He was buttoning the jacket now. 'Aye, I hear you, old woman,' he retorted. 'She's unharmed.'

'Bregetta,' she screeched, and finally Bregetta, with head bowed, went unwillingly to her side. The crooked hand fastened on hers, surprisingly strong. 'Now get out, and don't come back here hangin' around, for it'll do you no good!'

The sergeant's face was blank, though his dark eyes were angry. He raked his hand through his hair and opened the door. The two men straightened, looking bedraggled, but curious too as to why their sergeant had taken so long over so simple a matter and why the old woman was yelling. Bregetta saw the unmistakable answer in their eyes as they slid away from hers to the muddy ground.

'Thank you for the tea,' their sergeant said, soft enough for only her to hear, 'Bregetta.'

The door closed on him. 'What did he say?' the
old woman shrieked. 'Have you lost your senses,
girl? I told you he was dangerous. Stay away from
him; I've warned you, now, stay away!'

Bregetta pulled away. 'All right. I hear you, Ma.
I'll stay away. It was nothing, just a kiss. Nothing
to be worrying yourself about.'

But she could see her mother did not believe it,
sensing something of the emotion that had passed
between them. She was shocked to realise that she
did not believe it either. She had given him more
than her lips just now, and, whatever her mother
said, it was the beginning of something, not the
end.

Bregetta had hoped her mother would forget what
had happened, but when Molly came she broke into
a harangue about the sergeant and how he had tried
to rape her daughter.

'He did not,' Bregetta retorted angrily. 'He kissed
me, that's all, and it meant nothing.'

Molly looked uncertain. 'I didn't think him the
sort,' she murmured. 'Teddy says he's straight as
a die, which is something of a miracle.'

'Straight?' her mother cried. 'There's not one o'
'em as is straight. I've seen 'em lie and cheat like
the foulest road-ganger. Only the police is worse,
but they've had more practice.' She continued to
natter, but Bregetta pretended she didn't hear. No
doubt her mother knew all about Sydney at its
worst. But she was trying to interfere in something
that Bregetta did not want interfered with. Something she hardly understood herself.

'I'd best be going,' she broke in, brushing her
hair one last time and pinning it up. She had the
green gown on again—one of Madeleine's cast-offs.

Her mother sat up—a great effort—and shook her fist at her daughter. 'Remember what I said!' she cried out. 'He's dangerous. He'll take you and then he'll throw you back on to the heap.'

Bregetta went out and shut the door with relief. Teddy was there and accompanied her in a silence for which she was grateful. Some sailors, just off one of the ships docked in the bay, went past in a laughing, boisterous group. They would have plenty of money to spend if they had just been paid after their months in the Southern Seas chasing after the whales. They eyed Bregetta as she passed, but she pulled the shawl closer about her head, and felt Teddy's big hand close protectively on her arm. The sailors looked at Teddy and edged away. They were not in the mood for fighting; they were seeking pleasure.

'Heard from my brother again today,' Teddy said as they passed through the narrow lane to Gloucester Street.

'Oh, you mean Neil? How is he doing?'

Neil had travelled to the Hawkesbury River, north of Sydney, and bought land there. Not in the areas around Windsor and Richmond, already taken up by earlier settlers, and where prices for land and stock were far too high. But further to the north, where there was still untamed country to be had at reasonable prices, and maybe a fortune to be made. Teddy and Molly often heard from him. They were proud of his daring and ambition.

'Well enough, he says. At least he has work to do.'

'Things will get better here in Sydney.'

'How can they, with more emigrants pouring in every day and no work for them?'

Bregetta had no answer, and again they went on in silence. The tavern was warm and cheery after her mother's anger. She was glad to step into the light and receive the smiles of her customers. Will handed out tankards, smiling falsely at Teddy, while Bregetta slipped behind him and donned her apron.

She served ale and spirits to some merchants, laughed with a man who had won at the races, and commiserated with one who had lost. A group at a far table called for grog, and she carried the tray across, fending off a drunk's eager hands. The colony seemed to drink rum as if it were mother's milk. In the early days transactions had been made with rum instead of money and wages been paid in it. Many of the colonists still drank copious quantities of it each day. But at least Will sold good spirits, not the home-made grog in the sly grog shops that could kill a man at one sitting.

Bregetta set down the drinks and turned with a smile. It was then that she saw him, in the furthest corner, in the shadows. But it was him.

She almost dropped the tray in surprise. The dark eyes met hers, and his smile was secret as he bent his head over his drink. After a moment she went across to him, but it seemed as if her pleasure in the place was spoiled. She was not ready to see him again. She needed to think, to sort out her feelings, to recover from the last meeting. He was a soldier, after all, and she had been brought up to distrust that breed.

'What are you doing here?'

He looked up with feigned surprise. 'It's a tavern, isn't it? And I'm a paying customer.'

Bregetta bit her lip, eyeing him, between anger and bewilderment. Perhaps it was a coincidence,

and she was making more of it than... But, no.
The look in his eyes was no coincidence. 'My
mother would have a fit,' she whispered.

His eyebrows lifted. 'Is she coming here, then?'

Bregetta glared at his stupidity. 'She warned me
against you.'

He looked down at his drink, those absurd eyelashes sweeping his cheek. 'She's dying.' It wasn't
a question. 'What will happen to you then?'

Bregetta had often asked herself the same
question. But she always pushed it to one side,
frightened of any answers she came up with.
Perhaps he sensed her fear, for his hand came out
and took hers. She looked at the capable square
hand with its long brown fingers.

'I'll watch out for you,' he said softly.

Her hand trembled under his. She thought again
of all she had heard about the military, but
somehow the facts did not fit this man with his
black hair and eyes, and his stern, serious face.

Behind her, Will called out. She had to return to
the bar. But she watched him, and knew he was
watching her, there in the shadows, secret and silent.
For some reason the thought of him there made her
a little mad. She redoubled her efforts to please the
customers, and smiled at them with her eyes in a
way she would never have dared before. All because
he was there, watching her.

Teddy, in his corner, also watched her, but with
consternation. He had heard of girls going off the
rails at a certain age, turning into flirts and worse,
but he had never thought it would happen to
Bregetta. She was not the sort, somehow. He had
seen her speaking with the new sergeant and the
way the man's eyes followed her as though she had

them on a string. As though he would devour her entirely. And Teddy was worried.

'Bregetta,' Will's little eyes were angry, 'you're wasting your time with that one—serve the gentleman there. And, Bregetta,' as she turned away, 'Maddy wants to see you upstairs. And be quick about it. We're uncommon busy tonight.'

Madeleine was in her parlour, beautiful in a shot taffeta gown, her long fair hair combed sleekly back off her forehead, and a cashmere shawl artistically draped about her shoulders. She smiled and held Bregetta's hands, then frowned. 'You're pale,' she said. 'What's the matter? Is it Jim again?'

Bregetta rubbed her tired eyes and sat down. 'The man he hit died. It's murder now. And hanging, if they catch him.'

Madeleine looked shocked, and sat down too. 'They told you this?'

'The sergeant came again today.' She looked up, and her brown eyes were big and puzzled. She had to tell someone, and it might as well be Maddy. Madeleine was, after all, her best friend.

Madeleine's eyes narrowed as the story went on, and then she laughed softly. 'So you have an admirer,' she said. 'A soldier, too. Can't you do better than that?'

'He's a sergeant,' Bregetta murmured, annoyed.

'That's worse. A bully, no doubt as hard as nails. He'll beat you. What are you about, Bregetta, getting into such a mess?'

'I'm not. I——'

'He'll thrash you, this soldier,' Madeleine went on as if she hadn't heard. 'They all beat their women, you know. Because the officers beat them.' Madeleine took her hand and squeezed it. 'You can

do better than him. Wait and see. I'll find someone
for you. Someone rich and not too demanding. You
need someone to extract you from this tangle you've
got yourself into, don't you?'

'It's not like that!' she cried, and was surprised
at her passion. 'He frightens me, but not in that
way. He looks at me and I feel as if he could make
me do anything he wanted me to do. Because if he
asked it of me then I would *want* to do it. Do you
understand?'

Madeleine drew her breath in sharply, as if she
had been pierced with a needle, but her face was
calm and smiling when Bregetta looked up at her.
'You'd better go down now,' was all she said. 'Will
must be getting cross. I'll try and drop by this week
to see you and your mother.'

Bregetta nodded, and rose tiredly to her feet. She
felt so weary that she wished she could fall down
and never get up. But if she did that who was left
to look after Ma? She went slowly down the stairs
to the taproom. Madeleine had not been as helpful
as she had hoped. She had seemed almost angry
with Bregetta, as though she had done something
not to her liking, or not to her plans...

Back at the bar Bregetta went on with serving,
not daring to look over at the far table. It was late
when she finished and Will began to close up. Then
she looked, and the sergeant was gone. Teddy came
to take her arm, and she leaned on him gratefully.

'You've upset your ma,' Molly said when they
got back to the cottage. She looked worried. 'She's
not well, Bregetta. Will the doctor come out to her?'

'He won't come unless he gets the money first,'
Bregetta said drily. She looked at the sleeping form
of her mother. She looked tiny tonight, as though

only skin and bones were left, a dry and rustling bundle. She wondered again what would become of her when her mother died. Would Molly and Teddy take her into their tiny home when there was hardly enough room for themselves? Where else could she go? Will would not have her, even if Madeleine would. 'I will watch out for you': the words came back to her. She dared not think of them now, or what they meant. The weariness swept over her in waves.

When her friends had gone Bregetta sank down by the embers, half asleep already. She woke in the early morning, hearing her mother's moans and knowing she must get the doctor. Rising, she pulled a shawl about her shoulders, and slipped out into the chill dawn. Molly came, sleepy, at the knock on the door, and went back with her to the cottage.

'You're right,' she said to Bregetta when she had looked at her mother. 'You'd best go and see if he'll come. You'll be all right? Teddy's gone off to work.'

'I'll be all right. There's no one much about this time of day.'

It was true enough. As Bregetta hurried through the quiet mist-swathed streets she saw only prone bodies, and revellers too ill to do more than creep home. The doctor lived in Cumberland Street, and she roused him after pounding a long time on his door.

'You'll have to pay,' he told her sharply, and she handed over the coins Will had given her the night before. He slipped them into his pocket without a word and followed her out into the brightening morning.

Molly met them at the door, her face pinched with tiredness and worry. 'She's calling for your father, Bregetta. Thinks he's still alive.'

Inside her mother tossed and turned on the pallet, her face twisted with some inner turmoil. The hands that clutched the sheets were hot and dry when Bregetta lay her own hand over them, trying to give comfort. The brown eyes sprang open, clearing suddenly. She stared up at her daughter. 'Look after Jim,' she said. 'You were always the stronger. And take care,' she added. Her mouth twisted, working on things she wanted to say, but in the end she just contented herself with, 'Don't do what I did. You're a good girl, Bregetta.'

Molly's arm slipped about Bregetta's waist, and the doctor came over, distaste in his face, to examine the old woman. When he had finished he looked at Molly and shook his head. 'A matter of time only,' he murmured. 'No use in taking her to the hospital. Just keep her warm and comfortable. She'll not see out the day.'

'Not that we'd let her go to that place anyway,' Molly muttered, her arm tightening about Bregetta. Hospital in Sydney was only another name for death. But Bregetta didn't hear her; she felt a curious relief at the doctor's words. Her mother had been ill for so long. Bregetta had seen the way it was to be when the sickness had first come upon her, and had tried to pity her for her past and the hardships she had suffered, but it was hard to pity someone who went headlong into a mire of her own choosing. And, though she had loved her mother, she had been like a chain around Bregetta's neck, dragging her down. A chain made up of Bregetta's feelings of duty and love and compassion, all the stronger because it was of her own making.

'She's had a hard life,' Molly murmured, as if reading her thoughts. 'But there was probably not much she regretted.'

'No,' Bregetta smiled faintly, 'she tried so hard to be respectable, for my father. But it wasn't in her. She loved the life here in the Rocks, Molly. The nights spent drinking and talking, and the men. She was brought up to it; it made her feel safe. Reminded her of the times in London, I suppose, where people were held together by their poverty. I can't blame her for not being something she didn't have it in her to be.'

'Your father loved her, my dear, just as she was.'

Suddenly grief overwhelmed her, and Bregetta pushed past her outside. It was warmer now, despite the gusty wind which had come up and the clouds scudding across the sky. Bregetta took several breaths. After a moment she wandered down towards the waterfront to watch the ships swinging gently on their moorings, and the seabirds screeching on the mud-flats. The wharfs and warehouses were all but deserted, for it was a Sunday. The church bells rang out from the town, but Bregetta stood alone, watching the waves fetching up on the shore and knowing that a part of her life was ending.

CHAPTER THREE

BREGETTA sent a message to Will that evening that she would not come to his tavern, and why. Her mother lingered on, raving in her half-conscious state, as if determined to prove the doctor wrong— her last act of defiance. She was not in pain, but neither was she in her right mind. Bregetta tended her, trying to get her to take nourishment, keeping her warm and the fire stoked high. Darkness came down, and it was cold and wet again. It seemed appropriate, somehow. Bregetta slept, and woke suddenly, knowing there was someone in the room. For a moment she thought it might be the sergeant, and lurched to her feet. But it was a smaller man who bent over her mother's bed, with hair the colour of straw, and he was weeping.

'Jim?'

He turned, the tears unashamedly running down his cheeks.

'You risked much to come here,' she said. 'They're looking for you. You know it's a hanging matter now.'

He looked frightened. 'I know. It was an accident, Bregetta. I never meant to kill him. He was always taunting us, always threatening us with the gaol and the stocks, even said he'd bring the gibbet back just for us. We got into a fight—he'd been drinking and so had I. He was trying to choke me, and I pushed him, hard. He fell and hit his head on some steps. We were too frightened to touch him in case he was dead. We ran away.'

Bregetta sighed and knew she would believe him, whatever the truth of it. 'You must go before they come. Someone may have seen you. Some of the people around here will do anything for a few shillings...'

Jim looked at their mother, his face working. 'She's dying, sister. I can't stand it!'

Bregetta came to take him in her arms, and she knew her mother was right. She was the stronger of the two. 'She's beyond pain,' she said gently. 'She doesn't even know you're here. You must go— you're in danger. She would be the first to tell you that.'

He moved, and said, 'I've nowhere to go.'

Bregetta pushed him away, trying to read his eyes. 'You can't stay here.'

Jim moved back, wiping his cheeks, and then stooped to the fire, holding out his hands to the warmth. He was dirty, his clothing ragged and wet from the rain. She had never seen him look so haggard and tired. 'They'll catch me whatever I do. I've no money.'

Bregetta stiffened, but he met her eyes with a little smile. 'You think that's what I came for?' He shook his head gently. 'I'll not deny it did cross my mind. But not just for that, sister.'

'We haven't any,' she said fiercely. 'I spent some on the doctor, and when Ma dies I'll need the rest if she's not to go to a pauper's grave. Would you want that? Would our father?'

Jim grunted. 'Pa is not here to tell me what to do any more. Not that he ever cared for me. You were always his favourite.'

Bregetta moved angrily. 'That's foolish, Jimmy. Now you must go. There's a soldier... Sergeant Duncan. He's been here twice already, looking for you.'

Jim shrugged, though his eyes were wary. Then, with a sly look under his brows, 'You could ask Maddy. She'd help me.'

Bregetta frowned. 'I couldn't,' she whispered. 'It would put her in danger.'

He laughed. 'Maddy loves danger. Ask her for me. You can leave a message at the Black Dog, asking if she wants to help. Will you do that, Bregetta, or will you turn me in?'

Bregetta shook her head. 'You know I'd not do that.'

He smiled, and touched her cheek, then turned briefly to their mother before going to the door. 'Put the bar across when I'm gone,' he said. 'You should never have left it off, sister.' Then he was gone, silent into the night. Bregetta shut the door and barred it, cursing her tiredness for making her forget to do so before. She wondered how Jim thought Madeleine could help him. Money, she supposed. At one time they had been so close, and she knew Jim still hoped... Well, Will had been the better of the two in Madeleine's eyes, and perhaps she had been right. Jim was too wild to settle down, and certainly Madeleine would not be in the position she was now in if she had plumped for love rather than material comfort. Perhaps that was why she disliked Bregetta's new admirer... Bregetta pushed the thought away before it could properly develop. No time to think of that. Her mother was stirring again, and she must see if she would take some weak broth.

Molly came the next morning. 'You look tired to death,' she said, giving Bregetta a hug. 'Let me watch her awhile. Go for a walk.'

Bregetta readily agreed, for she would have to see Madeleine and this was as good a time as any. Besides, Will would be expecting her to return to her job, and if she did not do so soon he would find someone else. She must wheedle a few more days out of him.

Madeleine's servant-girl answered the door, her sloe eyes sliding over Bregetta and away. She led her into the parlour, and Madeleine rose from a chair where she had been sewing, smiling with delight. 'We had your message,' she said. 'Whatever has happened?'

After Bregetta had explained Madeleine poured them some wine and made Bregetta sit by the warm fire to sip it. 'What will you do,' she asked, 'when she is gone? Bregetta, you must come to us!'

Bregetta laughed. 'Will would be pleased with that! No, I cannot. And so you well know. Something will turn up. Besides, I have a favour to ask you that is more important than my future.' She looked into Madeleine's slanting blue eyes and sighed. 'Jim came last night. He needs help to get away. He seems to think you will give it.'

Madeleine stood up and turned to the window. Her back was stiff and straight, and she twisted her hands. Bregetta watched her with interest. Did she still have some soft feelings for Jim, after all?

'I . . .' Madeleine turned and bit her lip ' . . . I can give him money if that's what he wants. Will is always generous. But, as for helping him escape, I don't know what I could do. Will has shares in a trading vessel, but I could hardly ask him to take

Jim on as a seaman. He would be a little suspicious, don't you think?'

'I don't expect you to do anything. Jim has no hold on you to do so.'

Madeleine sighed. 'Hasn't he? Well, I'll give him money, but as for the ship... I'll try and think of a way to get him a place aboard, but that's the best I can promise. You must give him a message, tell him to meet me somewhere safe. And Will must not see him!'

Bregetta nodded. The wine was making her dizzy. She *was* tired to death, as Molly said. And yet she had no time to rest. After a moment she said, 'I can't come back to work for Will until Ma is...that is...'

Madeleine's warm hand covered her own. 'It's all right. I've told Will he must be patient, and if he needs help then I'll help him. He was furious,' she laughed, 'but he forgets that I helped him in the beginning when he had that horrid little place in Gloucester Street. Now he thinks I'm a lady and shouldn't soil my hands with such things.'

Bregetta smiled, but envy twisted deep in her heart. She was ashamed of it, for Madeleine had been good to her. She should be thankful for such a friend, not envious of her good fortune. Besides, would she like to spend her days, and her nights, with Will Tanner?

'I asked Will—about your sergeant,' Madeleine was saying.

Bregetta looked up, startled, and met the blue eyes. They were gleaming with mockery.

'His name is Alistair Duncan,' she went on with a sly smile. 'A Scot. He's in the 50th Regiment. He's a bachelor, but not much of a ladies' man by

all accounts.' Madeleine's eyebrows lifted delicately. 'Will says he's hard—I told you so!—but
honest enough. A shame, that, Will says. He had
a couple of good deals going with the last man—
gaming, you know. But no doubt time will change
him, mould him more to Will's liking.'

Bregetta looked away, plaiting her skirt between
her fingers. 'Was he here last night?'

Madeleine's smile broadened. 'Yes. He wanted
to know where you were, and Will told him.'

She looked up, angry. 'He shouldn't have. It's
none of his business.'

Madeleine shrugged. 'You'll have to give him the
right about, then, my dear, or he'll go on pestering
you forever. Besides, I've thought of just the man
for you. What about Francis Warrender?'

Bregetta looked at her in amazement. 'Will's
friend? Maddy, he's ancient!'

She shrugged a little peevishly. 'He's . . . mature,
certainly, but he has money and a fine house up in
Bridge Street. He likes young girls, Will says, and
he would certainly like you. He'd look after you.
You'd soon learn to get what you wanted out of
him.'

Bregetta shivered. 'No.'

Madeleine's face grew taut. 'You're ungrateful,
my dear. And a fool. There's no other way for the
likes of us. The only thing we have to bargain with
is ourselves, and we may as well get as much as we
can over the deal. Do you think I didn't hesitate a
little over my decision between Jim and Will? Do
you think I didn't wonder a little if the world would
be well lost for true love? But I knew that true love
could not compare with Will's money and what it
could buy me. When I am old and feeble I will look

back with satisfaction on my life, knowing I made
the right decision. I can't let you make the wrong
one.'

Bregetta stood up. 'I know you mean well,
Madeleine, but...I must think. My mother and...I
must think it over. Oh, I'm so tired.'

Madeleine's face softened. 'I'm sorry. Of course
you must. Here, I have some of Will's best brandy.
You look as if you need a nip. No, take it!'

Bregetta mumbled her thanks, tears prickling her
eyes. Madeleine hugged her, and she hurried away,
out into the cold street. Francis Warrender was old
and he smelt and, though he was rich, he would
drag her down into those depths from which she
had held herself up all these years. Bregetta
shuddered; perhaps she had too much pride to ever
make good as Madeleine had done. Her mother, if
she knew, would call her a fool.

Bregetta hurried down George Street, past the
long wall of the gaol, and up Essex Street—
affectionately known as Gallow's Hill—towards the
Black Dog. The alleys were meaner here—
dangerous. She climbed some narrow stairs, up to
the tavern. Four soldiers were gambling at the front
door, and a woman with a scar on her cheek
watched, shouting encouragement. Whalers had
been known to spend their entire season's pay here
in one night, and count it well worthwhile.

Bregetta opened the door. Sawdust on the floor,
rough forms and tables, the stink of rum and worse.
An evil-looking woman pushed her way through
the customers and asked Bregetta what she wanted.
Her eyes were sly in her pale face. But she took the
message without any surprise, pocketed the coin
Bregetta slipped her, and promised to pass it on.

Bregetta could do no more than she had already done. She turned down a steep little lane for home.

Molly looked up at her entry. 'No change?' asked Bregetta.

The other woman shook her head, her untidy hair falling down about her plump face. 'Worse, if anything, but quieter. She's slipping away. Did you see Madeleine?'

'Yes. She said I was welcome to stay there, when...if...'

Molly patted her arm. 'That's best, then,' she said. Bregetta did not have the heart to tell her she had refused Madeleine's offer. Molly seemed so relieved to have that worry off her shoulders. Instead she went to sit by her mother, holding the worn yellowed hand. Her mother would have thought nothing of taking up life in the Rocks, and yet Bregetta was made of different stuff. Her mother knew it too—why else would she warn off Sergeant Duncan? Or perhaps she just thought him not good enough for Bregetta, and that her daughter's beauty was more deserving of a man with money—like Francis Warrender.

The darkness drew in, and Bregetta dozed. Madeleine's brandy warmed her throat, and she managed to get her mother to take a few drops. The old woman was sinking fast now, and it was only a matter of hours. Her hands' restless dance had long ago ceased, and she lay still and quiet, hardly breathing. At the end, Molly was there, and they sat by the fire, thinking of the past. Teddy went for the doctor.

Then there was the funeral, and that mournful burial place south of Sydney called the Sandhills, where the dead lay in windswept silence. It all seemed a dream, and Bregetta felt as if she would never wake up. Molly fussed over her and made her eat, but she felt no hunger, nothing but a sort of dazed acceptance of the situation. The cottage was so quiet now, without her mother's complaining voice. It would take time to understand that she was gone.

'A girl on her own.' It was two days later, and Molly's voice broke in on her thoughts. 'You know it's too dangerous, Bregetta. What about Madeleine? Didn't you say...?'

Bregetta looked at her. 'With Will forever niggling at me? He'd have me scrubbing the floors and washing the dishes. I'll find something. Don't worry.'

Molly shook her head. She felt she must begin to talk to the girl about the future. Bregetta must begin to plan what she would do with the rest of her life. 'You'll have to come to us,' she said firmly. 'We'll fit you in somewhere. It's the only way.'

'No. please. I must think. Molly, please...'

Molly sighed, and patted her hand. 'I know you're tired, my dear. I know. It's just that you worry me so. Will will be expecting you back at work. You must...'

She went on and on. Bregetta knew she was trying to help, but wished she would stop. She didn't really know why she couldn't seem to make any decisions, and why she sat here as if waiting. What was she waiting for?

Outside a dog barked. Bregetta twisted her fingers. It was plain, as Molly said, that she must find somewhere else to live. It was true that her job at Will's tavern did not pay enough for her to move to Darlinghurst, with all its mansions, but surely there were better lodgings than this to be found? And another job, a better job?

Her fingers stilled their twisting. How many other women, and men, were looking for better jobs? Or any jobs, for that matter? Every week another emigrant-ship arrived, offloading its human cargo, and every week more people were disillusioned and destitute. What hope had she where they had failed?

'Bregetta?'

With a sigh she looked up at Molly, and opened her mouth to tell her she was right—she would move into Molly's house and do exactly as Molly said. The knock on the door came before she could speak, and was so loud that she started. Molly clicked her tongue in annoyance and went to open it. Beyond her friend's short, plump form Bregetta saw a red coat and dark hair. Him.

The black eyes flickered about the room and came back to rest on Bregetta.

'Sergeant Duncan,' Molly said sharply, 'what do you want here? This is a house of mourning.'

He didn't even glance at her; his eyes were still fixed on Bregetta. 'I'm sorry,' he said. 'I've been out to Parramatta for a few days, on military business. When did she die?'

Bregetta looked at her hands, folded tightly in her lap, and told him. Molly's eyes flickered from one to the other. There was an atmosphere here she did not understand. The girl's faintly flushed cheeks, the man's serious dark glance...Teddy had told her about that night at the tavern, but she had dismissed it as a young girl trying out her feminine wiles. Now, suddenly, she was uneasy.

'May I speak to Miss Smith alone?' he asked.

Molly hesitated, waiting for Bregetta to tell him to leave. But she said nothing. 'I'll be back in a moment,' Molly said at last, grudgingly brushing past him. She crossed the narrow lane and went into her own house, leaving her door pointedly ajar.

After a moment Sergeant Duncan came in and closed the door behind him. 'I would have come much sooner,' he told her, 'but, as I said, I had to go away. What will you do?'

Bregetta took a breath and said, 'I can stay with Madeleine, or I can stay with Molly. Or I can stay here.'

She felt his frown like a tangible thing. 'You can't stay here.'

'Why not?' and she met his look with lifted chin, as though daring him. 'Better than being a burden on Molly, or putting up with Will Tanner. I thought I might find another job. One that pays more money.'

'I came to offer you my help,' he said. Then he met the uncertain look in her eyes, and a faint flush coloured his lean brown cheeks. 'Not in the way you're thinking,' he retorted. 'I have some lodgings in a house in Kent Street. There's a spare room there; you could have it. And I could find you a job. I know people. They'd take my word that you were . . . respectable.'

Bregetta knew suddenly that it was this for which she had been waiting. Somehow she had known that he would come. The fuzziness of the dream in which she had been living for the past few days began to dispel.

His hand rested on her head, and she felt his fingers gently stroking the auburn tresses. 'It's not much,' he went on, 'but at least you'd be out of

this sewer.' His fingers paused, and suddenly he
dropped to his haunches beside her chair, his eyes
level with hers. He gazed at her in a sort of wonder.
'The only women I've ever known are either whores
or soldiers' wives, and they're more often than not
whores as well. But you...you...' And he shook
his head.

Her hand stole out to smooth his cheek. He
caught it, and, as if it was a game he'd won, kissed
her mouth. His lips were rough, bruising her own,
as though he wanted to memorise the touch of her.
He took a lock of her hair, where it lay on her
shoulder, and pressed it to his cheek. She watched
him with that same wonder.

'I'd have to tell Molly where I'm going,' she
whispered. 'And I'll have to stay on at Will's until
they find someone else.'

He smiled faintly. 'Aye, I understand all of that.
I'll come for you, later this afternoon. Have you
much furniture?' And he looked about in distaste
at the tumbledown room.

'No,' she said, and blushed.

'I'll bring a cart,' he said. Then, standing up,
'There's a woman who keeps house for me. Bates
is her name. Mrs Bates. She looks after the place,
me being a bachelor and she a widow. She's clean
enough and kind enough when it suits her.'

Bregetta felt her stomach sink, but managed not
to show her dismay. She nodded her head. 'It's not
my business if you and she are...I mean if you
have been her...' Embarrassed, she trailed off.

His laugh brought her head up, and he grinned
at her almost like a lad. 'We've not been lovers, if

that's what you mean. She's fifty or more. I've spent time with women, but it meant little. There's no one special in my life, Bregetta.'

He thought her a fool. Bregetta felt the colour run into her face. 'It is nothing to do with me,' she told him sharply.

His hand went out as if to touch her again, but he dropped it to his side. 'I'll be back later,' was all he said, and went out. Bregetta hurried to the door and watched him pick his way down the lane, through the refuse, and the people and dogs. A young boy said something to him, and he lifted his hand and pretended to cuff the child, ruffling his hair. Bregetta saw that he was laughing. It seemed a good omen.

Across the lane, Molly came out of her house and hurried over to Bregetta. She had obviously been watching for him to leave. 'What did he want?' she asked sharply.

Bregetta looked into the kindly worried face, and didn't know how to begin. 'Molly, don't be angry.'

Molly frowned. 'How can I be angry if you won't tell me what he said?'

'He's offered me a room. No, nothing else! And work, better work than Will's tavern. He knows people, respectable people, Molly! And I've agreed.'

For a moment she thought Molly was going to explode. 'Bregetta, you must not! Do you know what you're saying?'

'It's the best thing,' Bregetta replied stiffly, but her colour had risen. 'I'll have a room, which I will pay for, and when I find a better job I can move elsewhere. He has a housekeeper, Molly! An old woman—a respectable woman. It's only for a little while.' And, as Molly tried to interrupt, 'You said yourself that he was honest.'

Molly was wringing her hands now. 'He's still a man! You don't know anything about him. You hardly know him!'

'I feel as if I do,' Bregetta replied softly. 'I feel as if I've known him all my life.'

Molly looked at her, dismay drawing down the folds of her plump face, as if suddenly realising what she was fighting.

'I'm seventeen, Molly,' Bregetta went on, gently and implacably. 'I'm a grown woman. You know that girls far younger than I——'

'I know, I know,' impatiently. 'I was married myself at sixteen. But you're different, Bregetta. There's never been anyone serious before...'

Bregetta smiled in a dreamy way. 'No.'

Molly groaned with frustration. The girl seemed to have removed herself to a place where she could not reach her. 'When are you supposed to be leaving?' she demanded.

'This afternoon. He said he'd bring a cart for my things.'

'Oh, Bregetta, can't you wait until Teddy comes home? Perhaps he can talk some sense into you!'

Bregetta shook her head. 'Teddy won't change my mind. I'm going with him. It's for the best.'

For a time Molly continued to argue. And then she looked at Bregetta's face and suddenly all the fight left her. The girl wasn't even listening. 'You're as stubborn as your mother,' she said sadly.

Bregetta felt her eyes fill with tears, as if realising that this was the end of an era. 'I'll be back, Molly. This isn't goodbye!'

Molly hugged her. 'Take care, my dear,' she said. 'Do, do take care!'

CHAPTER FOUR

THE cart came rumbling. Bregetta heard it bumping and jolting before she saw it, and peered out of the door. It was a hand-held cart, like a large wheelbarrow—no horse-drawn vehicle could get through this narrow lane, which in parts was bare rock with rough steps cut into it. But the soldier who pushed it was not Sergeant Duncan.

Bregetta recognised one of the men who had come with him that first day. The soldier eyed her slyly but ducked his head at her politely enough—perhaps he had been threatened with dire consequences if he was rude. The people watched curiously from their doorways and windows. A baby bawled, a dog barked, a man laughed. Life would go on, with or without Bregetta.

There was little enough to put into the cart. She had given some things to Molly, and some others to her needy neighbours. It took only a matter of moments to strip the cottage bare. When Bregetta had finished she stood in the doorway, looking into the cold damp room which had been her home. She felt no sadness. There were memories here, but they were mostly unpleasant. She would not be sorry to be going. It was the end of one life, the beginning of a better one. She must tell herself that.

The soldier waited until Bregetta was ready, and they walked slowly down the lane with the laden cart. Some of the curious faces grinned and wished her luck; others turned away with envy, or disgust. She didn't care. She was escaping.

The soldier glanced across at her but didn't speak. There was a certain admiration in the way he noted her proudly raised chin and shining eyes. They turned out into a wider street, narrowly avoiding a water-cart.

'What's your name?' she asked at last. She felt a certain companionship with him as they walked slowly along.

'Eber, miss. Private Ebenezer Yates.'

'Where is your sergeant, Eber?'

The soldier's eyes were blue, and when he smiled he looked barely as old as herself. 'He had to go on duty,' he said. 'Said to tell you he'd be back before you leave tonight. He gave me this for you,' and he searched into his jacket and brought out a carefully wrapped parcel of brown paper.

Bregetta took it curiously and opened it with trembling fingers. It was a ribbon, the colour of the ocean at night—dark, dark blue. She smiled. It was a trifle, and yet...it made her feel very happy. As if it was a sign that she had done the right thing.

The boy, Eber, was staring stolidly ahead, but she was sure he had seen the present, and the smile.

Kent Street was mostly dilapidated, though some good houses stood towards the corner of King Street. The ordinary soldiers lived here, behind the barracks which ran through from George Street to York Street. Bregetta knew that most of them lived in brawling poverty, but it was better than the place she had just left.

They stopped in front of one of the good houses, a neat, narrow two-storey house, almost grand in comparison to what they had just passed. Bregetta looked up at the place, thinking how sober it looked, and saw a curtain at one of the windows twitch. Mrs Bates was watching. She took a deep breath, and turned down the short path to the front door.

It took time for her knock to be answered, and Bregetta knew that Mrs Bates was probably letting her wait on purpose. At last it opened slowly, and pale eyes looked out at her. 'Yes?'

Mrs Bates was short, with a dimpled face and blue eyes. She looked younger than her fifty years, though her skin was losing its firmness at jaw and throat. There was something forbidding in her expression, and suspicion narrowed her eyes.

Bregetta swallowed down her fears and forced a friendly smile. 'Sergeant Duncan has let me have one of his rooms, Mrs Bates. He told you about it, I'm sure. Just until I find something else, you understand?'

The blue eyes surveyed Bregetta a moment more, and then she opened the door wider with a jerky movement. 'He did tell me,' she said, and her voice was sharp with disbelief. 'You'd better come in,' she added at last. Bregetta went through into the cool, musty interior.

The room was upstairs, at the back, overlooking the yard and the washing-line. Other yards were all about, with their own washing-lines and their own small gardens. The room itself was small enough, but clean, it didn't smell of damp or mildew, and there were no gaps in the walls or holes in the ceiling. There was a bed, a hard, narrow thing, but better than what she had been used to. She turned to Mrs Bates impulsively.

'Oh, it's lovely. Thank you so much.'

Mrs Bates was taken aback, and regarded her a moment in amazement. And then she smiled, a reluctant half-smile, as though in the face of Bregetta's warmth and openness she could not help herself. Eber cleared his throat behind them, and brushed past with his arms full of Bregetta's possessions. Mrs Bates eyed them with amazement. Bregetta could almost hear her thoughts—Who is this slum girl? Why has he brought her here to my house? But all she said aloud was, 'There's a meal to be cooking,' and went back down the stairs.

After a moment Eber returned with another load of her things. She thanked him for his help and, when he had gone, began to sort out her belongings. When that was done she shook out the green gown and pulled it on. Her hair was tangled, and she spent a long time brushing the long shining tresses until they fell about her shoulders in a burning cloak. Outside, the evening was drawing in fast. It was chill, and without any wind to blow away the damp, clinging mist from the harbour. She thought of Jim and was ashamed that she had not thought of him earlier. Where was he now? Perhaps Madeleine had already seen him and given him the money which would take him to safety. It was his only hope. Bregetta shuddered. She had seen men hanging on the old gallows. It had been a pitiful sight. Oh, not Jim, not Jim——

The scrape of a boot outside on the landing brought her head around, her hair floating about her, and the sergeant was there in his white breeches and white shirt. He knocked on the half-closed door and stepped in, noticing her belongings put about. It was an unimpressive collection, but he smiled. The dark eyes ran over her in a way that was

possessive. Bregetta felt herself shiver, as though
he had physically touched her.

'Mrs Bates says dinner is ready,' he said softly.
'You'll eat before you go.'

It was not a question.

'Yes, of course.'

'I'll walk to Will Tanner's with you tonight.'

'I can manage.'

'Nevertheless,' and his voice was harsh. 'Are you
ready to eat?'

'Yes.'

'Come on, then.' He held the door wide, and
Bregetta brushed by him. He smelt clean, as though
he had been at pains to wash before he came to see
her. She went before him down the narrow creaking
stairs. Mrs Bates looked up from the bottom of the
staircase, and her blue eyes were cool, at variance
with her smiling mouth.

'Sergeant Duncan,' she said, and her voice
betrayed her fondness. 'Your favourite tonight. Beef
stew and dumplings, just as you like them.'

'You're a wonder, Bessy,' he said, and Bregetta
knew he was smiling as he stood behind her. They
went into the kitchen. The table was scrubbed and
clean, and the stew smelled good. Mrs Bates bustled
about, dishing it out—'An extra-large helping for
you, Alistair'—and handing them their plates.
Bregetta took a spoonful and forced herself to
smile.

'Delicious,' she said. 'You're a good cook, Mrs
Bates.'

The other woman gave her a complacent look.
'I may be a widow, Miss Smith, but I still know
how to see to a man's comfort. You'd be surprised

how many women there are who can't cook or keep a house in Sydney Town.'

Bregetta looked down at her plate again and felt anger knot in her stomach at the inference. 'I kept house for my mother for five years,' she replied softly. 'Ever since she fell ill.'

Mrs Bates must have eaten earlier, for she had no plate in front of her. 'Sergeant Duncan tells me you're respectable,' she said at last, and her blue eyes were pinned on Bregetta. Alistair made a movement, but she waved her hand at him. 'No, I'll have my say. If a man goes and brings a strange girl into his house he should expect his housekeeper to have something to say! I don't know anything about you, Miss Smith. You could be a trollop for all I know, and most likely are. But I'll not have any goings on in this house; do you understand what I'm saying? Well, if you behave yourself we'll get along fine. But if you abuse Sergeant Duncan's kindness to you then I'll make your life a misery.'

'Bessy!' Alistair Duncan looked surprised and angry.

'There, I've had my say,' the older woman said, and stood up from the table. 'Goodnight to you both.' And she stalked out into the hall and up the stairs. They heard her door close behind her, and then the silence.

Bregetta put down her spoon. She was no longer hungry. After a moment he put his hand over hers, and she looked up into his dark eyes. They were apologetic. 'I'm sorry,' he said. 'I didn't know she was going to say that. She doesn't know you yet. When she does she'll see she's mistaken the matter entirely.'

Bregetta shrugged. 'What can you expect? You bring a woman from the slums into your home. She thinks I'm out for all I can get. She sees me as an enemy you must be protected from.'

His hand tightened. 'She has no claim on me.'

Bregetta removed her own hand. 'Neither do I.' She stood up. 'I'd best be going if I'm not to make Will angry too.'

He rose. 'I'll walk with you.'

'There's no need.'

'I said I will walk with you.'

She closed her mouth and went out into the dusk. Birds were calling, going to their rest. The tattoo of drums and fifes was sounding, calling the convicts back to their barracks for the night. About them the clatter of humanity went on. A woman screeched from a house down the street, and some soldiers were hurrying to their duty. A horse pounded past them, the gentleman astride it singing at the top of his voice. Bregetta laughed and breathed deeply of the chill air. Her green skirts swished about her legs in a way which pleased her. They brushed against Alistair Duncan's white breeches and polished black boots. Her arm brushed his arm. She felt happy, walking with the tall man beside her, trying to match her dainty strides to his longer ones. Some passing soldiers shouted greetings, and he answered them. They seemed to like him. Bregetta looked at him sideways, under her lashes.

But he caught the look and smiled. 'I'm sorry about Bessy,' he said again. 'I'll tell her to go.'

Bregetta shook her head. 'Not on my account. She had more right to be there than I. We'll get on well enough together until I go.'

His eyebrows lifted. 'Where are you going?'

'I can't stay with you forever. It's not right, is it?'

He laughed at her, and then louder when she turned away from him with a flushed, indignant face. 'You worry about things not being "right",' he demanded, 'when everyone already thinks you're my woman?'

'But I'm not,' she said stiffly. 'And I've seen too many others used and then tossed aside to let it happen to me.'

He was silent for a long time. They reached the tavern, but, as she went to go inside, he held her arm. 'Tell me, Bregetta; what did it mean to you? When I kissed you and held you, and when you kissed me back? A child's game of some sort? I'm not a child—I've got ten years and more on you, you know. And I'm not one for games; I'm a serious sort of man.'

His dark eyes were hot and angry, but there was a question in them he needed to have answered. 'You don't understand,' she said quietly. 'I've seen what can happen to women. Madeleine offered me Francis Warrender, and if I'd wanted to be somebody's trollop, as your Mrs Bates puts it, I could have been his. I want more out of life, Sergeant Duncan.'

He laughed abruptly. 'You're too complicated for me,' he said harshly. 'I only know that I want you, whatever the cost and however long I have to wait.'

Bregetta said nothing, only pushing by him and into the warm, lively atmosphere of the taproom. He did not follow her, and she didn't know whether to be relieved or not. Will greeted her with a grunt and set her to work as if she had never been away.

The customers smiled as though they had missed her. Bregetta was glad to have something to keep her mind occupied.

It was late when Madeleine came down, and the place was nearly empty. Will was talking near the door, and there was no one to disturb them when Bregetta told her where she was now living.

'What did I tell you?' she mocked. 'Didn't I warn you what he was about?'

'It's not like that. He's being kind and ... he's a lonely man, I think.'

'He's a sly one, all right!'

'What do you mean?'

'Why, only that he was around here this afternoon, shouting drinks for all and sundry and pleased as pie. As if he'd won a wager with himself, or someone else.'

Bregetta shrugged, puzzled. 'Perhaps he had.' Was that where he had been when Eber had come to collect her? Drinking with his friends? Celebrating? She shied away from the thought that the cause of the celebration might have been her.

'I told you,' Madeleine was saying. 'I told you what he was about. Why didn't you come and stay with me?'

Bregetta shook her head and said nothing.

Madeleine smiled. 'I've heard nothing from your brother.'

'I'm sure he'll contact you when——'

Madeleine's warning look stopped her. Will was returning. They didn't have a chance to speak again. The sergeant came into the taproom shortly before closing. He sat down at a table near the door and folded his arms.

Will stared across at him, then transferred his look to Bregetta. 'A new protector?' he asked.

'He's a friend,' she said at last, trying to keep her tone cool.

Will snorted his laughter. 'Well, you and your friend can leave. I'm closing.'

Bregetta took off her apron, and came out from behind the bar. Sergeant Duncan stood up and opened the door for her. His smile was secretive.

Outside the chill air took away her breath. Bregetta wrapped her shawl about her shoulders, shivering. She felt dizzy from weariness, and was grateful when he took her arm firmly in his.

'You didn't have to walk me back,' she said at last.

'I wanted to.'

A group of drunken sealers reeled by, a woman in their midst. Alistair frowned at them but said nothing. They walked up into the narrow street, avoiding the black danger of the back alleys where thieves and murderers waylaid the unwary. Dogs were barking, and one of Sydney's ubiquitous goats clambered up a rocky outcrop.

The sky was clear, and the moon hung full and ripe in the darkness. Kent Street was already familiar, with its ramshackle cluster of cottages and rowdy occupants. The narrow house was dark and quiet, and inside lingered the smell of Mrs Bates' stew.

'Do you want some tea?' he asked her.

'Thank you.'

He had left a light in the kitchen, and the room was cosy with the glow from the lamp. The kettle was soon boiled over the heat of the embers. Bregetta sat at the table, letting weary contentment seep through her bones. The mug was hot against her palms, and she sipped the strong liquid eagerly.

He sat down opposite her, in the shadows, and his black eyes watched her. Self-conscious suddenly, she smiled. 'I never thanked you for your present.'

He shrugged. 'It was a mere trifle.'

But it had been more than that to her. It had bolstered her courage when it was flagging, and reinforced her belief that she was doing the right thing by coming here to his house.

'I know nothing about you,' she said suddenly, remembering Molly's words.

'As much as I know about you,' he retorted in his warm, deep voice.

'But you know much more of me! You've seen what my life is ... was, and you know about Jim.'

He leaned forward a little, into the lamplight. 'There's not much to tell,' he said after a moment, almost grudgingly. 'I joined the army when I was fifteen. I was a big, strong lad and looked older, and no one asked any questions. I already felt a man. I had kept my mother and sisters until then, and only left because my sister's husband took over the care of them. There was nothing for me in our village—no work but hiring myself out to the big farms, no prospects for anything better in the future. I could have gone south to the big towns and looked there, but I couldn't bear the thought of living in one of those dirty, crowded places. Perhaps I'd have had no choice if I'd stayed. Anyway, it didn't come to that. In October I was at the hiring fair, the Lowrin Fair it was, and there was a recruiting sergeant there. And I joined up. I've been a soldier for sixteen years now, and rarely regretted it.'

His life had been very different from hers. Bregetta thought of how he must have been at fifteen. Tall and dark-haired, already serious with the weight of so many responsibilities on his shoulders. And then, as a soldier, the experience of the years reinforcing that maturity. She wondered of the things he had not told her—the sadness of leaving home at fifteen, the gruelling life of a soldier, the hardships that had shaped him into what he was. She thought he was not a great one for confidences; he kept his feelings to himself. What had Madeleine said? He was 'not much of a ladies' man'. And yet there must have been women along the way... 'I've spent time with women,' he had said. Bregetta was surprised at the strength of the bolt of jealousy that struck her. She realised she could hardly bear to imagine him with another woman... kissing her mouth, holding her in his arms.

'What were you doing in Bathurst,' she asked him abruptly, to change the subject in her mind, 'before you came to Sydney?'

'I was in charge of one of the road-gangs there,' he said, and grimaced. 'Not the sort of work I like.' He spoke a little more, about Bathurst and its peculiarities. But Bregetta was suddenly tired, and she found her eyes starting to close. He laughed. 'You see?' he mocked. 'I've bored you to sleep. Go to bed. I'll see you in the morning.'

Upstairs, Bregetta lay down on the hard narrow bed, and was instantly asleep.

The next morning, when Bregetta came down, Mrs Bates offered her a half-nod before bustling about her business. It seemed, as she had said, that if Bregetta behaved she would tolerate her presence.

Alistair Duncan had already gone to the barracks. Bregetta made herself some breakfast. Her offer of help refused by Mrs Bates, she went out into a wintry Sydney morning. She had a few shillings left, and had already decided what she would spend them on. She found some cloth, rough to the touch but dark blue in colour. It was a close match to the ribbon he had given her.

Bregetta was a fair needlewoman, and when she got back to Kent Street she set about cutting out the cloth and making up a new gown. She hardly paused for lunch, and was still working when the evening came. She heard the door to the street bang, and his boots on the stairs—already she knew their sound. He knocked on her door, and opened it.

Bregetta smiled up at him from the stool, the half-finished garment spread about her. If he recognised the colour he didn't say so, only lifted his eyebrows with a, 'Good evening, Bregetta.' But the expression in his eyes belied the polite coolness of his voice. He looked at her as if the thought of her had carried him all the way home.

After a moment he went to the window and looked out. 'When you've had something to eat I'll walk with you to Will Tanner's,' he said. 'Has Bessy been——?'

'She's been fine.' Bregetta interrupted and, setting aside her work, stood up. He was watching her, dark against the fading light from the window.

'You sew,' he said.

'Yes. My father was a tailor before he bought his draper's shop.'

'I know.'

Her turn to raise her eyebrows.

'Your brother has some papers,' he told her, and his eyes flickered from hers. 'I've read them.'

Bregetta sighed. 'If my brother has done evil it's because he's been led into it. He was always my mother's darling. The more outrageous he became, the more she laughed. He didn't mean to hurt anyone; he——'

'Don't!'

It was said so harshly that Bregetta stared at him. He raked his fingers through his dark hair. 'Don't ask me,' he went on more quietly. 'I do my duty, Bregetta. I see you and that duty as two separate things.'

Bregetta put out her hand and touched his sleeve. 'I know that.' What did he think she meant to do? Trade herself for her brother's freedom?

His hand covered hers, and suddenly she was in his arms. His mouth was warm and caressing, and she thought again of sunlight through leaves. Bregetta's flesh tingled. It had never done so before. She remembered the inept fumblings of the few boys who had kissed her and tried to go further. Then she had been repelled or amused. But this was different. Now she was caught up in that desire herself, and understood a little of their desperation as she strained closer. He ran his hands through her hair, pressing his lips to the heavy silk of it, and his breath quickened.

'Ah, Bregetta, Bregetta,' he groaned.

The sound of a step at the door startled them. They spun about. Mrs Bates's closed, angry face seemed to hang suspended in the gloomy light of the landing. But, 'Your supper's getting cold,' was all she said, and she marched back down the stairs.

Bregetta looked at him in dismay, but Alistair was trying not to laugh. 'Come on,' he said, taking her arm, 'or you'll be late again.'

She *was* late again, and Will was none too pleased. Madeleine was upstairs entertaining some of Will's business friends, and Bregetta did not see her to ask of Jim. She did not dare ask Will. He had never liked Jim, she knew, and suspected it was because he and Madeleine had once been close. Will was jealous of the younger man. When the tavern closed Alistair Duncan was not there to see her home, but he sent Eber, the young soldier who had helped her move her belongings.

'He had to go to the barracks,' the boy told her in answer to her question.

'Oh,' and she bit back a sigh.

'Sergeant Duncan is a good soldier,' Eber added, as though her sigh had been a criticism of his character. 'Even the troublemakers respect him.'

Bregetta smiled, and now Eber was encouraged to go on. 'Some sergeants are always threatening their men with the lash if they disobey orders. It's nothing to get a dozen lashes for insolence. But Sergeant Duncan talks sense, and usually we listen. Though he can fight, too. I've seen him take a knife off a corporal who'd already ripped one man's belly, without getting a scratch.'

Bregetta liked listening to this young soldier's voice, and she liked the things he was saying. She was sorry when they reached Kent Street and she had to say goodbye. She was not so tired tonight, and took out her sewing and did some work on it. Alistair came home an hour or so later. Bregetta heard his footsteps coming up the stairs. They paused outside her door—she supposed he saw the light. She waited, her heart thumping, but after a moment he moved on. She didn't know whether to be sorry or relieved.

One of the soldiers' wives called on her the next day.

'I'm Mrs O'Leary,' she introduced herself, dark eyes curious. 'Corporal O'Leary's missus. We live down there,' she said with a vague gesture down the street. She shifted the baby on her hip. 'Young Ebenezer lives with us. He told us about you.'

Bregetta didn't quite know what to say, but the woman went on as if she didn't expect any reply.

'Your sergeant doesn't mix much with us.' And she slanted a long look at Bregetta. 'I've asked him time and time again to come down for a drink or something to eat, but he won't. Not the sort, I suppose. Pity, he's a fine figure of a man, your sergeant.'

Her smile was more of a smirk, and Bregetta wondered, before she could stop the thought, whether it was really Corporal O'Leary's baby she held on her hip. Her next words confirmed Bregetta's opinion of her.

'Lots of girls have been giving him looks, you know. But he doesn't look back. I was looking at him meself. Not that I'd steal another woman's man. As long as he's yours I'll respect that. He is yours, isn't he?'

Bregetta lifted her chin. 'Yes, he is.'

Mrs O'Leary smiled her sly smile, and then her eyes went past Bregetta. 'Mrs Bates!' she called in a voice the girl thought was friendly. Then, in an under-voice that only Bregetta could hear, 'Old bat. Guards this place like a bloody gaol.' And she was gone, back down the street from whence she'd come.

Mrs Bates made a sound in her throat. Bregetta turned to look at her, and thought she looked like a little bird, feathers all ruffled. 'That woman,' she said. 'A slut. She's been trying to get in here ever since Sergeant Duncan came. But she won't get past me!'

Bregetta's smile peeped out despite itself. 'She seemed to be trying to find out whether or not he and I were...' She paused delicately.

Mrs Bates eyed her narrowly. 'And I don't suppose you denied it? Well, it's only what I expected.' Suddenly she sighed, and the ruffled feathers settled back into place. 'I can see he's fond of you, Miss Smith. I've never known him to be so rash. He's never brought a woman back here before.'

'I'm fond of him, too,' Bregetta managed.

Mrs Bates gave her another long, piercing look, and then turned away. Bregetta went upstairs and allowed herself a big, wide smile.

Alistair was amused that evening when she told him. She had finished the blue dress, and wore it with his ribbon in her hair. The colour suited her milky skin and auburn hair. His eyes told her he thought her lovely, their dark warmth caressing her like the touch of his hand.

'I don't know how Will can keep his customers away from you,' he said sharply.

Bregetta smiled and unconsciously swayed a little towards him. 'They're usually very polite,' she whispered.

'The sooner you're out of there, the better,' he retorted. His hands closed on her trim waist and held her away from him. Bregetta looked puzzled. 'You know I want you,' he said harshly. 'Do you know what that means?'

Bregetta smiled gently. 'Of course I know.'

'I think about you all the time.' The confession seemed forced out of him. His hands tightened. 'I don't think you *do* understand,' he went on, more softly. 'That's why I'm trying to go slowly.' He let her go, and took a deep breath. 'Do you know what it does to me when you come close like that? And touch my arm? And when your voice goes low and husky? Bregetta, do you know how I feel?'

Yes, she thought. Because I feel like that too. As though she were walking five inches off the ground every time he came near her. Even the sound of his voice, his step on the stairs, could make her heart start to pound.

But he was going to the door. 'Come and eat,' he said, 'before I do something I'll regret.'

Later, they walked in silence to the tavern. She felt his need of her, and his iron control. He had told her he wanted her, but he would wait until she was ready too.

Madeleine sought her out at the tavern, and, when Will went below into the cellar for a keg of rum, leaned closer to whisper, 'I've seen Jim. He's gone. It wasn't so difficult, after all, to get him a place on the ship. I just greased a few palms. He'll be safe, for a time.'

'How did you see him, without Will——?'

'I slipped out. Down to the docks. I know my way about, Bregetta.' She turned away then, and her mouth was sad. 'He was the same. Sometimes I almost wish——'

'Hush!' Bregetta heard Will. The two girls exchanged a look, and then Madeleine was laughing.

'Remember what I told you,' she said, and tapped her arm. 'Take care with that soldier. He's not for you. You can do better.'

She was gone. Will glared at Bregetta and set the keg down, wiping his face with a handkerchief. She wondered if he'd overheard their talk, but all he said was, 'You'd best be going. I'll close up now.' He handed her a few coins, and she pocketed them with a nod of her head. Will cleared his throat. 'I've a mind to start another girl,' he said, and his voice was stilted. 'She was in yesterday, asking about work. She's been in the job before. At the Hero of Waterloo. I've heard she's quick, and she's reliable, which is more than can be said for some. You've been late every night this week.'

Bregetta looked at him angrily. She knew he was waiting. Waiting for her to beg for her job. He knew she was as capable and reliable as anyone, and he paid her a pittance. But anger made her unwise, and she said, 'Perhaps you should start her, then, Will Tanner. If you think she's so much better than me.'

His own anger surfaced and he shouted, 'Maybe I will!'

'Does Madeleine know what you're up to?' something made her add.

Will looked shifty. 'It's me that runs this place, not Maddy. And you keep your lying tongue away from my wife! I know what you're up to. Always goin' on about your bloody brother, tryin' to make me look small! I don't want you coming around here no more with your lies.'

So that was it! Bregetta turned her back and began to walk away. Her legs felt shaky. She had seen the hatred and resentment clear in his face, and it frightened her. But he followed, still shouting. 'You're like your mother, you are, girl! Just like her! A lying slut through and through!'

'Don't you dare speak to me so, Will Tanner!' she cried, rounding on him. 'You talk as if you were lily-pure yourself, when we all know how you've lied and cheated and bribed your way into the money. There are people who'd love to get a look at your books, Will Tanner. And I've a good mind to let them know what they say, that I have!'

He caught her arm and shook her like a rat. 'You bitch!' he spat. 'I've never liked you and your sly ways. I've told Maddy again and again that you was just livin' off us. Well you've had it now. You can get out and never come back, and, if you so much as breathe a word to anyone about my doings, I'll have you pickled in one of me barrels, down there in the cellar, and nobody will ever know.'

Bregetta tried to pull free from him, but his grip was too strong, his fingers digging into the soft flesh of her arm. His eyes were bulging with fury and resentment. He looked as if he meant what he said about killing her. She knew he was capable of it, to protect himself if not for revenge.

'I'm not afraid of you,' she breathed, but was.

He shook her again, and then flung her towards the door. She hit the jamb, bruising her shoulder, and slid to the floor, gasping with the pain of it. He started after her again, but as he did so the door beside her opened, and he froze.

'What the bloody hell is going on?' asked a cold, harsh voice.

Will Tanner's flushed face turned white, then red again. 'She's leavin',' he said, 'and so are you. Get out, lobster. I don't have to serve you.'

Alistair looked down at Bregetta's face, and the anger seemed to flare in him like tinder. He turned on Will Tanner and in two strides had him by the shirt-front. 'I asked you what was going on,' he said. Will was short, but he was broad and stocky. He struck out at the other man, catching him a blow to the cheek. Bregetta cried out, struggling to her feet. Will swung again, but the sergeant stepped back and his own fist came up under Will's chin and sent him crashing to the floor.

Blood spurted from his mouth, and he tried to rise, then fell back again with a groan. Sergeant Duncan stood over him, waiting, but when Will didn't move again he stepped away, his own hand going to his cheek.

Footsteps pounded down the stairs, and then Madeleine appeared, her blonde hair loose, pulling a wrap hastily about her nightgown. Her eyes were everywhere, and she seemed to understand what had happened without needing to ask. Slowly she came to where Will lay, and bent down to him, grimacing at the blood.

'I've sacked that trollop,' he said angrily, 'and nothin' you can say will make me change me mind. After what she said . . .'

Madeleine looked at Bregetta. This will change nothing between us, her eyes said. Then she looked away. 'Best go,' she murmured. 'Go now, before the police come and we're all in trouble.'

Bregetta would have spoken, but Alistair grasped her arm and pulled her out after him. The night air was cold, but she did not feel it. Nor did she see the vermin—rats and scorpions—in the gutter. He dragged her along the quiet street, and after a moment she began to hurry and stumble at his side.

'I've lost my job,' she said and bit her lip. The tears trickled down her cheeks. 'I've nothing now; nothing.'

His hand tightened roughly on her arm. 'He was paying you a pittance anyway. You'll find better.'

But she shook her head miserably. 'Madeleine was my friend; she was all I had.'

'If she was your friend then she still is, whatever Will Tanner might say about it.'

'How can she be? She has to look to herself, just as I do.'

'And what am I?'

Bregetta didn't answer him. They walked on in silence beneath the clear night sky. She could see all the stars, bright above. The Southern Cross lay on its side, just above the horizon, and there was the Scorpion overhead. Jim had known them all; some sailor had taught them to him. She shivered, thinking of Jim aboard a creaking vessel somewhere out on the dark sea. He would have plenty of time now to study the stars.

They reached Kent Street. Alistair Duncan had a key for the door and it opened silently into the dark house. He went past her, into the kitchen, and lit the lamp. It flared, and the light spilled over into the dim corners and neat shelves. Bregetta stood in the doorway, watching him.

'Will there be trouble,' she said, 'because of the fight?'

He turned and looked at her. 'None of my making.'

She saw now that his cheek was cut where Will
had hit him, and there was blood oozing. Bregetta
made a sound in her throat and came forward.
'You're hurt,' she said. 'I'll have to clean it. You
could catch a disease from Will Tanner; he's like a
mad dog sometimes.'

He smiled despite himself, and watched her
gather water and a bowl. There was no cloth to be
found and after a moment she lifted up her green
skirts and tore a piece off her petticoat. She dabbed
gently at his gash, frowning. She knew he was
watching her, but didn't dare to meet his eyes until
she was done. It was not a bad cut, but there would
be a bruise.

'They'll think you were brawling,' she said lightly,
and met his eyes at last.

Something in their blackness frightened her and
yet excited her. His hand closed about her arm and
he drew her down on to his lap. His mouth hovered
close, teasing, and then fastened on hers in a long,
deep kiss. Her arms slid about his neck, and she
kissed him back with a passion that tingled to the
very soles of her feet.

His breath stirred her hair, his hands sliding down
over her shoulders, and up under her breasts. She
gasped at his boldness, and looked into his eyes.
They shone with something that burned her like
fire. 'Are you my woman?' he asked softly.

Bregetta turned her face away, but he nuzzled at
her cheek, then began kissing her throat where she
arched it back. Passion was heating her blood as
no fire had ever done. She tingled and burned, and
knew he knew it too. His mouth slid down to the
neckline of her gown, and he began to unlace the
bodice, kissing her white flesh as he went. Her

breasts spilled out above the chemise, and he ran his fingers lightly over the warm flesh, then bent to kiss where he had touched. Bregetta caught her breath, and he was reaching up to kiss her lips. Her auburn hair made a cave about them, and he caught it up in his hands, pulling it back from her face.

'I've wanted you since the first time I saw you,' he said. 'I made a promise to myself that I would have you, even then.'

'I know.'

'I will have you, Bregetta.'

'I know.'

He swung her up into his arms, and carried her out of the kitchen and up the creaking stairs. She thought of Mrs Bates, and wondered if that woman was awake, and hoped not. They were already in the little room at the back of the house. The moonlight flooded in, covering the bed, and he lay down with her, his mouth hot and passionate.

Bregetta kissed him back, her fingers fumbling with his buttons, seeking the strong back and shoulders. He took off her gown, his mouth and hands finding her secrets, making her gasp and cry out with the hot wonder of it all. She felt his naked body against hers, pressing her down into the hard mattress. His black eyes were blurred with passion, and his mouth closed hard on hers as he took her.

Afterwards they lay together, still and close, her flesh to his. She fitted to his side exactly, as though they had been carved from the same piece of flesh—after all, Eve had come from Adam's rib. He had wanted her, he said, and now she was his. And yet it seemed right, and she loved him. She admitted it to herself slowly, and with pleasure. She loved him. She loved a red-coated soldier—he was all her world, and wherever he went she would want to be as long as she lived.

His hand stroked her rounded hip, and he bent to kiss her neck, breathing in the scent of her hair. 'Bregetta,' he murmured, 'you're like a flower, fresh and sweet. A bud—a new bud. I was the first.' It was not a question.

'There was never a man like you,' she dared.

He smiled his secret smile, and kissed her shoulder.

She was still, her heart thumping. She waited, hoping, but he said nothing of love. After a moment she half sat up, looking into his eyes. 'I don't mean to be a burden on you or anyone,' she said. 'You told me you'd find me some work.'

He smiled lazily up at her. His dark hair was tousled. He looked more relaxed than she had ever seen him. 'I'll find you work. Don't worry.'

'Don't worry' he said. Bregetta sighed. It made no difference if he loved her or not. She could not change her own heart—she would have had to cut it out. After a moment she stooped down and began to kiss his mouth with a growing wild abandon— as though she had burnt her bridges. He clasped his arms about her, and, laughing, rolled her over on the narrow bed, his strong brown flesh cleaving to hers.

CHAPTER FIVE

THE next morning Alistair was gone. Bregetta went slowly down to breakfast. Mrs Bates carefully avoided her eyes, though her manner was no different. If she didn't know for certain that they were lovers she suspected it. Bregetta was glad to go outside, into the wintry sunshine. She thought of going to see Madeleine, but knew it would be foolish to risk Will. So she wandered about the streets and past the high wall of the York Street Barracks, where she knew *he* would be. But she would not go in and ask for him, for she was not his wife—nothing more than another soldier's woman. The fact would hurt if she were not so happy.

She saw a group of soldiers standing near the gateway. One of them was Ebenezer, and she saw him recognise her. He said something to the others that made them all laugh. It might or may not have been about her, but it felt as if they were mocking her happiness. She hurried away into the anonymity of the crowd along George Street.

When she returned to the house it was afternoon, and Mrs Bates was nowhere to be found. Bregetta was glad, and went to her room. She sat for a long time and looked out of the window. Down in the squalid end of Kent Street they were having another party, or a fight. There was much yelling and screaming going on, and the sound of breaking glass or crockery. A woman ran out into the yard with

her bodice torn and her hair wild about her
shoulders, and a man pursued her and caught her.
They embraced in a wild display of passion, to the
cheers of others from the house, and then he led
her back inside. Bregetta shivered, thinking how
lucky she herself was to love a man who was straight
and honest, not one of the lecherous drunkards who
filled the barracks.

Alistair came at last, closing the door so softly
behind him that she did not hear him until he spoke,
and she spun around, the hair prickling at her nape,
as it always did at the sound of his deep voice.

'I've found you a job,' he said, and smiled as
her eyes widened. 'I helped the owner once with a
problem concerning her son. She owes me a favour.
It's a draper's—I told her your father had been in
the business. You're to go there tomorrow.'

She had been longing for him to come home, but
now that he was here she felt stifled with
embarrassment.

'Thank you,' she said, and looked down at her
hands as she sat on the bed. She remembered how
they had lain here together in the moonlight, and
her colour rose. After a moment he came and stood
before her. His hand went out and his finger stroked
her soft cheek, coming to rest on her lower lip.

'I can think of a better way to say thank you,'
he said.

Bregetta looked up and met his eyes, and was
lost. She would deny him nothing; he was everything to her. She stood up and slid her arms about
him and her mouth found his. His kiss was hard
and demanding, and he began to unpin her long
auburn hair. It fell down over her back, reaching

her hips. He unlaced her gown and slid it off her shoulders.

Bregetta shivered, and held his head fast to her, feeling the desire rush through her like a river after rain, unstoppable. He shrugged off his jacket and shirt, his chest shining brown in the dim light, his muscles rippling with every movement. His body was beautiful, she thought as he came towards her. Strong and beautiful.

'I can't stay away,' he said, and met her eyes almost ruefully. 'I was thinking of you when I should have been thinking of my orders and doing my duty. I can't keep my mind on anything but you.'

His kiss was savage, and his body pressed her back into the mattress. Bregetta welcomed his passion, returning it. The noise of the world outside faded. The words 'I love you' burned Bregetta's tongue, but she did not utter them. They were her secret until the day when he returned this feeling she had for him. And it would be soon, she was sure it would be soon.

His hands slid over her body with a kind of wonder, as though she were a dream he sought to make reality. She had never thought it would be like this when she loved a man. She had thought with distaste of Will and Madeleine, and with disgust of Francis Warrender, but never had she imagined it would be so wonderful, and so right, as though in the entire world there was only Alistair Duncan for Bregetta Smith, and no one else would ever do.

He kissed her creamy breasts, and she trembled. His thigh pressed between hers, and she quivered, her hair tumbling about them. His finger brushed her lips, and he smiled into her eyes. 'I'd like to wake up every morning to you,' he said. 'And come home every night.'

She stretched up to kiss his mouth and, when his body claimed hers, gave herself up to their passion.

As last he sat up and pulled on his shirt. She watched his back as he buttoned it, and wondered what he was thinking. She wondered if this marvellous thing between them would last forever, and if not... But she dared not let her thoughts wander so far, for they chilled her to the bone. So she lay, watching him dress, too happy and drowsy to do more than smile when he turned back to look at her lying naked on the bed, her hair a cloak about her.

'I have to go back to the barracks,' he said with regret. 'Will you be all right?'

'Of course. I have Mrs Bates to take care of me, haven't I?'

The dark eyes narrowed and he grimaced. 'Aye,' he said with a wealth of feeling. 'I'll see you a bit later, then.'

She nodded, and returned his soft kiss. She watched the door close. After a moment she rose, and found the ribbon he had given her. She tied it into her hair, and admired the effect in the glass. Her eyes were soft and heavy with secrets. Now it was not her own face that she saw, but a leaner, browner one, with dark eyes and strong chin and thin smiling lips.

The draper's shop was small but tidy, and there always seemed to be customers. Bregetta was quick and light on her feet, and a definite asset to the place. The owner, Mrs Muldoon, was a tall, stern

woman, with a grave way of speaking. She watched
Bregetta like a hawk, and, if she even for a moment
paused in her work, came swooping down, ordering
her to do that and do this. Bregetta felt as if she
were running all day long. But it paid double what
Will had given her, and it was pleasing work.

She had vaguely remembered her father's shop,
but she had forgotten the feel of good cloth: taffetas
and silks and crêpe de Chines, the soft brush of
velvet and the crispness of lace. To touch such
things gave her an almost sensual pleasure. She had
another gown to wear, of soft grey wool, worn over
a stiffened petticoat. And she was always neat and
tidy, with her hair pinned up sleekly off her long
neck, and her white collar crisply starched. 'Like
a little Quaker,' Alistair would whisper to her, his
dark eyes teasing, for he knew the truth.

He came, sometimes, while she was there. Mrs
Muldoon spoke to him gravely, and, though he
answered her seriously enough, he would find a
moment to wink at Bregetta and bring the colour
to stain her cheeks. Sometimes, in the evening, he
walked home with her, and she took his arm and
felt proud to be at his side.

He came to her room every night, eager as a lad.
If Mrs Bates knew, she said nothing, and kept her
distance. Alistair didn't seem to care about such
things, and he laughed when she mentioned it might
not do his career any good.

'Career?' he mocked once. 'What career? I've
not the money to make more than sergeant,
Bregetta. I haven't the influential friends to pull
strings, either, and I've no truck with bribes. They'd
get rid of me if they could. They like men who are

more malleable than I. No, I'll never be more than a sergeant.'

''Tis a shame,' she whispered, and smoothed back his dark hair. 'You're too fine for them, Alistair.'

He looked at her as if he would like to devour her, and she hid her face in his shoulder, breathing his clean, healthy scent. I love you, she thought, but still did not say it. Love me a little?

'I want you,' he breathed, and began to kiss her with passion.

They lived in a sort of a dream, where the outside world was little more than a slight, irritating interruption. And if Bregetta was not with Alistair in body then she was with him in mind.

Then, one evening, Molly and Teddy came to see her. She felt guilty that she had not been to see them, but so much had happened. It was as if they were as much a part of her past now as her mother and Jim. Molly hugged her, and she led them into the kitchen. Mrs Bates was upstairs in her room, as usual, and they had the place to themselves. Bregetta lit the fire beneath the kettle and made tea, talking about her new job. Teddy looked huge in the neat little room, and Molly bit her lip and peeped enviously at the tidy shelves and the shining pots and pans hanging from hooks above the fireplace.

'Where's Sergeant Duncan?' Teddy asked at last in a gruff voice.

'He's on duty. At the military hospital,' Bregetta added, smiling over her shoulder. 'But he'll be back soon.'

They exchanged a glance but said nothing. Bregetta poured tea into Mrs Bates's dainty cups, and laughed at the sight of one of them in Teddy's great paw. He seemed to realise the incongruity of it himself, for a smile touched his lips, and Molly chuckled, and the awkwardness between them was gone.

'You've done better than I'd feared,' Molly said, clasping Bregetta's hand with her own work-worn one. 'We didn't know what to expect when we were walking here this evening.'

'I asked in at Will's tavern for you once,' Teddy added, 'but the surly bugger'd say nothing other than that you was gone.'

'Alistair knocked him down after he'd given me the push,' she said with a reminiscent smile. Then, looking up at them, 'It *is* good to see you both!'

Molly sighed. The girl was even more beautiful than before, if that were possible. She had the sort of glow Molly could not mistake. Whatever this man, this soldier, was to her, he made her happy. 'Bregetta, will he marry you, do you think?' she burst out.

Bregetta's face changed, and she looked down into her cup. 'There's been no mention of it,' she said, and her voice was cool and prohibiting.

Molly blundered on. 'Surely you can ask him if he intends——?'

'No,' Bregetta warned her with a glance. 'If we marry it will be because he wants it, not because I wheedle and whine until he leads me to the altar out of sheer desperation. Besides, I am an independent woman now. I lead my own life.'

Molly shook her head. Independent, she thought, when it was clear as day that the man was her whole reason for living!

'The main reason we came,' Teddy said, breaking into the awkward moment, 'was to tell you we're leaving Sydney. We've had another letter from my brother Neil. He's offered me work up on the Hawkesbury, Bregetta. He needs help on the farm and he can't afford to pay for the labour. I can work for him, he says, and if we make money out of it we'll share. I mean to take him up. I'm sick and tired of struggling to survive at that shipyard, and of the stink of the place where we live.'

'We've written him about you,' Molly went on before Bregetta could reply. 'He knew you were alone in the world. He told us to bring you if you wanted to come. He knows you were always like a daughter to Teddy and me, us with no children of our own.'

Bregetta felt the tears sting her eyes, and blinked them back. 'You're kind,' she whispered. 'But, you see, I cannot go now. I have my work at Mrs Muldoon's and I have Alistair. I'll miss you both, though. Will you write to me?'

'Of course.' Molly was near to tears herself. 'We don't leave for two more weeks. We'll see you again, my dear, and say our goodbyes.'

The sound of the door's opening made them all start, and Teddy and Molly exchanged another of their looks. Nervously, Bregetta rose and smoothed her already neat skirts. He came down the hall and paused in the shadows of the doorway. He looked tired, and the dark eyes slid over the visitors with ill-disguised surprise.

'Alistair,' she said, the name smooth on her tongue, as though she enjoyed saying it. 'You know Molly and Teddy Field, my friends?'

'Aye, I know them.' He nodded, but still stood in the shadows.

'Won't you have some tea with us?' Bregetta asked anxiously.

For a moment it was as if he was going to refuse. And then at last he said, 'Thank you.'

He came into the room, and Bregetta saw his face was drawn, the strain showing in his tight lips and the dark shadows under his eyes. He sat down on the chair by the hearth, and took the cup from her hands. He drank the tea as though he needed it.

'Did you have a bad night?' Bregetta asked him, and Molly saw the softness in the girl's eyes and smile. The look he gave her back was mocking—harldy lover-like, Molly thought in dismay.

'Is it that obvious?' he said. Then, to the company in general, 'A fight broke out. A private who'd had his back flogged took exception to a corporal with a broken collar-bone. Everyone wanted to be in it.'

'You're not hurt?'

Molly winced at the way the girl fussed about him, expecting his temper to flare any moment, but he only shook his head and captured her searching hands in one of his.

'There were a couple of broken heads, but not mine, not this time.'

Teddy asked him a question, and they spoke together as men did. But he retained one of Bregetta's hands, holding it firm in his. Bregetta told him about Teddy's brother on the Hawkesbury.

'It's a wild and beautiful place,' Molly murmured. 'We'll be like the first people who set foot here at Sydney!'

'There *are* others there,' Teddy teased, 'but where Neil lives is still pretty isolated. There's no road through, so we'll have to go by river. Strand—that's the village near Neil's farm—is on the river. The land is hilly and mostly heavily timbered. The first settlers stayed mainly around Windsor and Richmond and Wilberforce, where the rich flood-plains lie, and they didn't need to clear land like that around Strand. But now, with the rush for more land . . .'

'Land,' Alistair repeated. 'Everyone is after land. And for one reason only: to make their fortune. Well, good luck to them, I say. And to you both.'

'It's not nearly as far away as those settlements down on the Goulburn or up on the northern rivers, but we'll not be visiting Sydney very often,' Molly said in a little voice.

Teddy winked at Bregetta. 'She'll be too busy to think of Sydney once we're there. Neil has been a bachelor so long, and used to living rough . . . Molly'll take one look at his place and reach for a scrubbing-brush!'

They laughed. The talk went on like this for a time. Bregetta noticed Alistair stifle a yawn, and gently squeezed his fingers. 'You're tired,' she said. 'Go up to bed. We won't mind.'

Molly was quick to agree. He rose with a grimace. 'I'm getting too old to brawl,' he said. 'I'd better go before I seize up entirely.'

'Goodnight,' Bregetta murmured, and, looking up, smiled.

He looked down at her, and something in his face made Molly catch her breath. And then he'd turned back to the others, murmuring conventional words. They heard his steps heavy on the stairs. After a moment Bregetta began to talk again, but Molly and Teddy did not linger. They made her promise, again, to visit them before they left, and went out into the street, Molly's diminutive form curved into Teddy's big arm.

'You know,' she said in surprise, 'I do believe he really loves her. Did you see the way he looked at her?'

Teddy grunted. 'You're as soft as butter, Molly!' he retorted. And, in the ensuing mock-argument, Bregetta was forgotten.

Alistair cajoled Mrs Muldoon into giving Bregetta the afternoon off. He seemed able to wrap her stern employer around his little finger. It was a fine day, with a wintry sun, and they walked in the Domain and gazed out over the harbour. He put his arm about her waist. A couple of nursemaids, passing with their charges, giggled, and eyed Bregetta with a curiosity that was mixed with envy.

'Would you ever leave Sydney?' Bregetta asked him, looking out over the water to Pinchgut Island, the clouds making patterns of shade and light on its flickering surface.

'One day, maybe, if my regiment left.'

The thought stunned her. She had forgotten he was at the mercy of an uncaring army. He touched her cheek, and she saw that his dark eyes were smiling. 'That won't be for a long while yet,' he told her. 'You'll be glad to be rid of me by then.'

Bregetta shook her head, but he stooped and kissed her lips before she could answer. His kiss told her what his emotionless voice had not. And she loved him so much that she thought her heart would burst, and did not realise that their days of happiness were coming to an end.

Madeleine brought the dark clouds when she came to see her at the shop. Bregetta had looked up, startled, at the sound of her voice, but at Madeleine's slight shake of the head managed to disguise her hasty greeting as a cough. She moved over to serve her, smiling her sweet, enquiring smile, as she did for every customer. Mrs Muldoon's hawk-eyes were watching. They bent their heads over some new bolts of muslin, and Madeleine whispered, 'Your sergeant told me where to find you.'

Bregetta flushed. 'He's not my sergeant.'

Madeleine's eyebrows lifted. 'That's not what he says.'

Bregetta's eyes met hers, wary. She had been hurt already over Madeleine's confidences. 'What does he say?' she asked slowly, as though against her will.

Madeleine bit her lip, uncertain, it seemed, whether or not to speak, and then she shrugged. 'Why not tell you?' she said, as if to herself. 'He comes to our tavern now and again, to sit and glare at Will. Will doesn't dare throw him out. He said once that he was breaking in a new recruit, but with such a look . . . it was clear what he really meant.'

Bregetta felt her heart go cold, and stood staring into Madeleine's blue eyes. Madeleine touched her hand in sympathy.

'It's just man's talk,' she said harshly, as if to try and repair the damage she had done. 'I didn't realise you would care so much.'

'What else does he say?' Bregetta asked in a surprisingly cool voice when her heart was breaking.

'Only that . . . oh, something about liking them carefree and . . . and misliking women who cling and whine of love and marriage.'

Bregetta looked down at the cloth in her hand, carefully refolding it. 'Thank you for telling me,' she said in that same cool voice.

Mrs Muldoon came closer, hovering. 'Is there something else you were wanting?' she asked Madeleine. 'We have a special bolt of silk damask just in.'

Madeleine smiled. 'Really? I should like to see it.' Mrs Muldoon went out to fetch it, and Madeleine winked at Bregetta and said, 'Jim sent a note. I have it at home. Will you meet me after you finish here? Will has to be away, so you'll be quite safe from his wrath, my dear. Will you?'

Bregetta nodded, and then Mrs Muldoon was back with the cloth, and they could not speak privately again. Madeleine fingered the cloth, but did not buy it, and when she left Bregetta felt Mrs Muldoon's suspicious eyes once more upon her.

She worked as usual throughout the day, and must have said all the right things, but her mind was repeating over and over what Madeleine had said. The words hurt like pins pricking her flesh. Her dream was destroyed. She *had* thought of love and marriage; she admitted it to herself. She had imagined herself always at his side, and he . . . he had only wanted her body. He boasted about it in front of others, and made her less than a woman. A thing, merely, a 'recruit' to be trained—her good and bad points discussed and laughed about—and then to be discarded. No wonder Eber and the soldiers had laughed at her outside the barracks that day! They must all know the joke. Everyone had known, except Bregetta.

She wondered what she could do. Confront him? But she shied away from such a thought; she was too proud to let him know how she ached. And what a naïve fool she had been. She had believed there was more to his words and his caresses than there had ever been. He had never once said he loved her—he had not lied to her with honeyed words. She had given herself to him of her own free will.

At least she had never told him she loved him. That was something she could hug to herself, safe from ridicule.

Madeleine was alone, as she had promised. Bregetta sat down uneasily, glancing about, expecting Will to pop up. But Madeleine only laughed and brought out her husband's best brandy. 'He's gone to see some man in Penrith,' she said. 'He won't be back for a couple of days, and I'm to mind the place and see that the girl he's hired doesn't rob him blind.' She laughed again.

Bregetta sipped the brandy. 'You said that Jim sent a note?'

Madeleine smiled. 'I have it here.' She passed the dirty piece of paper across to Bregetta. It was brief, saying he was going north and would be gone for a few months. He would keep in touch and if they ever wanted to reach him they were to go to the 'same place'—he didn't mention the name, but Bregetta knew he meant the Black Dog. She slipped the note into her pocket with a sigh.

'I hope he'll keep out of trouble now,' she said.

Madeleine laughed. 'He wouldn't know how.'

'You loved him once, didn't you?' Bregetta whispered. That word again.

Madeleine looked at her, and away. Her face was cold and hard. 'Love doesn't put shoes on your feet, or food in your belly. Love's a fool's thing. Jim knew that, as I do. We understand each other too well for lies.'

Bregetta eyed her slyly. 'But it was to you he came for help... and you helped him.'

Madeleine shrugged her shoulders angrily. 'For old times' sake,' she said. Then, suddenly, the bad mood vanished and she laughed again. 'Well, he's gone, and good riddance!'

Bregetta finished her brandy and felt the fire of it warm her cold heart. Madeleine looked a moment at her tragic face, and then repeated softly, 'Love is for fools, my dear. A trap for the unwary. You should not fall into it.'

'No.' Bregetta straightened her back. 'I... Did Sergeant Duncan really say those things you told me?'

Madeleine smiled over the rim of her glass. 'Do you think I would tell you lies?' Then, blue eyes narrowing, 'You know I only do what I do for your own good, Bregetta. I'm trying to help you. You know that, don't you? I've always tried to help you. I wish you would reconsider Francis Warrender. We could be neighbours, and you'd have a carriage and pretty clothes. It would all be so... suitable.'

Bregetta shrugged her shoulders in an echo of Madeleine. 'Men!' she said, to show her disgust of them. 'I don't want to hear any more about them!' And inside she cried, I thought *he* was different! She told Madeleine about Teddy's and Molly's visit.

Madeleine was quiet for a time, and poured herself another brandy.

'If you went I would have no friends,' she said.

'Nonsense,' Bregetta cried. 'You have many friends; you're always telling me——'

'None who have known me from childhood, like you. From the times when life was not so easy. My friends now are friends of fortune, Bregetta.'

'Well, it is unlikely I will go,' Bregetta said, awkward with Madeleine's sudden sadness. 'I may find lodgings elsewhere and...'

Madeleine smiled now. 'I'm glad you're going to leave him,' she said eagerly. 'It's much better, you know. It's the sensible thing. That's what I told myself, when Jim and I... It was the sensible thing.'

Mrs Bates met her in the hall when she returned to Kent Street, and sniffed. 'Sergeant Duncan's been looking for you,' she said.

Bregetta clenched her hands to control the feelings that that name aroused. 'Where is he now?' she asked.

'I don't know,' Mrs Bates replied. 'He had to go out, he said.' Her eyes met Bregetta's. 'I've changed my opinion of you,' she said. 'I think you really care for him. But that doesn't mean you're good for him. He was upset about something this afternoon; very quiet and withdrawn—you know? Something to do with you, it was.'

Bregetta frowned as Mrs Bates disappeared into the kitchen. Upstairs, she closed the door and leaned against it. Madeleine, and now Mrs Bates, both wanting her to leave. Only it was Alistair who would soon do the leaving if what she heard was the truth.

With shaking fingers she lit a candle. Perhaps he had already gone. No, that was foolish. He had been looking for her. He would come back, and then ... maybe he wanted to say he was sorry. The thought was like balm on the angry hurt inside her. Perhaps he would kiss her and say he loved her after all, and it would all be as it had been so short a time ago.

Bregetta sighed and rested her head in her hands. After a moment she remembered Jim and reached into her pocket for the note. Jim's illegible scrawl stared back at her. She was bent over it, concentrating on reading—Jim's writing was so bad—when the door opened behind her.

He stood in the shadows, and his dark eyes took her in from head to toe. The note crackled in her hand. She thought of slipping it back into her pocket, but knew that would only make her look more furtive.

'Where were you?' Alistair asked in a quiet voice, and something in it filled her with dread. As if he had thought her gone for good. Perhaps that was what he wanted.

'At Madeleine's,' she said at last, and as casually as she could began to refold the note. 'Mrs Bates said you were looking for me.'

He moved without her hearing him, and his hand came out and fastened on her wrist, strong but not brutal. She looked up into his dark eyes like a rabbit before the fox. Slowly, slowly he unbent her fingers, and the note fell to the floor. He stooped and picked it up.

The candle wavered. He bent down on his haunches, level with her, and began to read. Madeleine's name was on the top. She watched his face go still and hard, the lines deepening at his mouth and between his brows. At last he looked up and his eyes were black and empty as the night sky.

'Where is this tavern he speaks of, where he leaves messages for you?'

Bregetta said nothing, only staring back at him.

His voice was a rasp now, soft and angry. 'Is this why you've stayed here with me? To keep me from your brother's heels? To lull me into letting him escape?'

She shook her head, but he didn't seem to notice. The candlelight danced over his face as he watched her, making strange hollows where his eyes were, and for a moment she thought she saw pain in the twist of his mouth.

'You told me you didn't know where he was,' he went on. 'That was one lie. How many others have you told me?'

Bregetta moved her hand. A tear trickled down her cheek. 'How could I tell you? You would have hanged him. He's my brother.' And her voice cracked.

'Perhaps I could forgive that if you hadn't sold yourself to me to better help him escape,' he said bitterly.

'No.' But the word was insubstantial, as she was.

He stood up, and she looked into his harsh, closed face, knowing that nothing she could say would change his mind about her.

'I'd better go and see if I can trace him,' he said. The contempt in his voice stung her like a lash.

The door slammed behind him, and she heard his steps hurrying down the stairs and out. The front door also slammed. There was silence. Bregetta stared into the place where he had stood. He wouldn't catch Jim now, she knew it. Madeleine would not tell him. But his escape had cost a terrible price. For a moment she didn't move, feeling her heart breaking, and then a great shudder came over her, and she covered her face with her hands. She had been a fool, he had used and discarded her just as Madeleine had warned. He had believed the worst of her, and she had not dared to tell him the truth—that she loved him. He would have slapped the word back into her face. He knew nothing of such emotions. He was an empty man, caring for nothing but his duty and his own pleasure. She had thought she'd found her true love, a man to be proud of; instead she had found her destroyer.

He did not come back that night. In the morning Mrs Bates looked at her with curious eyes, no doubt wondering what had happened. Bregetta didn't enlighten her, and left as usual for work. She hoped, despite herself, that he might come in and it would be the way it was before. He would wink at her, his eyes aglow with secrets. But he didn't come.

She went straight to Madeleine's that evening, knowing she must learn what Madeleine had said.

Madeleine's face was white and grim. 'Your sergeant is a determined man,' she said. 'He's like a terrier—he'll keep after his prey until he has it.'

Bregetta took her hands in a strong clasp. 'You said nothing?'

'Nothing. I pretended ignorance as to his whereabouts. How did he know?'

'He saw the letter.'

Madeleine looked at her in disgust. 'He was angry, dangerously angry. What did you say to him?'

'Nothing. He drew his own conclusions.'

Madeleine turned away, picking up her brush, and began to stroke her long hair. It shone pale gold, long and fine as silk. 'What will you do now?' she asked, looking at herself in the mirror.

Bregetta sat down on the bed. 'Nothing. What can I do?'

Madeleine smiled. 'You could tell him to go to hell.'

Despite herself, Bregetta laughed. 'When will Will be back?'

'Tomorrow or the next day. Come tomorrow. If he's here I'll leave a cloth hanging out of the window.'

Bregetta nodded and stood up. She felt weary, as though she were walking through water, forcing her limbs forward against the current. Madeleine's eyes narrowed; her face had grown taut. 'Go home, Bregetta,' she said quietly. 'Get some sleep. It'll be better in the morning. You'll see.'

Bregetta walked slowly back to Kent Street in the growing darkness. She felt like a pale moth in the gloom—a ghost. At least Jim was safe, she told herself.

The sound of laughter rose gaily, and there were many lights spilling from one of the soldier's shanties. A horse went by recklessly, the rider swaying in the saddle. Music rose and fell, and there was the splinter of furniture and more laughter. It was coming from the O'Leary place, and Bregetta thought of the dark-haired, sly-eyed Mrs O'Leary with sudden foreboding.

Mrs Bates met her at the door. 'He's upstairs,' she said, and her eyes were almost compassionate.

'Asked where you were. He's in a mood. Never seen him like it before.'

'Mrs Bates——'

'That slut was over here before—you know the one I mean. Wondering when *he'd* be home, she was.' Mrs Bates folded her arms over her bosom. 'I told her to clear off, but she just laughed.'

'I think they're having another party,' Bregetta said. Then she took a deep breath and started up the narrow stairs.

Alistair was washing in the basin by the bed, his coat spread neatly on the chair, his shirt unbuttoned at the front and rolled up at the sleeves. He turned as she entered, his hair dripping from the water he was sluicing over it. After a moment he began to dry himself with meticulous care.

'You were at Mrs Tanner's,' he said. 'Why waste your time there?'

'You're not very kind to my friend,' she replied quietly.

A breeze stirred the curtain at the window, chill from the harbour. Bregetta shivered, and from force of habit moved to close the casement. His voice halted her.

'Leave it! I need some fresh air. The stench of the hospital is with me yet.' Then, when she didn't answer, 'She's your friend, not mine. Why should I be kind to her?'

He sounded angry, impatient with her, as though she were a child swinging at his coat that he wished would go away.

'She is *my* friend,' she said again, trying to make him understand that because Madeleine was *hers* he should be kind to her and like her, for Bregetta's sake.

'She's from your past,' he retorted. 'I thought that was over and done with.'

Bregetta frowned. 'She loves me,' she tried again.

And now he turned and threw the towel down on to the bed. The look on his face was a mixture of disgust and savage mockery, as though she had said something only a naïve child might say. 'Love?' he repeated, and shook his head slowly. 'I know nothing of that. It's a word mouthed by fools and women when they can't get what they want, or have lost it. It's a grasping, greedy word, Bregetta. It wounds and tears and hurts, and draws blood like a bayonet. No doubt you will say you loved your mother, and that was why you remained with her in squalor and misery all those years.'

'What should I have done? Left her to die alone?' she whispered, her eyes big with shock and dawning fear. Then, swallowing, 'Do you love no one, then, Alistair Duncan? Is there no one in this world who you can say you love?'

He looked at her in the lamplight, his eyes black and unreadable, and the smile on his mouth was not pleasant. 'Why?' he said clearly. 'Did you think I loved *you*?'

She didn't know what to say. It was if he had fashioned a knife for her heart, and she had helped him to plunge it in. He did not love her. He wanted her, and she pleased him—*had* pleased him, she amended to herself—but he did not love her. After a moment she swallowed again. 'No, I don't think you love me, Alistair. Love is something I don't think you're capable of.' She moved to the door and paused with her hand on the latch. Tears were close, but she held them back, and her voice was cool and firm when she spoke. 'I'll find other lodgings tomorrow.'

She paused, as if still hoping he would speak and draw her back into the room...but he said nothing, and she closed the door.

In her own room, she stood and let the tears flow down her cheeks. 'Did you think I loved *you*?' he had said. Oh, how he hurt her! So much that it caught in her chest like a hand, squeezing her heart. Why should he speak so bitterly? She had denied him nothing, had never hurt him. Why had he turned on her so?

It was as if he had changed utterly, or perhaps she had just never known the real man until this moment. Madeleine had tried to warn her; she had told Bregetta what he had said in the tavern, how he had treated her name and made of her the kind of woman she had always sworn she would not be. But she had not listened, so caught up had she been in the web of love. She had seen everything as she wanted to see it. Not as it had been.

She sat there a long time before she heard the banging on the door downstairs. Then Alistair's voice swearing and his steps going down. There were voices, and laughter. Bregetta stood up, uncertain. In the end curiosity and a need to stop her agonising thoughts sent her out on to the landing.

'For God's sake,' Alistair was saying, between anger and exasperation, 'I've just come off duty——'

'Then you'll need to come and have a drink with us, Sergeant.'

The voice was low and seductive. Bregetta came softly down the stairs. From the safety of the shadows she could see the group at the door.

Alistair had his back to her, but beyond him there were a number of other soldiers, and a woman. It was the woman who stood at the forefront, and the lamplight from the second-storey window showed her with hands on her hips, head thrown back in what could only be invitation. Mrs O'Leary.

'I'll make you more than welcome,' she said, and laughed softly.

Bregetta made an instinctive movement. Maybe it was the swish of her skirts, or maybe he just sensed her, but Alistair turned to look into the shadows where she stood. She thought she saw his dark eyes gleam as they met hers. It was only one breathless moment, and then with a harsh laugh he had spun around and caught the woman about the waist. Laughing, they led him away.

Bregetta's hand gripped the stair-rail so tightly that her fingers ached. Behind her, Mrs Bates peered down the stairs, clutching a shawl about her nightgown. 'I can't understand it,' she muttered. 'What's got into that man?' She brushed past Bregetta, and hurried to close the door, which was swinging ajar, letting in gusts of cold air. She looked up at Bregetta in the darkness.

'I'm sure he'll be back,' she said softly.

Bregetta felt her pity like a blow, and turned away before she began to cry. Once in her room, she started to bundle together her few personal belongings, leaving any heavy items. The tears were trickling down her cheeks, but she brushed them away. Mrs Bates stood in the doorway and watched her.

When Bregetta was finished she turned to face the other woman. 'I must go,' she said, avoiding her eyes.

'What will I tell him?' Mrs Bates asked her.

Bregetta shook her head. 'He knows.' Then, with a nod, she passed by Mrs Bates and down the stairs. She thought she heard Mrs Bates call out 'Good luck' as she reached the street.

She knew the way without thought, avoiding the dangerously narrow alleys, hiding in a doorway as a loud drunken group of sailors passed by. Molly's house was dark and it seemed that she knocked for ages before anyone came. Then Molly appeared, her face sleepy, eyes opening wide with shock. She pulled Bregetta into the house with a cry of, 'Bregetta, what is it? What's happened?'

CHAPTER SIX

BREGETTA dissolved into sobs, falling into her friend's warm, comforting arms. Molly held her against her large, motherly bosom, patting her shoulder. Teddy, bleary-eyed, peered around the dividing curtain and vanished again when he saw who it was.

Bregetta's tears turned to hiccups at last. Molly went to stir the embers in the hearth and put the kettle on the hob to boil. 'Here, sit down, love!' she said, and pushed Bregetta into a chair. 'Lord, you're in a state, aren't you?'

Bregetta sat down, and Molly knelt awkwardly before her, rubbing her cold hands. 'What is it?' she asked, and yet seemed to know, for she went on almost at once. 'Ah, he's not worth it. None of them are, bloody lobsters.' And yet she had really thought that he loved the girl ... He even fooled a sharp one like me! Molly thought with disgust.

Bregetta laughed despite herself, and with a shaking hand wiped her tears. Molly set to making some strong, sweet tea, and handed her a mug. Bregetta sipped, letting the brew scald her lips and throat, trickling down to warm her chilled body. 'Ah, I loved him,' she gasped. 'I did love him.'

Molly looked at her with sympathy. 'I know,' she soothed. 'I know you did, my dear.'

'I want to come with you and Teddy,' she said at last, when she was calm again. 'I can't stay in Sydney Town.'

Molly nodded. 'Can you tell me?' she asked.

Bregetta met her eyes. 'I made a mistake,' she said. 'I was a fool, that's all. I'll not be one again. But I can't stay here. I can't see him again.' Her voice cracked.

Molly patted her hand. 'No, you won't have to. You'll come with us. You'll be ready?'

Bregetta nodded. 'I've money to pay my way.'

'I know you have, love.'

She found Bregetta some blankets and left her in the glow of the fire. Bregetta sat there a long time before she slept. It was as if her heart was cold in her chest. A burnt-out fire, only cinders and blackened ashes remaining where once the flames had raged and shone with an unbearable heat. As her love for Alistair Duncan had burned and shone, and now was dead.

Why had he done it? It was as if he found something contemptible in her which she had never known was there. As if he hated her, and yet she knew in the beginning he had not hated her. 'I want you,' he had said. But once he'd had what he wanted it was no longer to be cherished.

If only I understood, thought Bregetta, then I could put it behind me and begin my new life without the bad memories. If only I knew why everything went so wrong!

Mrs Muldoon was not pleased with her leaving, but could not dissuade her. 'You make a good draper's assistant,' she said. 'You have a feel for the merchandise. I'd even think of a shilling extra if you stayed.'

Bregetta shook her head regretfully, knowing this was indeed a concession on Mrs Muldoon's part.

'I have to leave. Family reasons,' she added cryptically, and looked down at her hands.

Mrs Muldoon sighed. 'Oh, well, I suppose if you've made up your mind to it——'

'I have. I'm sorry.'

She took her wages gratefully, and then went down the narrow lanes and passageways to the Black Dog, and left a message for Jim to tell him where he could reach her. Then there was Madeleine.

Teddy came with her that evening, and when they saw no cloth hanging from the window he went into the tavern for a drink while Bregetta went to see her friend. Madeleine was shocked and sad that she was leaving. 'I wish I could help,' she said.

'You already have.'

'Not enough, it seems. Perhaps Will could be persuaded to give you your job back. We could be as we used to be. And then, Francis Warrender is... Oh, why don't you stay and let me help?'

Bregetta shook her head. 'I will never have anything to do with another man.'

Madeleine blinked, and then laughed as though she was startled. 'Oh, come now! You're being dramatic. You'll see. In a little while you'll be just as——'

But Bregetta only shook her head again. She said, 'I'll write. And I suppose I will see you again, one day.'

Madeleine went to her wardrobe, and after a moment drew out a gown of peacock blue. 'Take it,' she said sharply. 'You can wear it to win a rich husband, or else trade it for money or food if things get desperate.'

Bregetta felt tears in her eyes. 'You are the best friend I could ask for,' she whispered. 'Oh, Maddy...'

But Madeleine's laugh was sharp, and her face a little pale as she shook her head. 'The best friend?' she murmured. 'Well, that's still to be proven, isn't it? One day you may not think so.'

'Madeleine?' Bregetta frowned and stood up. 'What do you mean?'

'Only if one day you hear something about me that is...if perhaps I have said things or done things which... Oh, damn, it was all for the best, after all! Take care, Bregetta, and write as often as you can.'

'Of course I will.'

They embraced briefly, and then Madeleine had pushed her away with a laugh. 'I must go back to the taproom or that girl will have robbed Will blind.'

It was only left for Bregetta to murmur again her thanks, and leave.

Teddy didn't say much on the way home, and when she showed him the dress he merely lifted an eyebrow, as if wondering at Madeleine's motives, and puffed on his clay pipe.

'She is my best and kindest friend,' Bregetta said sharply.

Teddy shrugged. 'She always liked everyone to think so.'

'What do you mean?'

'Bregetta, she was always jealous of you, girl. Eaten up with it. Didn't you know that?'

Bregetta shook her head angrily in denial. 'No. You wrong her. Without her I don't know where I would be now. Dead, probably.'

'Rot. You're made of sterner stuff than that.'

Maybe he was right, she thought later. Not about Madeleine, but that she was stronger than she had thought. She had thought she would die when Alistair . . . But she hadn't, and now she was setting out for a new place and a new life.

The boat cut through the water. Bregetta looked out over the bow, the fresh breeze whipping her hair about her face. They were almost at their journey's end.

They had made the first part of it by dray from Sydney to Windsor. The rattle and bump of the vehicle had become almost familiar to Bregetta, as had the nightly ritual of setting up camp. She had heard hair-raising accounts of escaped convicts attacking travellers, though they were less common since Governor Darling had formed a special force of soldiers to track down the bushrangers back in the 1820s. But Bregetta still felt fortunate that they had escaped unmolested, though Teddy carried a gun.

They had reached Windsor at evening, and Bregetta had admired the settlement with its straight, neatly laid-out streets and old stone buildings. It had been one of the earliest villages in the colony, after Sydney, and had become important when it had been found that food for the colony could be grown better on its rich river-flats than about Port Jackson and Sydney Cove. The land here was rich and lush—and already taken.

They had stayed the night in an inn—luxury after camping out. Their goods and chattels were stored in the stables, the hens in their cages protesting loudly. Neil had sent a list of things for them to bring to save him the price of transportation, and they had done their best.

The next morning they had boarded their boat, and set off downstream for Strand.

Bregetta pushed back her hair, and looked about with pleasure. The cold wind stung some colour into her pale cheeks, and her eyes almost regained their old sparkle.

The country had gradually changed from lush flat plains, thickly cultivated, with little settlements dotting the landscape between the lone farmhouses, to undulating hills and valleys, timbered right down to the water in some cases. This was the land no one had seen the need to settle, until now. But at the latter end of the 1830s land hunger had sent men and women into places previously passed over, as well as far out into the unexplored wilderness.

'Nearly there.' Teddy came up beside her and smiled.

Bregetta smiled back, and he was pleased to see she was almost back to her old self. He had been furious when she had come to them so distraught, and had threatened to go and give the sergeant a piece of his mind. But she had been even more distraught at that and made him promise not to approach the man.

'It's not his fault,' she'd insisted. 'He never promised me any more than he gave. It was I who imagined there was more. Please, just let it be forgotten.'

So they had forgotten, or pretended to forget. And, if sometimes Bregetta cried in her sleep in the night, no one mentioned it the next morning.

Ahead of them the river widened and swept in a graceful curve. As they came around it, Bregetta saw the little bay with its jetty protruding out into the water.

Strand, or what they could see of it, clustered back from the jetty. Timber buildings and a narrow street carved out from the surrounding bush. There were some stretches of cleared land along the riverbank on the other side, and crops growing. Horses cantered, and children, paddling at the edge of the sandy curve of the river, waved.

As the boat drew in to the jetty, people flocked towards them, seeking goods they had ordered or cargo the captain might have to sell. And it seemed he did have cargo to sell, for soon barrels and boxes were being unloaded, and there was much bargaining going on.

Molly and Teddy were busy seeing to the unloading of their own small cargo. Bregetta picked up her bundle, and looked about her.

The people of Strand were plainly dressed, relatively neat and businesslike. The men wore wide-brimmed hats, fustian jackets and trousers, and, almost without exception, full beards. The women wore serviceable gowns, shawls, and were brown of face despite their bonnets. Children clung to their skirts. Obviously life here was not easy, and the bush was not kind to new settlers. This was not Sydney, where everything was at one's fingertips. Here things must be grown, or made, or occasionally bought from a captain with a cargo.

One of the men—he had the darkest, lushest beard she had seen—came towards Bregetta, and Teddy stepped forward. The man hesitated, and

Bregetta smiled at his expression as he took in Teddy's size.

'I'm looking for Neil Field,' Teddy said.

The man's teeth showed white through his black beard. 'You must be his brother!' And he held out his hand. 'I'm James MacDougall; I'm the blacksmith here.'

A few of the other townspeople, finished their bargaining, had also wandered over. One of them, a small, dark-haired woman, James MacDougall introduced as his wife, and two girls of about Bregetta's age as his daughters. Molly was soon making friends. It seemed the boat's arrival was Strand's excuse for a get-together.

James MacDougall called over a boy of about twelve or thirteen and instructed him to go and fetch Teddy's brother. And then Bregetta, Teddy and Molly were taken to the inn, incongruously called the Rose, to wait.

The inn was primitive—really just the front room of the owner's house—but cosy, and Teddy drained his tankard with relish while Molly asked Mrs MacDougall some questions on housekeeping in the bush, and Bregetta made somewhat difficult conversation with the two daughters. They seemed young to her, and very serious. The elder, Katherine, was the prettier, and, though she did return Bregetta's friendly smiles, even Bregetta soon ran out of things to say. She was glad when the boy clattered into the inn, and behind him came Neil Field.

Bregetta almost laughed aloud. Neil was as small as Teddy was big—a little, skinny man with steel-grey hair and kind eyes. Molly ran to hug him— he was more her size—laughing and exclaiming.

Teddy picked him up with a great roar of laughter. At last they drew Bregetta forward to be introduced.

'She's more than welcome,' Neil winked. 'The more willing workers I can find the better for me. Though we'll have all the young lads hanging about the place like bees around a honey-pot.' And he laughed as the colour rushed into Bregetta's cheeks.

Molly protested, half scolding, half laughing herself. They made their farewells to the MacDougalls and the others who had followed them to the inn, and made their way out to the cart Neil had driven in from his farm. It was only a moment's work for them to load their belongings on to it. Teddy, Neil and Molly squashed up on the seat, while Bregetta sat up in the back, and they started off down the rough, pitted track which served as a road.

Strand, Bregetta decided, consisted of a straggle of houses, an inn, a blacksmithy and a church, all centred around the jetty, their main link to the outside world. Outside the little town the hills broadened out, and there were cleared areas of crops and pasture for cattle, sheep, horses and pigs. Small cottages or huts were built at regular intervals. And, beyond it all, the bush closed in, like a cupped hand, ever-threatening to close.

Bregetta felt the strangeness of it. She had always lived in Sydney and this was alien to her. She sat among the bags of seed and flour and sugar, with a keg of treacle digging into her back, looking about her as the winter sun shone through the grey-green leaves of the trees.

Behind her, Molly was questioning Neil about Strand, and he answered with a trace of laconic amusement.

'Twenty families at most,' he said, 'counting the outlying farms like mine. There are other settlers over the river, and Mr Gordon has a big station a mile or two downstream, where he runs his sheep and cattle. He's the big man around here. He was the magistrate for the Hawkesbury River area, but he's retired. Though he still has lots of friends... powerful friends, in Sydney.'

Molly sniffed. 'He's not an emancipist?'

'Good God, no!. He's no government man. Pure merino, our Mr Gordon. But he's keen to see Strand go ahead. Wants a road to join us up with the Great Northern Road so that his bullock waggons can carry his wool back to Sydney, and he can run his cattle to market. And that would mean *we* could take our own maize and wheat to market instead of paying the river-boats to do it. All the more profit for us.'

He paused for breath, and flicked the horse with the reins. 'Here we are,' he said. 'Home. This is the farm.'

Neil's farm was large in comparison to what they had passed. The paddocks that ran down to the road were mostly cleared, though there were still some tree trunks to grub out. On a rise, up above the open land, was a slab cottage, with a barn and various animal pens near by. Behind all that rose two rugged-looking hills, covered in timber.

Neil had done most of the work himself, apart from a lad to mind the animals, though in the early days he had had a couple of assigned convicts to help him. But convicts were more trouble than they were worth, he said, and, besides, it was difficult these days to get any, what with transportation on the decline and so much land being opened up...

Bregetta climbed down stiffly from the cart and smiled at the lad, whose name was Peter. He was too shy to answer her greeting. She looked about her, shading her eyes to gaze up at the bush-covered hills that rose behind Neil's farm. The sun was setting, and birds were wheeling. A wild dog howled eerily, and Neil's dog started barking in response, pulling on its rope. Bregetta felt very weary, but there was a certain peace inside her. As if she had been right in coming here. She would make a new start among the people of Strand, and maybe in time happiness would come to her again. Perhaps there would be another man who... But the thoughts were too painful, and she put them away until she could bear to look at them again.

Work on the farm was hard. They rose at dawn, and did not stop until the daylight had gone. Neil was still in the process of clearing land, and there were trees to cut down, haul away, and the roots and stump to be grubbed out and burned before the seed could be properly planted in the dusty soil. Some settlers just sprinkled their precious seed among the stumps of the trees, but Neil said they had time to do it properly before the spring.

The women worked as hard as the men. There were meals to cook, clothes to wash and animals to feed, as well as unpleasant jobs like making candles and soap. Neil's cottage was, as Teddy had predicted, a rough affair.

It was made of horizontal slabs of wood, which were fastened to strong posts and battens, and had a veranda at the front to keep out the worst of the sun. Inside, the walls of the two rooms were bare. The roof was built of wooden shingles, reinforced

with spares and rafters. With the wooden shutters
over the windows and the door closed it might be
rough, but it was cosy.

For cooking there was a fireplace in the main
room, with a camp oven and a couple of pots. Neil's
diet had consisted of meat, damper and tea, and
Molly set about adding a bit of variety to that. She
used eggs from hens she had brought, she bullied
him into purchasing a milking cow, so they had
fresh milk and cream and butter, and she started a
garden of vegetables behind the cottage—the main
foods grown in the area appeared to be cabbages,
potatoes, pumpkins and water-melons. In Windsor,
they had been told, the peaches had been so
plentiful that they were fed to the pigs. There was
a creek running through Neil's property, but in the
drier times it became no more than a dry riverbed
with a few deeper water-holes.

Molly also set about trying to make the cottage
more 'homely', as she put it. She covered the bare
walls with calico, and the earth floor with suitable
wooden planks. She was appalled at Neil's idea of
furnishings, and the men were soon put to work
making frames for the beds and a table with forms
to sit on. Molly sewed curtains for the windows,
and the various fribbles she considered necessary
to make the place habitable.

'Your wife is a wonder,' Neil would say, shaking
his head in awe. 'A real wonder.'

And Teddy would agree, his eyes gleaming with
amusement.

Winter had turned to spring, and the trees
blossomed with sweet, bright flowers, dripping a
syrup which drove the little native bees and the
bright-coloured birds mad, and Molly's seedlings

came poking green through the soil, promising good things to eat. Bregetta helped to tend them, as well as helping with everything else. She did not shy away from hard work, and even worked with the men, grubbing out stumps.

They had built a lean-to on to the cottage to fit in the extra bodies. Bregetta had a hard little bed in one corner of the cottage, divided from the rest of the room by a screen of calico sacking. But she was usually so tired at night that she fell on to it without thought or care for privacy—the strange silence of the bush had long ceased to frighten her, and she no longer allowed herself to think of *him*. Alistair was locked deep in her mind, and she told herself he might as well be dead.

The lad, Peter, slept in a canvas tent under the big trees at the back of the cottage, with his gun and his dog, ever watchful of the penned animals. He was younger than Bregetta by a year, and an ex-convict. He smiled at her and blushed when she spoke to him, but he treated her with the same respect he gave Molly.

'You're not sorry you came?' Molly asked her one day, straightening her aching back and wiping the perspiration off her brow. They were working in the garden. The pumpkins were running amok, and the peas and beans looked lush and green.

Bregetta looked surprised and shook her head. 'There's nothing for me back there,' she said. 'And I feel as if I'm doing some good here, helping Neil.'

Molly smiled at her. 'You're a good girl, Bregetta.'

'Are you sorry?' Bregetta retorted.

Molly grimaced tiredly. 'I was at first. Such a state it was in! But now...well, Teddy's happy, and so am I.'

Sometimes they went into Strand. The MacDougalls were always glad to see them and the two daughters claimed Bregetta as their friend, which rather surprised her. But they were hardly lively companions, lacking the caustic wit of Madeleine. Life to them was a serious business and not one to joke about. Occasionally there would be a dance, or a picnic, or a 'do' on at the church. And everyone went and was determined to have fun. It wasn't often the people of Strand were able to put down their tools and be merry with their neighbours, and they made the most of it.

Bregetta enjoyed these get-togethers. She did not lack for partners, but something about her set her apart, and when she did not respond rapturously to their overtures her suitors would melt away. All, that was, except Maurice Gordon.

Maurice was the son of the local station-owner, and spoke with a plum in his mouth—or so Teddy would have it. He had been to a good school in Parramatta, and his father hoped to make a gentleman of him. But he was at home for the moment, helping his father with the station, and learning how to run it. For he was an only child and it would all be his when his father died.

Bregetta had met Maurice outside the church one Sunday after the service. He came up to Neil and murmured some pleasantries and asked to be introduced. He was about twenty, with fair hair and blue eyes and a wide, warm smile. He was not handsome, but he was so friendly that no one ever noticed.

Bregetta was wearing her green gown, with her hair plaited and wound like a rope about her head. She was glowing, her skin turned to gold by the sun and her new outdoor life, and freckles sprinkling her nose. She was laughing at something Molly had said when he first saw her.

'My father always says you're the best farmer hereabouts,' he told Neil, a little condescendingly, Bregetta thought. But Neil only smiled and looked pleased.

'Your father takes an interest,' he said. 'How is your mother, Mr Gordon? Still ailing?'

'I'm afraid so.' But his eyes were on Bregetta. 'My mother is an invalid,' he said, as if for Bregetta's benefit. 'Are your parents still in Sydney, Miss Smith? It's a wonder they would allow you to come so far without them.'

'I'm an orphan, sir,' she replied softly.

'She's near enough to our own daughter, anyway,' Molly said stoutly.

When they were leaving Bregetta glanced back over her shoulder. He was still watching her. It amused her, and pleased her vanity a little. It was not so much of a surprise when a few days later he called upon Neil at the farm.

Molly had the cottage finished to her satisfaction by this stage. They had a scrubbed table and forms, with a few extra chairs, and the pots and pans hung gleaming over the big hearth. But still it could never be called elegant, and Bregetta wondered what he thought of it, being a gentleman and used to better. But if he was dismayed he did not show it. He sat down with a pleased smile, and accepted their tea and Molly's maizeflour cakes as if he had never dined in any other way in his life.

Bregetta bent to the hearth, stirring the soup Molly had simmering in the big pot, while Maurice and Molly chatted behind her. His mother was worse, it seemed, and his father was busy down at Wilberforce. Did they know a bolter had been caught there? The convict had bolted into the bush about two months ago and survived on wild animals and fruits and what he could steal from the surrounding farms.

'Poor chap,' he said with genuine feeling, 'he was as thin as a rail when they caught him. Still, they have to learn that such things will not be tolerated here. A sentence must be served in full.'

Molly nodded. Teddy stuck his head around the door and, after greeting Maurice Gordon, said to her, 'There's a tinker out here. Has all manner of bits and pieces. Are you wantin' something or shall I send him on his way?'

Molly jumped up. 'I'll take a look,' she said, and after a quick glance at Bregetta went out. Bregetta felt herself freeze. There could be no mistaking that look.

Maurice cleared his throat. 'The weather's been fine these past weeks. But we need rain for the crops. Otherwise they'll be wilted in the ground even before the summer heat.'

Bregetta nodded in what she hoped was a knowledgeable manner. She looked at him with steady eyes and he met them, and looked away. He seemed not to know what else to say, and suddenly the situation amused her enough to make her lose her stiffness. She also realised that she felt a little sorry for him. It was true she had no love to give him, but she could be a little kinder to him.

'I suppose it's as you say,' she replied gently. 'But I love the spring. So much new life. All the new animals and the new plants. The bush is alive with colour. It's like a miracle after the dreariness of winter.'

'You're very poetical,' he said with a smile which was totally without mockery. Then, 'Are you related in some way to the Fields?'

Bregetta shook her head. 'My father was a great friend of the family. He owned a draper's shop and he was an Irishman—perhaps that's where the poetry comes from. He died when I was still young. I have a brother, but he is away at present.'

Outside she could hear Molly's laughter. Maurice gestured to the door. 'Would you like to see what the tinker has to sell?'

Bregetta smiled. 'Yes, I would!'

'I suppose you miss Sydney,' he said as she went out of the door, 'with all the shops and people. Strand must seem a poor thing in comparison.'

'I do miss it, but I love it here.'

Outside there stood a rickety hand-cart, and a dirty little man with white hair was laying out trays of goods for Molly's inspection. His cart jangled with pots and pans, and there were some parcels of cloth as well as small boxes and kegs, packed neatly. Bregetta peered into one of the trays, holding back a loose lock of hair which threatened to sweep the lot on to the ground. There was a brooch—a trumpery thing, but she admired it. She held it up and asked the tinker how much. He eyed her slyly.

'A shillin', missy.'

She put it back down. She said it was too much.

Molly chose some cloth and a new pot. The tinker packed up with a muttered word, and set off back

to the road. Maurice also said his farewells, and
rode off on his thoroughbred horse, dust flying.
Molly looked after him and said, as if to herself,
'Fine young man, that. Would be a good catch for
some lucky girl.'

Bregetta sniffed. 'Some rich young lady, who
speaks properly and knows how to act in polite
society and will do him proud. Doesn't sound like
me, Molly, does it? So don't go getting any silly
ideas.'

Molly looked at her with big, hurt eyes. 'Me?'
she said, and flounced off. But Bregetta saw the
other woman watching her with dreamy eyes, as
though spinning schemes, and she was worried.
Maurice Gordon's world and the world of Bregetta
Smith were far apart. Besides, she had had enough
of romance. It was not the tame, sweet thing she
had once thought, but a wild animal which savaged
you with cruel, angry fangs and would not let go,
no matter how you tried to shake it off.

Bregetta wrote to Madeleine when she had time,
and sent the letter off on the boat which usually
came to Strand every month, bringing goods to sell
and carrying goods the townspeople wanted to sell
at market. She told Madeleine about the hard work.
She made some joke about Maurice, and said that
she was saving her dress for the right moment. Let
Madeleine believe she had forgotten.

The spring drew on. Maurice called again, and
she saw him at one of the impromptu dances in the
town. Bregetta stood up with him, and enjoyed
herself. He flattered her, and squeezed her rather
tightly. It was not marriage he was thinking of,
Bregetta decided, despite Molly's fond hopes. He

would never marry such as she—his family would
not allow it.

During the dance he slipped her outside into the
moonlight, and she let him kiss her once, but
pushed him gently away when he tried to do it
again. 'Bregetta,' he sighed, gazing down into her
face. And he slipped his hand inside his jacket and
brought out the brooch she had admired the day
the tinker had come. Bregetta laughed in delight.

'Your diamond brooch, ma'am,' he said, teasing
her.

'Glass, more like,' she retorted, but pinned it
carefully on to her gown.

'I'd give you diamonds if you'd like them.' His
face was suddenly very serious, but Bregetta
shrugged it all off with a laugh and a joke, and
brushed past him into the dance. On the way home
Molly noted the brooch. She made no comment,
but Bregetta saw her lips fold into a satisfied smile,
and sighed.

It was a warm day. The perspiration clung to
Bregetta's body, dripping down between her
shoulder-blades and making her gown stick uncomfortably. She eased her back, straightening up
from where she had been working in the garden.
The sun blazed, and, even with her broad-brimmed
hat to protect her, she could still feel her skin
burning.

There was a man walking up the track towards
the farm. For a moment she thought that she knew
him. That quick, slouching walk, the bright colour
of his hair... He drew closer, and then, pausing,
looked up. He had a bundle tied to his back, and
the clothes he wore looked old and ragged. Some-

thing about him made her heart beat faster and her breath catch in her throat ... Jim.

The hoe was thrown aside, and Bregetta lost her hat as she flew down the track and into his arms. He swung her about, laughing, and she kissed his cheek. 'Jimmy!' she cried. 'I thought for sure I'd never see you again.'

He was laughing. But he looked thin, and there were lines on his face that had never been there before. He took her hands hard in his and looked at her. 'Ah, you're looking as fine as ever, sister,' he murmured. 'Do you think I can come in, just for a minute?'

'Jim, you can come in, of course you can! Molly!' she called. 'Guess who's here?'

Molly came hurrying out, hair as untidy as ever, and stopped short in the doorway. Bregetta saw her face close in on itself, and realised with a jolt that not everyone would be welcoming Jim as freely as she did herself. Then Molly was coming forward, holding out her hands. 'Jim,' she said softly. 'It's good to see you, lad. Come in and wet your whistle.'

Jim came forward and squeezed her hands. 'Thank you, Molly,' he said, and the words seemed to come from deep inside him.

Once indoors he drank down their tea and wolfed up the bread and cold meat as if he had not eaten for a week. Molly and Bregetta exchanged glances. 'Where have you been?' Bregetta asked him gently.

Jim shrugged, and avoided their eyes. 'Here and there, a bit of work occasionally when I could get it. You know how it is.'

Molly sat down, and put her hand over his. 'You're not thinking of going back to Sydney, lad?'

Jim shook his head. 'No. I hear they're still after me there. That bloody Sergeant Duncan would love to see me at the end of a rope.'

Bregetta made an involuntary movement, but did not speak. The name sent a shaft of pain through her that took her breath, like a stitch, when one ran very hard.

'What then?' Molly was asking.

'I was hoping,' and he paused and looked rueful. 'I was hoping maybe I could stay on here a while. Oh, Molly,' and he put his head into his hands, 'I feel as if I've come to the end of the road. I know I was mad to do what I did. I'm that sorry about it all. If only I could have a chance to start again.'

The contrition and pain in his voice were genuine. They could not doubt that. Whatever had set Jim upon his wild course was gone, and a new, wiser man now stood in his place. Bregetta bit her lip, looking at Molly. After a moment Molly stood up. 'I'll need to talk to Teddy and Neil,' she said. 'Rest here for a time, Jim.'

She went out. Bregetta smiled at him. 'I'll make you up a bed,' she said, getting to her feet. 'You'll need a good rest before you answer any more questions.'

But Jim put out his hand and stopped her. His eyes were suddenly very hard. 'Madeleine said something about that redcoat,' he said. 'I didn't believe her at the time. Was it true?'

Bregetta looked away, and his hand dropped.

'I swear if I ever set eyes on him again I'll kill him!'

'Enough!' Bregetta cried, angry herself now. 'I've heard enough of killing. I thought you were changing your ways?'

Jim looked crestfallen. 'You don't understand,' he said sullenly.

'No,' she retorted, 'I don't.'

She was sorry afterwards, but it had had to be said. It was no good carrying a grudge for something that was over and could never be changed. They must make a new life, far from Sydney and all the memories it held.

Teddy and Neil spoke to Jim quietly after their supper, but whatever he said to them must have convinced them, and they agreed to keep him on at the farm. Neil needed as much labour as he could find, and he could not afford to pay them anything other than board and lodgings. Besides, the boy, Peter, was leaving for Windsor, where he had a brother, and they would soon be short-handed.

Bregetta took a walk with Jim in the dusk, and, though they didn't have much to say, she was glad to have him by her side again.

'I miss Madeleine,' she said. Birds flapped over the trees, looking for their beds. Cicadas hummed, and somewhere an animal called to its mate.

Jim looked rueful. 'So do I. I loved that girl, Bregetta. I made a mess o' that and all.'

Bregetta did not have the heart to remind him that Madeleine had never had any intention of marrying him.

'I miss Ma, too,' he went on softly. 'I wish I'd been there, when she——'

'She wasn't conscious,' Bregetta assured him. 'And you saw her once, putting yourself in great danger. She's at peace. She'd been sick so long, Jim. It isn't fair to wish her back to that.'

'I know, I know. I'm just thinking, there are a lot of things I have to make up for, aren't there?'

Bregetta pressed his arm. 'We'll be happy here,' she told him firmly, and it was only later, in the darkness of her makeshift bedroom, that she woke from dreaming of cold rain on the window and the warmth of Alistair's body against hers, and wept.

CHAPTER SEVEN

SUMMER came, hot and sultry. They worked on, and Jim was accepted in Strand. No one knew him there, and he went under the name of Jim Mallory—as long as the truth remained hidden he would be safe. Neil said he was a hired farm-hand, and if anyone doubted it they said nothing. He had put on flesh, and worked harder than any of them. It seemed, in truth, that he had turned over a new leaf, and Bregetta was proud of him.

He was amused at Maurice's infatuation with her, and teased her about it. 'I can just see you, up at the big house, calling the magistrate "Papa" and telling him you've got a bolter for a brother.'

'Don't!' cried Bregetta. 'Not even in jest.'

But he ruffled her hair and laughed. 'You'd make a fine magistrate's daughter-in-law!'

'It's not marriage he has in mind,' she retorted.

Jim shrugged. 'Stranger things have happened.'

The letter from Madeleine came just before Christmas. Neil and Teddy had been down to the monthly boat to pick up their supplies, and brought back a letter for Bregetta. It was short and to the point: 'He's been to see me. He knows where you are. Take care.'

Bregetta folded it carefully and looked blindly out of the window at the hot, sullen bush. Jim, watching her, took it gently from her and read it slowly, mouthing the words. He looked up with a frown. 'What is it? What does it mean?'

125

Bregetta looked at him blankly for a moment, and then forced her voice out in a jerky way. 'He's going to seek me out. Why is he coming?'

'Who? Bregetta, you're making no sense!'

'Sergeant Duncan,' she whispered. 'He knows where I am. He still wants you, Jim. If he comes... You must go now!'

Jim looked down at the letter for a moment, and then shook his head. 'No,' he said, and there was a new firmness and determination in his voice. As though the boy had finally become a man. 'I won't run any more. If they find me so be it. Though I doubt even he'll come this far. There must be more pressing matters in Sydney. I'm hardly a master criminal...'

'Yes.' Bregetta swallowed with relief. 'Yes, of course. He has to do as they tell him. He can't just travel up here when he wants to.' And yet there was something frightening in that message, and she could not be at peace. After a moment she stood up, throwing the letter into the fireplace, where the fire always smouldered, ready to cook their meals and heat their water, no matter what the temperature outside—it was too difficult to re-light with Neil's flint and steel if it went out.

The paper crackled and glowed, then curled up into ashes. Jim watched it, and then reached out to take her fingers hard in his. 'Don't worry,' he said, 'I'm as sly as a fox. I'll not be hanged for a long while yet.'

But she shuddered, and could not echo his laughter.

One Sunday Maurice suggested she come out with him in his boat. 'I'm not an expert,' he told Molly, 'but I can promise not to upset it.'

Molly agreed readily enough, as she did with anything Maurice said, and Bregetta looked forward to the outing. The boat was small, with a single sail, and Maurice seemed adept at handling it. It was a hot day, and they set out into the river, catching the faint breeze that blew across the surface, the bow sliding smoothly through the glittering water.

It was cooler on the river, and Bregetta leaned back, her broad-brimmed hat shading her face, enjoying it very much. Maurice smiled at her, his eyes screwed up against the glare, and steered the boat out into midstream. Other boats dipped and skitted about them, and it was almost like a tiny Sydney Harbour.

After a time she noticed a much larger boat coming up-river behind them, and Bregetta shaded her eyes, watching its slow progress. This was not one of the private sailing sloops of ten to twenty tons, which sailed to Sydney by sea, taking the produce of the farmers to market, or the grain down to the flour-mill at Pitt Water and bringing back the coarse flour. This vessel was much bigger, perhaps forty tons, and it looked old and battered. Something about it struck her as ominous.

Maurice followed her look. 'Must be the government transport my father was speaking of,' he said. 'Soldiers for the new garrison. Looks pretty old; probably due to be turned into a prison hulk.'

Bregetta felt her heart go still in her breast. 'Soldiers?' she repeated.

'Yes. Didn't you know? They're to set up a garrison and a barracks in the town. Convict labour. My father's finally had his way. There's to be a new road to join us up with the Great Northern

Road to Sydney. My father's been pushing the idea
for years, and now the place is doing well enough
for the governor to think it'll be worthwhile. It'll
probably bring more settlers, too. My father hopes
to get the convicts over to our place for a time to
add a bit to the house.' He laughed self-consciously.

'I didn't realise.' Bregetta fanned herself with her
hat—her hand was shaking and she sought to hide
it. 'A new road, you say?'

'Yes. And they'll clear some land, I expect, for
a few public buildings. A court-house and so on.
Sometimes they're hired out to settlers, too, to clear
farmland.'

'Where have they come from?' Newcastle, she
thought. There was a convict settlement at
Newcastle for those who had committed second
offences.

Maurice looked surprised. 'Sydney, I expect.
Does it worry you, having a chain-gang in the area?
I'm sure they'll be locked up tight at night; no threat
to the people.'

Bregetta forced herself to smile. Her mother had
been a convict—what would he think if he knew
that? She watched the transport come slowly into
the bend of the river, and drop anchor in the deep
water there with a rattle and groan of the chain.
Men rushed about on deck as the old boat swung
around, but another anchor at the stern held it fast.
Bregetta shaded her eyes again and saw the red coats
of the soldiers, and heard their faint shouts across
the water. But Maurice's little boat was moving
further along. A sudden breeze had caught her sail,
and the craft scudded before it, passing by the
transport and moving on, until there was only un-
broken, rugged bushland on either side of them.

Bregetta sighed. What had she expected to see? She dared not answer that question. But for some reason she began to find Maurice's conversation tedious, and could hardly conceal her impatience until they turned again for Strand.

Maurice brought his boat into the jetty, and helped Bregetta out—evidently the transport drew too much water to come so close. Bregetta shook out her skirts, and shaded her eyes again. There was still much going on on deck. A couple of smaller boats had been lowered alongside the transport, and Maurice said the man in charge would probably be coming ashore to visit his father. He took her arm, hurrying her towards his horse and sulky, which he had left by some trees near the smithy.

'My father will be looking for me,' he said with a sigh. 'I shall take you home, Bregetta.'

'It's been lovely,' she said, and meant it.

'Will I see you next Sunday?' he asked her, and looked into her eyes.

She smiled. 'And the one after if you wish.'

His smile was full of warmth, and she was ashamed. His lips touched hers lightly. Perhaps, thought Bregetta, as they trundled and bumped their way along, it would be no bad thing, after all, to have a new road.

Jim was outside, and Bregetta went to find him as soon as possible. He was sitting in the shade of some trees and looked up at her sleepily, putting aside his newspaper. It was the *Sydney Gazette*, an old one, of course. New ones were like gold outside Sydney.

Bregetta knelt down at his side. 'There's a transport in the river,' she said. 'Soldiers. With convicts. Maurice says they've come from Sydney to build a new road.'

Jim raised an eyebrow. 'So?'

'They might find you, arrest you——'

'I doubt they'd send a ship to bring me in,' he retorted, humour lighting his eyes.

'Jim, please, this is serious!'

'Only if you make it so. No one here knows me; I would have to be very unlucky indeed to find anyone on that ship who did. Unless you are thinking that our Sergeant Duncan is aboard.'

Bregetta met his eyes bleakly.

'Sister, why should he follow me so far?' he asked her. 'It would not further his career to come out into the wilds after *me*, now, would it?'

'He said once that he had no career,' she returned bitterly.

Jim looked away. 'I know nothing of that. I suppose your knowledge of the man is better than mine.'

The anger in his voice reminded her of what he had said. She grasped his arm urgently. 'You must promise me,' she whispered, 'if he *is* here you will stay hidden. He must not find you, no matter what he says or does to me.'

Jim's eyes gleamed, but after a moment he shrugged. 'As you say,' he muttered, and, rising, walked past her and into the cottage.

Molly only shrugged when Bregetta told her. 'More redcoats,' she said, and went on with her baking. Bregetta began to feel as if she was really making more of the thing than it deserved. So what if he knew where she was? And so what if a transport ship had arrived? Why should he come so far from Sydney for so little a reason? Jim was right: she was being foolish.

The summer heat was oppressive, and she longed for it to break in a storm. Christmas Day was very hot, and they sweltered over plum pudding. It seemed foolish to be indulging in such a meal just because it was the done thing on the other side of the world, and yet Molly wouldn't hear of changing it. 'It's tradition,' she said stubbornly. 'Anything else wouldn't be Christmas.'

Afterwards, Bregetta went outside, wondering what Maurice was doing. She could see him, sitting down to a lavish, groaning table with his big red-faced father and pale invalid mother. She saw him smiling and chatting, always friendly, always kind. Perhaps he was thinking of her.

Neil's dog had followed her out, and she bent to pat it. She found a stick to throw, and the dog fetched it, waving its tail excitedly. She laughed, knowing what Neil would say—'That dog's for work, not play!' as he did to Jim when he made a fuss of it.

There were clouds building in the sky now. Great dark ones, promising the storm that had so far failed to come. The sultry air made even breathing a chore, and Bregetta wiped her brow with the back of her hand, reaching down to pat the dog again. It growled suddenly, low in its throat, and the hair on its back bristled. The flesh on the back of Bregetta's neck prickled as if in sympathy. Startled, she swung around.

The horse and rider were close behind her, near to a stump which had yet to be dug out. The red jacket showed up bright in this place of greys and greens and sullen skies, and his dark chair clung damply to his forehead. His black eyes raked over her in a way which brought blood stinging to her white cheeks.

'Sergeant,' she said, and for some strange reason her voice was as cool as if he had only left this morning.

'Bregetta,' and his voice was harsh. After a moment she managed to turn away, bending to soothe the dog, which was still growling. Once she no longer had to meet those dark eyes she found she was able to breathe again. Carefully, she began to edge her way towards the cottage, which she could see through the trees to her left.

'You're a long way from Sydney,' she said, still in that cool voice.

'I came on the ship.' Alistair was following her, step for step, urging his horse forward. And she knew in despair that he had no intention of allowing her to escape. 'We're to set up a garrison in Strand, and quarters for the convicts. You're to have a new road, Bregetta, whether you like it or not.'

'Poor work, I should have thought, for a man of your...talents,' she said softly, stingingly. 'I thought you didn't like road-gangs.'

'I take what I'm given,' he said. 'Besides, the posting suited me. I had business to attend to here in Strand.'

She met his eyes again. They were darker even than she remembered, or perhaps, before, they had warmed to a lighter colour when they had looked upon her. Now they chilled her with their emptiness.

'I hope you haven't wasted your time,' she managed.

'I think not,' and he smiled. It was a thin, mocking smile, not really a smile at all.

Neil's dog suddenly heard some animal in the
bush and went bounding after it with much crashing
of undergrowth and snapping of twigs. They both
turned to watch it go. His horse moved restlessly,
but he held it with an iron hand.

'Are you the Bregetta Smith that Mr. Gordon's
son speaks of so highly?' he asked softly.

Bregetta lifted her chin. 'I expect so.'

'Do you think he'd still admire you if he knew
what you had been to me?'

She looked up at him, angry now, and raised her
eyebrows. 'What was I to you, Sergeant? Forgive
me, but I thought I was less than nothing.'

Anger sparked in his eyes, and his lips thinned.
'Do you mean to marry him? He'll not have you,
you know. His father wouldn't allow it.'

Bregetta laughed suddenly, loud and harsh.
'Well, maybe he'll just *have* to allow it. If the thing
is already done even he can't alter the law to undo
it!'

She was goading him, she knew, but somehow it
gave her pleasure to see the anger in his face after
so long. She took a step towards him. 'I don't know
what you want from me,' she said, 'but you'll get
nothing willingly. Now go, before I call Neil's dog
back and put it on to you.'

He looked at her a moment longer. 'I'll go,
Bregetta. But I won't be far away. Remember that.'
And then he turned and rode away. She watched
him until he disappeared into the bush. And then
she slumped down on to the ground and put her
hands to her face as all the strength went out of
her.

After a time she pulled herself together. She had
faced him, and he had only been a man after all,

not the terrifying spectre she had created in her mind. He could not hurt her unless she allowed him to. Perhaps he would not seek her out again—but she knew that hope to be a vain one.

The others could see that something was wrong when Bregetta returned to the cottage. Jim looked at her, shocked by her pallor. Molly rose, taking her arm. 'What is it, love?'

She told them softly, without pause. They looked as if lightning had struck them. 'That man!' Molly whispered. 'You were right, Bregetta. He's dangerous. What are we to do?'

Teddy cleared his throat. 'We'll do nothing,' he said. 'As far as anyone else knows, Jim here is just a farm-labourer employed by Neil. And, if he keeps low and doesn't wander into town, why should your sergeant become suspicious?'

Bregetta moved uneasily. 'I can't help thinking he will search every house until he finds him.'

Molly shook her head. 'He can't do that. Maybe you're wrong. Maybe he's come here by accident; maybe it's nothing to do with Jim.'

Bregetta looked at her for a moment. 'He said he had business in Strand. I took that to mean with Jim, or questioning me about Jim. I... No, that must be what he meant!'

Later in the evening, when the storm had tired itself out with showy lightning and growls of thunder and the rain had cooled the thirsty earth, Molly sought Bregetta out. 'You don't think there is more to it than Jim?' she asked softly. 'You don't think that maybe he's come to see you?'

Bregetta said nothing. He wouldn't do that. He hated her. But what if he had come for her? He had all but destroyed her once. Did he mean to do the job more completely this time?

Molly gripped her arm. 'Don't let him near you,' she spat. 'He's hurt you once—don't give him the chance to do it again.'

Bregetta shivered and wrapped her arms about her own body. 'I know all that, Molly; you don't have to tell me. But he... I'm afraid. When he looks at me I remember... This afternoon I feared...but I made myself angry to withstand him. I don't know what will happen if we meet again.'

Molly shook her, angrier than Bregetta had ever seen her. 'Don't say so! He's got no hold over you unless you give it to him. Think of Maurice. That boy loves you, and he'd marry you, given a little encouragement.'

'Oh, Molly, how can he? He's as far above me in station as the moon and stars. Oh, he likes to dream, but the truth is he'll marry some girl from Sydney, of good family, who his father thinks is suitable.'

But Molly shook her head. 'We'll see,' was all she said. 'We'll see.'

The work at Strand went ahead. Bregetta could see it progressing when they went into the town on Sunday to church. The soldiers and their convict charges attended too, filling the little building to overflowing. Bregetta was a bundle of nerves, remembering what he had said and his angry face. But he did not even bother to look in her direction once during the service, though she found her own eyes constantly straying to his dark head.

Afterwards, when most of the congregation stood outside and chatted, the place buzzed with talk of the soldiers. The MacDougall girls were almost animated, and their mother had the same glint in her eye that Bregetta saw in Molly's when she looked at Maurice Gordon.

'It'll be wonderful to be able to drive to Sydney, or even to Windsor, instead of going by boat,' Katherine said.

Mrs MacDougall patted her daughter's arm. 'Katherine gets so seasick,' she murmured.

Annie Petty, the minister's sister and house-keeper, came up and nodded at them in a manner she thought befitted her station. Miss Petty also taught the younger children of the settlement the basic skills of arithmetic, writing and reading.

'Poor souls,' she said. The group dutifully turned and watched the convicts clanking past in their grey and yellow uniforms. They looked a grim, lean lot, mouths drawn down with bitterness and hardship. Only the twice-convicted were put into the road-gangs, and usually the harder the job the more hardened the convicts. Bregetta wondered idly at what degree the Strand road was classed.

'Very nice,' Mrs MacDougall was saying. 'Came to tea.'

'Really.' Miss Petty lifted her fine eyebrows. 'I had heard some of his men were making nuisances of themselves at the Rose.'

'Oh, he put a stop to that,' Mrs MacDougall went on, as if it were at her instigation.

'And you invited him to tea?' Miss Petty sounded mildly astonished.

Katherine MacDougall looked earnestly at her. 'He refused at first because he didn't want to put mother to any trouble. But when mother insisted he accepted very prettily.'

Molly gave Bregetta an expressive glance. There was a silence until Miss Petty began to speak of the weather. Bregetta found her mind wandering again, and her eyes searched over the groups of people. She didn't realise what she was looking for until she found him. Alistair was over near the church door, speaking seriously with James MacDougall, the blacksmith. Bregetta felt her eyes fasten on to him despite herself—like a starved kitten on to a saucer of milk, she thought bitterly—and there was an ache in her stomach that had nothing to do with her lack of breakfast.

He was as tall and strong as ever, his dark hair a little longer maybe, and untidy at his collar, and his tanned face frowning. There was a great emptiness in her heart at the sight of him. He had been her life and her love, and he had destroyed both.

Suddenly he looked up, his own dark gaze coming to rest surely upon her, as if he had known, all along, exactly where she was. The distance between them contracted to nothing. Bregetta felt her head spinning. And then the blacksmith had reclaimed his attention, touching his arm, and he looked away again, leaving her cold and afraid, remembering what Molly had said.

'Bregetta,' Molly's voice whispered in her ear. She followed the other woman's gaze and saw that Maurice had now joined James MacDougall and the sergeant. They spoke for a moment, and Maurice glanced across at Bregetta. Then he was, unbelievably, drawing them towards her own little group.

Bregetta had the absurd desire to turn and run. Instead she stood, frozen, while Maurice came near, smiling and laughing, all unknowing what he was doing to her. Mrs MacDougall greeted them with a pleased look, surreptitiously edging Katherine forward.

'You haven't met Captain Duncan,' Maurice was saying to Molly, and they all smiled and nodded, as though they didn't know very well who he was. Bregetta wondered suddenly why he had kept their acquaintance to himself; she supposed he did not think it warranted mention.

Molly muttered under her breath, 'Captain now, is it?' but luckily no one heard her above Mrs MacDougall's loud voice.

Bregetta forced another smile, looking at Maurice only. 'It'll be pleasant to have a good road to Sydney, won't it, Mr Gordon?'

'Indeed it will,' he agreed readily.

Molly was fanning herself with ill-disguised impatience. She kept glancing across the grass towards a group of men among whom were Teddy and Neil, trying to catch their eye.

'Miss Smith and I saw the transport arrive,' Maurice was saying to Alistair Duncan. 'We were out sailing on the river. We must do it again, Miss Smith.'

She gave him her best smile. 'That would be nice. But you're always so busy with your father.'

'Business,' he said as though the word were poison. He glanced at the soldier. 'Not that I begrudge learning all there is to know about my inheritance,' he went on in his irrepressible way. 'But I see my whole life mapped out before me. I want to do other things, I want to see the world. I expect,' and he turned to the soldier again, 'you've seen the world, Captain Duncan?'

Alistair lifted his eyebrows. 'I've been up and down the length of England and Scotland,' he said. 'And I've been to Ireland, and to India. If you call that the world...?'

But Maurice was looking at him with undisguised envy, while Katherine's expression was rapt. Bregetta might have laughed aloud if she had not felt so disturbed by his presence.

'And now you've come to New South Wales,' Maurice was saying. 'How I wish I could join the army. But I fear my mother would be distraught if I even suggested such a thing.'

Bregetta could see by the look on Alistair Duncan's face what he thought of this confidence, but he said nothing. She remembered what he had told her of himself, joining up at fifteen, and before that being the man of the house to his mother and sisters. To him, such as Maurice must be slightly contemptible.

'Are the Indians very savage?' Katherine MacDougall asked quietly. 'Are the women very beautiful?'

Miss Petty made a noise like a snort, but Captain Duncan smiled down at the girl and answered her questions seriously. 'The Indians are very much like other men. But yes, the women are beautiful, though I've seen as beautiful here in New South Wales.'

A faint flush came into Katherine MacDougall's cheeks. Bregetta felt herself turning to ice, despite the heat of the sun above them.

'Indian women are very modest,' he went on. 'It is part of their way of life to be unassuming, and to serve their husbands.'

'Ah,' Miss Petty broke in, 'perhaps New South Wales women should follow their example, then, Captain! I've seen them brawling in the gutters in Sydney, filthy and drunken. It appalled me, but I believe it is so much the norm there that passers-by hardly gave them a second glance.'

Molly, flushing in outrage, retorted, 'You are speaking of a certain class of woman, Miss Petty. We are all respectable women here!'

'Of course,' little Susan MacDougall responded, looking suitably concerned.

Alistair Duncan half smiled, and his glance fastened on Bregetta. The insult was clear in his eyes. 'Of course,' he echoed softly, and mocked her.

Maurice seemed to notice nothing. He took Bregetta's arm in his with a smile. 'I dare say your Indian ladies are very striking, Captain,' he said, 'but, if it comes to beauty, I'm sure you would agree they could not surpass Miss Smith here.'

Alistair's face was hard with distaste. 'I am not much of a man for the ladies, Mr Gordon.'

Even Maurice was momentarily set back. Miss Petty stepped into the breach. 'What, is there no one you have left behind, Captain, for whom you have tender feelings?'

Bregetta could almost hear the MacDougall women collectively holding their breath.

Alistair laughed harshly. 'The army teaches one many things, ma'am, but displaying tender feelings is not one of them!'

'Captain!'

The voice boomed out across the church ground. Mr Gordon was coming towards them; Maurice hastily unclasped Bregetta's arm. His father was a big red-faced man with a wide girth. 'My wife has asked that you join us for luncheon.'

Alistair smiled. 'I'd be pleased to, sir,' he said. 'How is Mrs Gordon?'

'Well enough, Captain. As well as can be expected. Still pining for Sydney, I fear.' Mr Gordon nodded at Molly, evidently not remembering her name. He eyed Bregetta more favourably, but she thought she detected a certain sternness come into his expression after a moment. Perhaps he had already heard of his son's predilection for her company.

Alistair said, 'If you'll excuse me, I'd best give my men their orders before I leave.' He nodded slightly to the group and turned away. Mr Gordon watched him go.

'Good fellow, that,' he said. 'Couldn't have found a better man for the job. Of course, they had to dangle a promotion in front of him to get him out here. Not the sort of place a good soldier would come to willingly, you know.'

He nodded at them in his turn, and, with a frowning glance at his son, went towards his carriage. Maurice gave an apologetic smile and followed. Some of the soldiers were laughing in a group with some of the women from the town, but the latter drifted away as Captain Duncan approached them.

'He doesn't seem as though he means to embarrass you,' Molly said uncertainly when they were alone. Bregetta didn't have to ask her who she meant.

'Perhaps he will do it over dinner with Maurice and his parents.'

Molly bit her lip. 'I hadn't thought of that. Oh, no, surely not? Would he do something so petty?'

Bregetta frowned. 'You were willing to think worse of him before. Why have you changed your mind?'

Molly shrugged uneasily. 'I don't know. Perhaps because Mr Gordon thinks well of him, and because it seems that the only reason he came here was to get a promotion to captain.'

Bregetta shook her head slowly. 'He said nothing of promotion when he met me at the farm. Then it was only "I had business in Strand". Don't trust him, Molly. He's not to be trusted.'

A few days afterwards, Maurice rode over. He seemed unchanged towards Bregetta, and she could only conclude that Alistair had not told Maurice anything of their mutual past. In fact, he called the captain a 'capital fellow'. Bregetta tried to look suitably impressed, but something in her face betrayed her. Maurice, puzzled, asked, 'Don't you like him? Why?'

Bregetta shrugged. 'He seems harsh. I pity his men.'

Maurice frowned. 'I've heard he is very fair with them. Surely you don't dislike him for being a good soldier? I'm sure he admired you!'

Bregetta stared to think he thought her so shallow she could only like a man if he admired her. Had Alistair's poison already begun to work?

'He said you were too beautiful to be hidden away in this wilderness, and I agreed with him,' Maurice went on, preening himself a little.

Bregetta frowned. 'I'd rather you didn't discuss me with him.'

Maurice was puzzled. 'But——'

'I just don't care for him,' she said haughtily. 'Please, let's not spoil the day by talking of him any more.'

Maurice, all contrition, took her arm in his. A breeze stirred her hair, and Bregetta shaded her eyes against the sun. 'You know how much *I* admire you,' he said.

Bregetta smiled, stepping up on to a fallen log and springing lightly to the ground.

'Bregetta.' Suddenly he was serious. He looked down at her. 'Will you marry me?'

She looked into his kind, wistful face and was very tempted. But she knew she could not do it; her conscience would never let her. She liked him, but she would never make him happy. He would alienate himself from family and friends, and for what? A woman who was unable to love him, or anyone, ever again.

'It wouldn't work,' she whispered, and saw his eyes grow dark with hurt. 'Maurice, your father——'

'My father would learn to love you; how could he fail to?'

'Oh, Maurice,' she whispered, 'you know I'm not what he wants for his only son.'

Maurice's mouth grew mulish. 'That's not important. It's what *I* want that matters.'

Bregetta looked at him and realised how very young he was and how spoiled. He thought that because he wanted a thing it was his to take. Time, and life, would show him the error of his ways. It was not for Bregetta to do it. She had too soft a heart to hurt him. She forced herself to smile.

'Perhaps you should speak to him,' she said gently. 'See what he says.'

Maurice brightened. 'All right, if you think so. And if he agrees?'

Bregetta lifted her chin. 'Then I'll say yes,' and she knew there was no chance of that.

Maurice caught her to him, and gave her a kiss on the mouth. 'He'll agree,' he said boldly. 'I'll make him!'

The days passed in work. Storms came at night, shaking the cottage with thunder and spearing the darkness with great forks of lightning. And sometimes, when rain followed, the world was fresh for a time, until the steamy sun came up the next morning. Mosquitoes came with the dusk, making their lives a misery, and only the burning of dried cow-dung seemed to keep them away.

Neil and Teddy had gone into Strand, taking Molly. There was a deal of work going on in the town—the convicts were completing a community hall for the people. Jim and Bregetta were alone at the farm, Jim out clearing some bush at the back of the cottage, Bregetta inside cooking. It was hot again, and her hair stuck to her forehead in little tendrils. She heard a horse whinny and looked up with surprise from her work. Had they returned already? She had not heard the cart...

The bright doorway filled up, and Alistair stood there, dark against the glare. Bregetta felt cold, despite the temperature inside the kitchen, and her hands, covered in flour, stopped their kneading of the dough. His smile mocked her, while his black eyes met hers.

'Miss Smith,' he said, 'I'd hoped to find Mr Field here.'

Bregetta forced her hands to begin kneading again, forced herself to concentrate on the familiar, soothing motion, and she was able to look away from his handsome, dangerous person. 'They've gone into town.'

'I've business to discuss with him,' he went on after a moment.

Bregetta lifted her eyebrows in an imitation of him, and, though she was pale, looked him in the eyes. 'What business would that be?'

He stepped further inside the room. He was a big man, and had to duck his head. He folded his arms. She looked up at him. 'We need stone to make a road,' he said. 'There's some suitable stuff in the hill behind this farm. I'm to quarry it and pay Mr Field.'

Bregetta couldn't believe it. That was what he had been doing in the bush that day! Not seeking her out, or spying on her, as she had mistakenly imagined. She should have known it. He would not pursue her. It was over. Her fears had all been groundless and foolish. She should be light-headed with relief. Why, then, did she feel as if she wanted to cry?

'I hope he refuses,' she said viciously. 'I don't want to see you every day.'

He smiled at her, still mocking her. 'You won't. I don't mean to dig the rock myself. I'm only over-seeing the operation.'

Bregetta looked up to reply. Behind Alistair a figure had appeared in the doorway. Jim. Bregetta felt terror strike at her heart. Alistair started to turn, following her gaze. Before she allowed herself to think she put out her hand and grasped his forearm, and her voice was soft and strange.

'Alistair...'

He froze and looked down at her hand, then up into her face. And then his other hand came up and fastened on her nape. He pulled her forward towards him, and his mouth closed on hers. Bregetta groaned, feeling the passion wash over her. Her lips clung, and she felt his fingers slide up through her untidy hair. The kiss seemed to go on and on. And it was only by sheer power of will that Bregetta reluctantly began to pull away.

When she moved Alistair thrust her back as though she burned him. Behind him, Bregetta noted with dizzy relief, the doorway was empty again.

'I saw your friend Mrs Tanner while I was in Sydney,' he said suddenly, as if that should mean something to her.

Bregetta put a shaking hand to her hair, trying to tidy it. 'Madeleine? Is she well?'

'How should I know?' savagely.

Bregetta blinked, trying to pull herself together. 'If you mean she told you where I was, I know. She wrote to me.'

He looked at her strangely.

Bregetta began to pound the bread dough. 'Did you enjoy your Sunday lunch?' she managed.

'Thank you, yes,' he replied, and his voice was cool again. As detached as hers.

Bregetta began to roll the dough out. 'You must miss Mrs Bates's cooking,' she said huskily.

He took so long to answer that she looked up. There was a strange mixture of expressions on his face: anger and possibly pain. Anger won. 'She was right about you, at least.'

Bregetta felt the colour leave her face again. 'I never asked you for anything,' she whispered. 'It was you who turned from me. I saw you, that last night, go with that . . . woman.'

'She was my corporal's wife,' he said furiously.

'And that made it all right?'

For a moment she thought he was going to throttle her, and then he flung around and out, slamming the door behind him so violently the whole cottage shook. She heard his steps outside, then the horse's hoofs pounding away down the track.

After a while she sat down heavily. Her legs were so shaky that she didn't think they would hold her up any longer.

'I still love him.' The words came out without conscious thought. It was the truth, and she knew it with a sudden deep despair. She had thought her love had been torn from her when she had left Alistair and Sydney. But it had never gone; it had just been hiding, awaiting the chance to show itself again. Evidently, her love, once given, was the sort that was constant. She could no more change it or turn it off than she could become as hard and grasping as Madeleine had when she'd wed Will Tanner.

Only *he* must never know, Bregetta thought desperately. I have my pride. How he would scorn me! And what a fool he would think me to still love him after all he had done.

Jim appeared in the doorway. He stepped forward and his face was grave. 'He's gone,' he said. 'He looked like the very devil. What did you say to him?'

'That's not important,' said Bregetta. 'But you are! You must leave, Jim. You can see that now, can't you?'

He shook his head. 'I can't, Bregetta. I'm tired of running away.'

She took his hands. 'Just for a little while! Until he's gone.'

Jim shook his head. 'This is the last place he'd think of finding me.'

'Oh, Jim, we can't risk it!'

He looked sullen. 'And what of the risks you take? Do you think I like the thought of my sister and that bloody lobster——'

'It meant nothing,' she said with a shrug, returning to her dough. But he caught her chin and forced her eyes to meet his.

'Nothing?' he repeated with soft anger. 'And that's why you look like you've just had a dozen lashes?'

'Leave it, Jim,' she said harshly, and pushed his hand away. 'It's my business. I'll get over it.'

Jim said nothing, but sat brooding while she finished the bread. A short while later the others returned. Captain Duncan had spoken to them on the road, and Neil said, 'What could I do but agree? He also told me he'd buy any milk or other provisions we had to spare to add to the convicts' rations. It was a good deal, and we need the money.'

Bregetta looked at her brother. 'I've told Jim he should go.'

Neil cleared his throat. 'I've something to say about that. I was talking with Mr Gordon in the town. He's looking for a man to watch his sheep on a run he has some miles out. I said I could spare you, Jim.'

Jim looked as if he would like to argue, but Molly took his arm. 'It's best,' she said, shaking it slightly. 'Just for the moment. You can come and visit us when it's safe. You know that. But, for safety's sake, you must go.'

Even Jim knew when he was beaten. Finally, he agreed.

'You can go tomorrow, first thing,' Neil said. 'I'll take you over; that way you'll get there safely. You're a good lad,' and he patted Jim on the back. 'I'll have you back here the moment we know it's safe.'

Jim grinned despite himself. 'You'll not keep me away,' he retorted.

With Jim safe, out on a far run of the Gordons' property, Bregetta felt more able to relax where his safety was concerned. Otherwise she went about her tasks hardly knowing what she did. Her life seemed to be out of her control. Maurice had asked her to marry him, and the truth about Alistair Duncan had finally surfaced from the black depths to which she had sent it. She loved him, and nothing had changed after all.

'Fool!' she whispered aloud, and slopped the precious water she was carrying from the water-holes to dampen Molly's little vegetable garden.

Fool. After all he'd done to hurt her, after her flight to this place, after her determination to make a new life, he had only to look at her, to kiss her, and she was back in the run-down cottage in the Rocks, meeting his dark eyes across the threshold, and in love.

She sometimes caught Molly glancing curiously at her, as if she sensed something was wrong. But she said nothing, and neither did Bregetta.

CHAPTER EIGHT

WELCOME rain had arrived the day they set out for Strand, Bregetta and Molly, for a visit to the MacDougall women. Molly had become quite friendly with Mrs MacDougall, and the latter sometimes came out to Neil's farm to visit them.

Strand was going about its usual business. Bregetta could see the new convict-built garrison and barracks. They would be starting on the road very soon. She had heard that the convicts were presently out at the Gordons', doing some building and clearing. Even Alistair Duncan was not immune to pressure from the higher echelons, she thought sourly.

Mrs MacDougall welcomed them, and ushered them in. 'James is out in the smithy,' she said. 'He has new shoes to put on the Reverend Petty's horse.'

Bregetta smiled at the two MacDougall girls. Katherine was wearing a new dress of deep red, and the colour suited her dark hair and rather sallow skin.

They sat down to tea, and Mrs MacDougall produced some biscuits. Molly was delighted with them, and listened as Mrs MacDougall gave her the recipe.

'Maurice Gordon likes you very much,' Katherine said to Bregetta softly. Her grave eyes were even more grave than usual.

'We are good friends,' Bregetta replied after a moment.

'He's very rich, I understand,' Mrs MacDougall broke in. 'If you were to marry him, Bregetta...' Her daughters were aghast at such bad manners. Their mother looked at them crossly. 'Well, it would be a wonderful thing, wouldn't it?' she retorted.

'Wonderful,' Molly sighed, and eyed Bregetta slyly.

'He's only a boy,' Bregetta murmured. 'He's too young to be married.'

'Oh, certainly,' Katherine agreed. 'He's not a man of the world, like Captain Duncan.'

'Oh, no,' agreed her sister Susan enthusiastically.

Bregetta caught Molly's eye and didn't know whether to laugh or weep.

'He came here to dinner last week,' Mrs MacDougall went on. 'And such a coincidence! It was his favourite, wasn't it, Katherine?'

Something clicked in Bregetta's mind and she spoke without thinking. 'Stew and dumplings.'

There was a silence. 'But...how did you know?' whispered Katherine. They stared at her, and she recollected herself with a jolt.

'I just guessed. I'm sorry. Was I right?'

'Yes.' But the MacDougalls continued to eye her with uncertainty.

Molly clicked her tongue at Bregetta when they left. 'Why did you say that?'

Bregetta shrugged angrily. 'It just slipped out. I was tired of listening to them singing his praises. I wasn't thinking.'

Molly shook her head. 'Is it any of your business if those silly girls are setting their caps at him?'

'Of course not. They can have him with my good wishes!'

Molly looked at her a moment more. Then she said in an odd voice, 'Well, you'd best remember that, because here he comes.'

Bregetta swung around.

Two soldiers were coming towards the smithy, and one was Captain Duncan. The other was a smaller man with brown hair.

'Mrs Field, Miss Smith,' Alistair greeted them coolly. He turned to his companion. 'This is Corporal White, who has just arrived from Sydney. Corporal White, these two ladies are from Neil Field's farm, where the quarry is to be. That is, as soon as Mr Gordon allows us to have our men back.'

The ironic note in his voice was not lost on Corporal White. He smiled as he nodded to Molly and Bregetta. 'Well,' he said, 'it was his influence that brought them here in the first place. Perhaps he thinks he deserves first pick. You know what these squatters are like; think they're master of us all.'

Molly giggled, but Alistair looked at Bregetta and said, 'Take care what you say, Aaron. Miss Smith is a particular friend of Maurice Gordon.'

Bregetta glared at him, while Aaron looked at her quizzically. Then he smiled. 'I can understand a man wishing to become a particular friend of Miss Smith's,' he said.

Bregetta ignored that, and asked sharply, 'Are you on your way to see the MacDougalls? We won't keep you.' She moved towards the cart, Molly hurrying along behind her. But, as she grasped her skirts in one hand and went to climb up, she felt two strong hands clasp her firmly about the waist.

Before she could say anything Alistair had lifted
her up and placed her on the seat.

Bregetta looked down at him. Her face was
flushed and furious, but he met her stare with eyes
as cool as ice, his eyebrows raised enquiringly.
Molly and the corporal were on the other side of
the cart and momentarily out of earshot.

'How dare you?' she whispered.

'How dare I what? What's wrong with you?'

'Leave me alone.'

'It was you who offered yourself to me the other
day.'

'Offered—you are mistaken.'

His face went hard. 'I know,' he said with feeling.
'And I've suffered from that mistake ever since I
met you; I wish to God I never had!'

'That makes both of us,' she told him in a harsh,
breathless voice. 'I see the curtains twitching in the
MacDougall house. You'd better put on your best
face, Alistair, or Katherine won't like you any
more.'

He laughed strangely. 'Good God, are you
jealous?' he asked in a queer, shaky voice.

Bregetta froze him with a look, and, taking up
the reins, started the cart with a jerk. Molly, only
just aboard, squealed as she sat down hard. After
she had settled herself she glanced uneasily at
Bregetta. 'What did he say?' she asked.

'Nothing.'

Molly let out her breath. 'Have it your own way,'
she snapped.

They drove home in silence.

Bregetta gradually felt the anger leave her. Why
had she lost her cool control? Was she jealous, as
he had said? Jealous of Katherine, who obviously

longed for his ring upon her finger? And perhaps
he was quite keen to put it there. Things could not
go on like this. It was intolerable.

A couple of days later Corporal White visited the
farm. Bregetta wanted to dislike him, but found
him so pleasant that she could not. He had
twinkling eyes and a ready laugh, and soon insin-
uated himself into Molly's heart.

'You'd find it quiet here, after Sydney,' Teddy
said, gulping his tea.

Corporal White grinned. 'Very. But we get out
a bit, and I've been to the MacDougalls' for tea a
few times.'

'Ah, yes,' Molly teased. 'The Misses
MacDougall...'

Corporal White grinned again. 'I'm afraid I'm
only second best at the moment, but I'm hoping to
change that.'

Bregetta wondered if Alistair knew he had a rival
for Katherine's heart.

'How's the Gordon place going?' Neil asked.
'Finished the building yet?'

'Yes. That's why I'm out here. To have a look
at the site for the quarry and decide where we'll put
the convict camp.'

'Where's Captain Duncan?' Teddy asked stiffly.

'Paperwork.' Aaron White grimaced. 'We have
to keep them informed back in Sydney. You
wouldn't believe the number of forms he has to fill
in, and the number of reports he has to write up.'
He glanced at Bregetta as if to say more, but
changed his mind. She had the strangest feeling that
he was making excuses for his captain, who should
have been there in his place.

On the following Sunday, after church, Maurice again came over to Bregetta. He looked sullen. 'My father wants me to go to Sydney,' he said when he was able to speak to her alone. Molly was chatting with a group of the townswomen, and Neil and Teddy were looking at some horses over at the smithy with a view to buying one. 'He says I'm being a fool,' Maurice added with disgust.

Bregetta made a soothing noise. 'Perhaps,' she ventured, 'it's for the best.'

He looked almost angry with her. 'I won't go,' he said. Across the church grounds, his father fixed his eye on him. Maurice hastily turned away. 'I won't go,' he repeated more quietly. 'He'll just have to get used to the idea. If I stand firm he'll give way. He must.'

Bregetta said nothing. She glanced again at Maurice's father and saw that he was speaking to one of the farmers, who had his back to her.

'Will you come?'

'What was that?' Startled, Bregetta turned to him.

'I said will you come to afternoon tea? My mother is having an "at home" afternoon. Captain Duncan is coming, and the corporal, and some of the townspeople.'

'She hasn't asked me——'

'There will be plenty of others there. And *I'm* asking you. Please. I'll come and fetch you.'

Bregetta opened her mouth to refuse, then, Why not? she thought. Let Alistair see she was as sought after as the MacDougall girls, and certainly not still wearing the willow for him!

Molly was excited by the news. 'You must wear your blue dress,' she said. 'The one Madeleine gave you. You haven't worn it yet.'

Bregetta opened her mouth to refuse, then closed it again. Why not? she thought again.

Molly looked at her suspiciously when she agreed, but said nothing. But when Bregetta appeared in the dress she cooed with admiration. 'You look a real picture,' she sighed. 'He won't be able to resist you.'

Bregetta knew guiltily that the 'he' in her own mind was not the same man as in Molly's.

The peacock-blue colour suited her well. The bodice was low-cut and, though a little firm for Bregetta's more ample proportions, showed off her figure beautifully. The waist was nipped in, before the skirts flared out, rippling about her to the floor. There were ribbons at the front of the bodice, and lace on the hem. It was the most feminine, frivolous dress Bregetta had ever worn.

Maurice came to collect her in his sulky, and they drove out into the warm afternoon, Bregetta tying her bonnet firmly under her chin. Maurice kept glancing at her, his eyes on the way the blue of the fabric enhanced her creamy skin and the shining auburn of her hair. Occasionally he touched her arm and smiled, as though afraid she would disappear. Bregetta smiled back, but she felt sad. She did not want to destroy this fairy-tale romance of his, but she knew, as he did not, that men like him did not marry women such as she. Oh, maybe if she were desperately in love with him she might go with him to Sydney, force his father's hand . . . but she did not love him.

She had never seen the Gordon homestead before, and found it large and intimidating. There were verandas at the front, and an upper storey with white shutters on the windows which looked down over the paddocks and the road to Strand, while views of the Hawkesbury were to the other side. There was a garden all around, full of English shrubs and trees and flowers. Behind a freestone wall, an orchard was bursting with fruit, and parrots and lorikeets squawked and screeched as they had their fill.

Bregetta swallowed, taking it all in, and wondering if after all she dared to be so bold. 'Are you all right?' Maurice asked her.

'Yes,' and she smiled and took a breath. There was nothing to lose, after all.

'Come on,' he said, and took her hand.

The drawing-room was full of people, but they all hushed when Bregetta stepped over the threshold—a tribute to her beauty rather than her daring. Maurice's hand on her arm tightened, and he drew her forward towards a little woman reclining on an over-stuffed sofa. 'Mama,' he said in a voice that was a little breathless, 'this is Miss Bregetta Smith. Miss Smith lives with the Fields, on their farm. I *have* mentioned her.'

After a moment Mrs Gordon held out a languid hand. But her eyes were anything but languid. They were as sharp as needles and as cold as ice, and they ran over Bregetta in a way which was as insulting as it was rude. Bregetta, flushing, lifted her chin as she took the hand and bobbed a little curtsy. The little woman smiled faintly, as though she had eaten something not quite nice. 'You're charming,' she said. And then, with a little grimace,

'Maurice, dear. Please fetch me my shawl. I seem
to feel the cold even on the warmest days!'

Maurice went off at once, like an obedient little
puppy-dog, Bregetta thought. It was obviously Mrs
Gordon who ruled this roost, invalid or not. She
was smiling at Bregetta again. 'Such a dear, sweet
boy,' she said softly, for Bregetta's ears only. 'So
well-meaning. One has to be so careful he isn't taken
advantage of. People can be so unscrupulous, can't
they?'

Bregetta said nothing.

Mrs Gordon smiled again. 'How do you find life
in Strand, Miss Smith?'

'I'm enjoying it, Mrs Gordon.'

Mrs Gordon gave her a faintly astonished look.
'Good heavens, are you? I find it tedious beyond
belief. The only conversations I seem to have are
about sheep and maize, or someone's latest prize
bull. I long for my circle of friends in Sydney.'

Her voice drawled to a close as Maurice returned.
After a moment of solicitous settling of the shawl
about his mama, and making sure she was comfortable with her numerous cushions, he moved
away with Bregetta. She took a dainty cup of tea
from the uniformed maid, and sipped it carefully,
trying to still the angry quivering in her stomach.
What did it matter to her if Mrs Gordon was rude?
She didn't want her son anyway!

She looked about her and noticed a number of
townspeople she knew. They nodded at her, some
with secretive smiles—as if they were on her side,
but would not say so before the Gordons. After a
moment James MacDougall and his wife came over.
Maurice listened to them politely, and Bregetta
smiled. 'You look a picture, my dear,' Mrs

MacDougall said after a moment, eyeing Bregetta's dress with some envy. 'The colour does suit you.'

'Thank you.'

'Katherine and Susan are out in the garden. Corporal White offered to walk with them.' They spoke a little longer, before Mrs MacDougall saw someone else of her acquaintance and went away. Maurice and James MacDougall were still deep in conversation and, bored, Bregetta moved to the windows. The view over the gardens was refreshing, and a faint breeze stirred the curtains. She wondered what it would be like to live here. To be waited on by servants eager to do your bidding and never to soil your hands with manual labour again. If she were Maurice's wife all those things would be hers. She could understand, suddenly, why Madeleine had married Will Tanner. The temptation was great.

She wondered why Madeleine had not written again. It was some months since her last letter. She realised she missed Maddy's smiles and rather acidic humour. She missed the busy streets of Sydney and the bustle of life, the drums and fifes beating a tattoo, calling the government convicts to their barracks, the red-coated soldiers on their horses, the merchants and the sailors, the never ceasing commerce. Would she ever go back there? If she was Maurice's wife she would go back in style. She would go to all the best shops and buy only the best. Maurice would let her do as she wished; she was the stronger of them, that she knew already. She felt much older than him, even though she was the younger in years. Perhaps, she thought, it *would* work. Perhaps his father would come around, and they could marry in a fashionable church.

Perhaps... The picture came to her unbidden: she
and Maurice kissing, she in Maurice's arms, in an
intimate embrace. And suddenly she shivered in
disgust and misery, knowing the foolish games she
was playing with herself.

'Are you cold, Miss Smith? Perhaps, like Mrs
Gordon, you are delicate of constitution?'

Alistair's voice was soft behind her, but the
sarcasm in it belied the solicitous words. Bregetta
started, but did not turn. She stared directly ahead
of her, into the garden. There was an orange
butterfly fluttering about a white lilac bush; it
wandered aimlessly about the blossoms, as if un-
decided on its choice.

'I didn't realise you'd be here this afternoon,'
the soft, deep voice taunted. 'I wouldn't have
thought you were on Mrs Gordon's guest-list.'

Bregetta refused to look at him. 'I am a friend
of Maurice's,' she said at last. 'He asked me to
come.'

'A very dear friend, I'm sure,' he retorted, and
his breath fanned her nape as he bent closer.
Bregetta closed her eyes. She could smell the clean,
fresh smell of him, and the memories threatened to
overwhelm her.

Then his voice went on, suddenly harsh, 'Have
you seen your brother, Bregetta?'

Startled, she turned and looked at him. He was
gazing beyond her, out into the garden, his dark
hair falling, a little untidy, across his brow. Then
the dark eyes came back to hers, and she thought
she saw her own white face reflected in their depths.

'Why do you ask such a thing?' she demanded.

'He's a wanted man.'

Bregetta bent her head to brush some imaginary speck from her dress. 'And do you think I'd tell you if I did see him?'

His lips curved faintly. 'No. Your idea of truth and mine differ greatly, Miss Smith. It is my duty——'

'Oh, yes, you're very good at doing your duty, aren't you, Captain?' she mocked. 'But do you really think I would deliver my brother into your hands? So that you could hang him to punish me for some imaginary wrong I have done you?'

'There was nothing imaginary about it,' he said stiffly.

'Alistair,' she whispered, and bit her lip. For now his face had become even harsher, and his gaze was full of contempt as it rested on the creamy swell of her breasts above the low-cut bodice of the blue gown.

'Still using your looks to catch the men? There is a name for a woman like you.'

'If you can do unpleasant things to get a captaincy, surely I can do the same for a rich husband?'

She went to move past him, but he caught her arm in a punishing grip. Suddenly they were so close that she could see the lines about his mouth, and the fine creases at the corners of his eyes from squinting into the glare of the sun. 'So you admit it!' he said in a savage whisper. 'It was the truth!'

Angrily Bregetta shook her arm free. 'I admit nothing. I don't know what you're talking about.' And she hurried away with a swish of her skirts to find Maurice.

Maurice gave her a harassed look and turned back to his father. Mr Gordon looked grim. He nodded only briefly at Bregetta, and she could see that Maurice took that as a personal insult. She touched his hand and whispered, 'I should go.'

Mr Gordon was listening, and caught the gist of this. He said in his booming voice, 'You must leave, Miss Smith? A pity. It was nice to have met you.' His eyes gave the lie away.

'I will drive you back,' Maurice murmured angrily.

'You will do no such thing,' his father retorted. 'Your mother wants you here, to help with the guests. You know how delicate she is.'

'Please,' Bregetta murmured. 'It doesn't matter. I can drive myself.'

The scene was becoming ugly, and several people near by were looking at them, trying not to listen too obviously.

'Father, if you think I will allow Miss Smith to go home alone you are sadly mistaken.'

Father and son glared at each other, neither of them prepared to back down. Suddenly another voice intervened. 'I'm about to leave, and I'm going that way. I'll drive Miss Smith home.'

Bregetta's hands clenched into fists, and she prayed that Maurice would overrule him, that he would protest and lead her manfully from the room ... but when she glanced at Maurice she saw to her dismay that he was actually looking relieved that the situation had been taken out of his hands and he would not have to openly defy his father.

'Capital idea!' Mr Gordon was saying. 'Maurice, there are some things we must discuss. Say your goodbyes to Miss Smith.'

Maurice gave Bregetta a long look, while she tried to convey to him her unhappiness with the outcome.

And then he was turning away to follow his father out of the room. Bregetta stood watching him go. A strong, warm hand gripped her elbow, and a soft voice said, 'Come, Miss Smith. This is no more pleasant for me than it is for you.'

Angrily Bregetta walked out of the room. She already felt as if she had been made to look a total fool. And now, to have to ride home in the company of a man with whom she had only just had the most terrible argument... She spun around on the drive, glaring at him. 'I'm not riding pillion with you!'

'What a nasty thought,' he retorted coldly. 'I'm sure they won't mind if we borrow the sulky. After all, I'm doing them a favour.' One of the servants went to the stables to have it brought around, and Bregetta stood waiting a moment in stony silence. But her anger had hold of her, rushing through her in an exhilarating tide, and she was loath to give it up.

'Why did you say you'd drive me home? What did you mean, "doing them a favour"?'

'I could see that you were causing an embarrassing situation. I offered a way out—by removing the embarrassment.'

'By——' Bregetta didn't trust herself to reply.

The sulky was brought around, and she moved to climb up, but his hands came around her waist and he lifted her up as if she were nothing but thistledown. The touch of his hands remained long after he had removed them, and Bregetta tried to hide the colour in her cheeks by arranging her skirts with angry little jerks of the cloth. As he climbed up beside her she sat stiffly and as far as possible from him on the narrow seat. But he seemed neither to notice nor care, and set the horse at a trot down the driveway and out on to the road to Strand.

The afternoon was still and hot. The trees drooped their grey-green leaves, and the dust rose in clouds from the horse's hoofs and the sulky wheels. Above them in the blue sky the sun beamed down, offering no respite.

'You can't seriously mean to marry him,' he said at last in a harsh voice.

'We've already discussed it once this afternoon. I don't want to talk about it. It's none of your business.'

'His father is dead against it.'

Angrily she shrugged her shoulders. 'He'll come around.'

He looked at her strangely. 'He means to send the boy to Sydney until he gets over his...infatuation for you.'

'And I suppose you just can't wait to tell him what sort of woman I am?' she demanded, her eyes flashing.

But when he looked at her there was no answering anger in his eyes, only that emptiness that so frightened her. 'I don't tell tales,' he said, and turned back to look over the horse's ears and down the road. Bregetta was glad he could not see the effect he had had on her.

'Anyway,' she went on, trying desperately to rekindle her ire, 'I could marry him without his father's consent.'

'He's not of age.'

'He will be in less than a year.'

'Can you wait that long? Or would you marry him anyway, and hide out in some little love-nest in Sydney until his birthday?'

Bregetta didn't reply, watching the passing scenery. She felt sick inside, saying such things, knowing what he must think of her. Though he already thought her so bad that nothing could make a difference to him. And, if he was to know that it was really him she still loved, it would be worse than anything he thought of her now.

A lock of her hair slipped out of its pins, and she pushed it back impatiently. 'Where did you get such a dress?' he asked her suddenly, and she saw that he was watching her in a way that was more puzzled than anything else.

'From Madeleine,' she said wryly, and watched him under her lashes. 'She told me I could catch a rich husband with it, or else sell it for food if I was starving.'

He smiled as wryly as she. 'So you chose the husband? When you put it like that perhaps I can't blame you.'

Suddenly it was as if the walls they had built up between the present and the past were lowered. Bregetta looked at him without anger. 'Why did you come here?' she asked softly.

He was still smiling, but his eyes were dark and empty. 'Don't you know?'

She shook her head slowly from side to side, more hair falling loose about her shoulders. 'No,' she said. 'I don't. I thought it was because of Jim, but now I'm not sure. Molly thinks you came because it meant promotion. Is that why?'

For a moment he said nothing. They had reached Strand, and drove through the quiet little town. The garrison and convict quarters looked square and stolid, as befitted military buildings. The convicts were now beginning work on the road. Bregetta

wondered how long the work would take, and if
Alistair would be here until it was finished. What
would she do when he had gone back to Sydney?
The thought gave her physical pain. Having him
here, even if he hated her, was better than never
seeing him at all.

'They offered me the job,' he said finally. 'I think
someone wanted to get rid of me; someone with a
bit of power. And it was worth their while to dangle
a promotion in front of me if I would take it and
go. I told you once I didn't take "sweeteners", but
this time I thought, Why not? And I took up their
offer, and came out here. I had nothing to lose by
it.'

'Strange that we should both end up in such an
out of the way place,' she murmured, as if to
herself.

A cockatoo flapped overhead, white wings
against the blue sky.

'I hoped never to see you again,' she went on,
as though digging at a wound.

He gave her a hard look, and suddenly drew the
horse to a stop. Bregetta held her breath. Would
he murder her now, out here in this lonely place?
she wondered. Would her body ever be found? And
then he was turning to her, and his dark eyes were
strangely vulnerable.

'I thought of you during the voyage here,' he
said. 'I lay awake at night in the dark, and thought
of you. It was as if you were inside my mind and
I couldn't escape. I thought of that last night in
Sydney.'

'You hurt me,' she whispered.

'I meant to.'

'That woman——'

'It was a coincidence,' he said softly. 'She was just there, and...and then, suddenly, *you* were there and I wanted to hurt you. It seemed as if it was meant. Only I didn't touch her. I couldn't. I came back but you were gone.'

Bregetta stared at him, wondering whether to believe him or not. And yet there was no guile in his eyes, only that curious blankness. 'But why?' she breathed. 'Why tell me this now?'

'Perhaps it's easier to tell now, when it's over,' he said, and looked away.

Bregetta felt the tears prick her eyes, and blinked them back before he could see them. Over for him, maybe, but not for her. Never for her.

'I never told you,' he was saying, and she struggled to listen. 'When I was your age, seventeen, I met a woman. The wife of a fellow soldier. We had an affair. I thought I loved her—that word! I thought she loved me—she was a lot older than I was. But eventually I found out she was just amusing herself with me, just a game to pass the time, stop the boredom. And then her husband discovered it. I was ready to fight him for her safety, for her...honour,' and his mouth twisted on the word. 'But he refused. I was too young, he said. A dupe. He didn't fight dupes. It was the final insult. I told myself I'd never become that involved with another woman, and I was glad of that vow many times when I saw others suffer and made to look fools.'

Bregetta's hand went out to touch and comfort, but he looked at it as if she repelled him, and after a moment she dropped it to her side. 'I'm glad you told me,' she said at last. 'I understand a little better. But still not——'

He smiled wryly. 'I think you understand more than you're willing to admit.'

She shook her head, but said nothing as he started the horse moving again.

'I didn't come here after your brother,' he said. 'But if I find him I'm bound to arrest him. You see that?'

She bowed her head, wondering if he had seen Jim after all, and was warning her.

'He's a murderer, Bregetta. He's not outside the law.'

'It was an accident,' she whispered.

'That's for a court to decide.'

'Do you really think they would be lenient to someone who's killed one of their own?' she retorted bitterly.

He said no more, for they had reached the gate up to Neil Field's farm. Molly came out as they drew up at the cottage, her arms akimbo. Bregetta jumped down to the ground without waiting for any assistance. She shaded her eyes and looked up at him. 'Thank you,' she said stiffly, and meant for his confidences, and his warning about Jim.

Molly murmured something about coming in for refreshment, but she was unwilling, and he refused ironically and turned the sulky back the way they had come. Molly bit back a sigh, looking at Bregetta's flushed cheeks. She had gone to the afternoon tea with Maurice, and come home with the captain. It made no sense. But all she said was, 'Your brother's here.'

Bregetta rushed inside, and Jim rose from the table. 'Oh, God,' she said, 'he'll catch you yet.' And burst into tears.

When she was calm again she sat quietly with Jim's arm about her. He looked tanned and well, and his ready smile was warm. But he wanted to come back to the farm. 'Mr Gordon is a good employer,' he said, 'but he's not my friend. How long will I have to stick it out with the road being built? It'll take months...a year maybe.'

'Captain Duncan may not stay here all that time,' Molly soothed him. 'He might return to Sydney, and give the job over to someone else.' Her eyes narrowed at Bregetta. 'I certainly hope so.'

But her worries seemed groundless. Bregetta did not have a chance to be alone with Alistair again during the following weeks. She saw him on Sundays, and occasionally he came to the farm, now that the convicts were working at the quarry, but it was always to speak with Neil or Teddy, and he barely nodded at her. It was as he had told her—it was finished.

Maurice, too, was busy. His father was making sure he didn't have a spare moment. He was always off on errands to the furthest corners of his father's property, and only once did he have a chance to spend a few hours with Bregetta. He was still angry, still determined that his father would give in to his wishes. Bregetta nodded in sympathy but said nothing to encourage him in the hope. She knew it was only a dream. Maurice would grow out of his unsuitable love and be very glad in a year or two that he had escaped such a coil.

'He deserves better than me,' Bregetta retorted when Molly asked how things were progressing.

'Better?' shrieked Molly. 'Where would he find someone as beautiful and kind as you? And someone who so obviously has his best interests at heart? Or are they your interests, Bregetta? Are you more concerned with someone else?'

Bregetta made an impatient sound. 'That's over. It was nothing.'

'It didn't seem like nothing the night you came to my house, crying as if your heart would break.'

But Bregetta refused to be drawn, and Molly had to be satisfied.

A further letter came from Madeleine. Jim was visiting when Bregetta opened it, and they both puzzled over it. Will Tanner had been taken to the George Street gaol. Evidently, he had been found guilty of selling a drunken customer to one of the whaling ships as a crew member—this was known to happen in some of the taverns and grog shops. Bregetta knew of one that had a cell beneath the taproom, where a drunken man could be kept confined until he was collected by the captain of the ship. But Will had never practised such things, at least not when she was working for him. Madeleine went on,

'Of course he is innocent, but he is always making deals, and perhaps has got into something too deep. I know everything will be all right, but I worry. He tells me he will be out as soon as the court has finished with him, but I wonder. He has never been popular, and, although there are many others who bend the law, he may be made an example of. Of course, I have been to our friends for help, but it seems in times of trouble they melt away like butter in the sun.'

She added that the girl he had found to replace Bregetta had had her hand in the cash-box and run off with an ex-convict. 'The worst mistake he made was to turn you off,' she wrote, and there was something prophetical in her words.

Jim scratched his head. 'She may be right,' he said. 'Will isn't exactly the most popular chap in Sydney, is he? He knows too many things about too many people. It worked for him while he was in business, but, now he's locked up, those same people may not be keen to see him free again.'

'Poor Madeleine,' Bregetta said. Madeleine and her chaise-longue and her rich, doting husband. What would become of her, with Will in prison? Would she run the business on her own?

'Write to her,' Jim said suddenly. 'Tell her, if the worst comes to the worst, to come to us.' Then, remembering where he was, he looked embarrassed. Neil laughed.

'It's all right,' he said. 'She can come. But she'll have to work, and maybe I'll need some of your wages, Jim, to feed her!'

Jim smiled. 'She saved my life,' he said softly. 'She can have everything I own.'

Something about the way he spoke the words made Bregetta glance at him sharply. He still loved her, despite what had happened. What was it about the Smith family that they must love so truly, and so constantly? She wished for both their sakes that it was not so.

CHAPTER NINE

As MARCH drew on, with its cool, sharp nights and warm, sunny days, a long-awaited event arrived. There was a dance in Strand, at the new convict-built hall, to celebrate its construction. Everyone had been looking forward to it for weeks. The women supplied refreshments, under Miss Petty's watchful eye, and the men were on their best behaviour, though Bregetta noticed them slipping outside at various intervals, where no doubt a supply of the 'strong drink' Miss Petty so abhorred was secreted.

Bregetta wore her dress from Madeleine. The colour again set off her special beauty, and her hair, pinned up, was like a halo about her face in the lamplight. Molly eyed her fondly. 'I hope Maurice will be there,' she said and stiffened, ready for a fight.

Bregetta opened her mouth to argue, and then gave up and laughed instead.

Teddy winked at her, putting a big arm about his wife. 'This woman has a one-track mind,' he said. 'You just have fun, my girl.'

The soldiers were there, being very proper and correct, though some of them, Bregetta thought, looked like proper reprobates. But Corporal White came over to them, smiling.

'Miss Smith, you put the sun to shame.'

She laughed. His eyes went beyond her, and Katherine MacDougall joined them. Corporal

White's smile became tender—Bregetta wondered if Alistair Duncan knew yet about his rival. Evidently Katherine didn't, for her first words after greeting them, were, 'Is Captain Duncan here?'

Aaron White sighed ostentatiously. 'And I was hoping I would do,' he said.

Katherine flushed, and didn't know whether to smile or try and explain herself. After her few stammering attempts Bregetta came to her rescue.

'He's teasing you. Now tell us, where is Captain Duncan?'

Corporal White raised an eyebrow at her. 'Paperwork, he says. Perhaps he'll be along later. Where is young Mr Gordon?'

Bregetta had a good idea his father was making sure he was well out of the way, and Maurice had yet to openly defy his father.

The dancing began, to the sounds of an improvised band consisting of one man with a fiddle and Miss Petty on her piano. Corporal White drew Katherine MacDougall out into the sedate dance, winking at Bregetta over her shoulder.

'What is the matter with that man?' Molly asked.

'I think he's trying to cut out Captain Duncan,' Bregetta retorted, and avoided Molly's eyes.

A few of the soldiers had disappeared outside, and when Neil came to claim Bregetta for a dance his breath smelt of the strong beer brewed at the Rose. He swung her about so enthusiastically that she was glad to escape back to Katherine MacDougall's side. Bregetta looked at the other girl, noting her high colour. Katherine was fixedly watching Corporal White dancing with her sister. Did Bregetta detect a hint of jealousy in her eye, in the twitch of her fingers on her shawl? Perhaps she was not as indifferent as she seemed.

'Corporal White is very entertaining, isn't he?' Bregetta said at last.

Katherine smiled. 'Yes. If it weren't for...' But she bit her lip and coloured even more at having spoken her thoughts aloud. 'He thinks you're lovely,' she went on hurriedly. 'He told me so.'

Bregetta laughed. 'Did he? Well, we both know what he thinks of you!'

Katherine looked at her with big eyes, and there was a sadness about her that told its own tale.

'But your heart is already taken?' Bregetta whispered, and it was as if her own flesh had turned to ice.

'I don't know,' Katherine replied seriously. 'I think it must be. Is it so obvious?'

'Only to me,' Bregetta lied. She wondered suddenly if she should warn the other girl, tell her that Alistair Duncan was not a man to trust with your heart. And yet perhaps he loved Katherine? Perhaps if she was to speak it would ruin their chance of happiness? Bregetta sighed; it did not seem to her as though he had loved Katherine the day he had driven Bregetta home from the Gordons'. He had not appeared to be capable of loving anyone, let alone this young, serious girl before her.

After a time she contented herself with, 'You'd be better not to depend on one man too much, Katherine. And Corporal White is very nice.'

Katherine smiled and nodded, but Bregetta doubted she gave her advice a second thought.

Some soldiers had returned to the hall, and Bregetta noticed that one in particular was very unsteady on his feet. Other men were going out quite openly now. The dancing, despite Miss Petty's efforts, was becoming wilder. Loud laughter came from some youths in a corner. A lone man did a jig—good lord, was it Neil?—to the applause of the others.

Someone came and claimed Katherine for a dance, and Corporal White returned to stand by Bregetta. He watched Katherine for a moment, her petite figure clasped in a bear-hug by some farmer's son. 'Do you think I have a chance?' he asked softly.

Bregetta turned to meet his twinkling eyes. What was it about her that she must play the confidante tonight? 'You're more her age,' she said at last. 'And you're *very* attractive.'

He laughed. 'But will that drive Captain Duncan from her mind? I fear the impression he's made is too good.'

Bregetta looked away. 'I can't help you, Corporal, other than to wish you luck.'

He leaned closer. 'But I thought it was to both our advantages, Miss Smith, if Miss MacDougall favoured me?'

Bregetta started, and the face she turned to him was pale. 'Oh?' she managed. 'Why is that?'

Aaron White scratched his chin. 'I know I shouldn't . . . but, damn it, I will! Miss Smith, I'm almost certain Captain Duncan does not feel anything other than a brotherly affection for Katherine MacDougall. I'm almost certain he has eyes for someone else altogether.'

Bregetta forced herself to straighten her shawl about her shoulders with particular, finicky care. She felt shaky, and wished for a chair.

'Don't you want to know who I mean?' he went on in a puzzled voice.

'Not particularly.'

The youths in the corner were laughing even more wildly. One of the soldiers went over and began to talk to them. Their faces darkened with anger.

'But Miss Smith——'

'Corporal White!' and she turned to him stiffly. 'If you think you can win Katherine by setting Captain Duncan on to me like a...a dog on to a rabbit, you are——'

A shout startled them into turning. Corporal White swore under his breath and darted across the room, pushing his way through the crowd of dancers to reach the corner. The soldier and one of the boys—a big, bull-headed lad—were locked together. Another couple of red-coated soldiers were running to join in. Their faces were flushed with drink. Miss Petty left her piano and began to make distracted little movements with her hands. 'Do stop!' she cried. 'Please, gentlemen...'

The brawl, because that was what it had now become, certainly did not consist of gentlemen. They rolled and yelled and struck at each other with a mad determination. Most of the men in the room were keen to join in, and even one or two women jumped into the fray, pummelling at the backs of the aggressors. Bregetta saw Corporal White leap into the midst of it all, his actions more indicative of joining in than of putting a stop to it.

She edged away towards the door, hoping for escape, but was knocked flying by the sprawling body of a youth. She lay for a moment, trying to collect her wits, and then struggled up through her skirts and petticoats and hair.

The fight was everywhere. Women were screaming and, depending on their nature, either joining in or huddled around Miss Petty's piano. A soldier fell to his back beside Bregetta, and sat up, shaking his head groggily. He had blood trickling from a cut on his temple, and Bregetta made a sound of disgust. He turned and seemed to notice her for the first time, and fumes of beer gusted over her as he said, "Tis an angel, by God! A blessed angel!'

Then, before she could reply, he grabbed her within his arms and began to kiss her. Her screams, hardly begun, were muffled. But she struggled, flaying her arms and hitting at his head and back until finally he released her. He looked at her in a puzzled, muddled manner while she continued to hit at him.

Then suddenly a shadow fell over him, and he looked up. A hand gripped the front of his jacket and hauled him to his feet. Alistair Duncan's angry white face came close to his, and then he shook the man like a dog did a rat, before tossing him to one side. The soldier hit the wall and slid slowly to the floor.

Bregetta tried to stand up, her skirts hampering her, wondering if she would be treated with the same swift justice. But the hand that grasped her arm was firm rather than harsh, and Alistair lifted her carefully to her feet. Bregetta tried to push her hair back into some sort of order. 'I . . . he . . .' she stammered. But he wasn't listening. He looked over her head at the sea of brawling men, then pulled her back towards the piano.

Miss Petty clutched at him with claw-like hands, but he ignored her. He put Bregetta bodily into the corner by the piano and looked sternly into her face. 'Stay there,' he said. 'Don't move.' Then he was gone, back into the fray.

Bregetta saw him again, briefly, through the mêlée, and then there was a gunshot. The sound of it was deafening in the little hall. More screams from the women—Miss Petty looked distracted. Then silence. Alistair was standing by the door with a smoking pistol held above his head. His face was grim.

'All of my men,' he said. 'Out!'

For a moment no one moved, and then red-coated soldiers picked themselves up from all over the room and began to stumble and crawl towards the door, alone or with the help of their companions. Corporal White, sporting what would soon be a black eye, paused as if to say something to his commanding officer, then changed his mind and went out into the darkness.

The rest of the men also began to pick themselves up, shamefaced, many looking the worse for wear. Molly shrieked and rushed to Teddy, who had a split lip and a torn sleeve. Neil appeared to be unscathed, though he was decidedly unsteady on his feet.

'You'd think they'd know better!' Miss Petty cried angrily. 'Like a lot of children. Well, that is the last time I will allow the hall to be used in such a way!'

Among the groans and protests Bregetta moved to the door. She looked out and, because it was a clear night, saw the dark group of the soldiers moving *en masse* towards the barracks over the street. She felt an absurd stab of disappointment. Alistair had gone. Slowly, Bregetta went down the

steps, and had reached the bottom one when the
dark form stepped up towards her, startling her,
and *his* voice asked sharply, 'What is it? Are you
all right?'

'Yes,' she whispered. 'I ... Are you?'

She was standing with her back to the light from
the hall, and by the faint glow that fell on his face
she saw that, though he looked grim, he was
unmarked.

'Corporal White says he tried to stop them,' he
remarked, ignoring her question.

Bregetta opened her mouth, then shut it again.
She remembered seeing Aaron White leaping into
the fray more with an eagerness to be a part of it
than to stop it. But it was not for her to tell tales.

Alistair eyed her narrowly a moment, but didn't
go on with it. 'The man who assaulted you will be
punished,' he said.

'I think he was drunk,' Bregetta murmured, and
suddenly the whole episode seemed amusing to her.
She covered her mouth with her hand, 'He thought
I was a ... a "blessed angel".'

He frowned at her. 'I'm glad you can laugh about
it,' he said coldly. 'I don't find it so funny. Nor
will he.'

'Oh, Alistair,' and she put out a hand and
grasped his arm, 'it was nothing. Or at least ... you
came to my rescue. Don't make too much of it—
people might actually begin to believe you care what
happens to me!'

He was looking at her, his eyes so dark that she
was startled. Her heart began to thump. She felt
the muscles under his jacket contract like iron; then
his hands came up and he caught her about the
waist and swung her down the last step. She felt

the wooden wall of the building against her back, and smelt the grass and the river and the clean scent of him as he pressed her hard against the hall and began to kiss her.

At first Bregetta was so startled that she did nothing. But then the warm, hard pressure of his mouth against hers, and the heat of his body, moulding to hers, stole over her. She felt as if she too had drunk too much beer, her head spinning, her blood singing. Her hands clasped his head, fingers twisting in his hair. His mouth moved down over her throat to the swell of her white breasts above Madeleine's gown, and she pressed him to her, her breath harsh in her throat. His lips came back to hers, and she met them eagerly, fumbling with the buttons of his jacket and sliding her palms up over his chest. The flesh was warm and hard with tensed muscles, and his heart shuddered. She pressed her mouth where a pulse beat at his throat.

Everywhere he touched was lit like fire, and she knew that in a moment they would both lose control. Already he was running his hands over her hips encased in Madeleine's gown... She felt herself shaking. His hand impatiently brushed aside the soft material and touched her bare thigh.

'It's too bad!'

The voice came from near the door. They froze. Footsteps came closer, then halted. 'Miss Petty, please!' someone cried, further back in the hall, and the footsteps retreated again. Bregetta let out her breath and put a shaking hand to her face. Alistair Duncan stepped back and smoothed his fingers through his hair. She could see his white face in the starlight.

'I'm sorry,' he said, in a quiet, strange voice. 'I would have taken you then if she hadn't——'

'Alistair——'

'And you would have let me.'

She met his eyes, and then turned her face away. 'Yes,' she breathed. 'I would have let you.'

'I won't come near you again,' he said. 'I meant not to touch you after...but somehow it happened.'

She didn't give an answer, but he didn't wait for one. He was buttoning his jacket.

'I have to go in and apologise for my men. Will you be all right?'

'Yes.' Her voice was husky. 'I'll wait here.' She moved to turn away, her body brushing his. He made a sound, half a groan, half a laugh, and, gripping her nape, plundered her mouth again with his.

'For God's sake, go,' he breathed. 'Now!' and gave her an ungentle push in the direction of the vehicles.

As she stumbled away she heard his voice raised in the hall. 'Ladies! And...gentlemen?'

Tears were on her cheeks, hot and stinging. Her body ached with her need of him. She reached the church and sank down on the grass, lifting her face to the sky. He was right, she would have let him take her. She had no defence against him. She loved him, and only him. She felt stripped and bare of the shell she had built up since Sydney, as though she was as vulnerable to his kisses and his cruelties as she had been in the beginning.

People were leaving the hall now, their voices drifting out towards her. Bregetta stood up, wiping her face, glad of the darkness to hide her disarray, and moved across to the group. Molly saw her and took her arm.

'Are you all right?' she breathed beneath the chatter. 'I saw that drunken soldier grab you but I couldn't get to you, and then Captain Duncan came.'

'I'm all right.'

Teddy came up and put an arm about her. 'What a night!' he said with a laugh. 'It's almost worth being in disgrace.'

Molly clicked her tongue crossly.

Katherine MacDougall took Bregetta's other arm. 'Captain Duncan was wonderful,' she sighed.

Bregetta harshly echoed Teddy's laugh. Corporal White, it seemed, had lost ground over this in Katherine's eyes. But Aaron White was not so easily beaten. As they reached Neil's cart, he came hurrying over to them.

'I'm sorry, I had to see to the men,' he said breathlessly. 'Are you all right?'

Katherine looked pleased and embarrassed, as he was looking directly at her. 'Yes,' she said in a soft voice.

'Miss Petty will need persuading to do this again,' Molly snapped. 'Come on, Neil. I want to go home.'

Aaron White took Katherine's arm. 'I'll escort you back to your mother,' he said, and, as he passed Bregetta, grinned at her in the darkness. Bregetta didn't know whether to laugh or cry. He imagined he was doing her a favour, as well as himself. If only he knew it was Captain Duncan he should be petitioning, not Bregetta.

*   *   *

Somehow, Bregetta had known nothing would change. 'I won't come near you again' Alistair had said, and so he hadn't. He avoided her so assiduously that she could not even speak to him. And she grew depressed. Especially when she saw him on Sundays, smiling down at Katherine, his demeanour quiet and attentive. As if he was courting her, Bregetta thought bitterly.

He would not even look at Bregetta. If his eyes happened to catch hers they slid away as if he was afraid of being drawn into a spider's web. He seemed determined never to be so close to her again that such a thing as had happened could reoccur. If only she could speak to him! If only he would hold her and ... He must feel something for her to have acted so the night of the dance. It couldn't be just desire. And yet why was he so determined to avoid her? Why was he afraid of what he felt for her—if it was fear? It made no sense. Oh, if only she could see him alone again!

Corporal White called a number of times, until Molly asked Bregetta if perhaps she had a new suitor. But Bregetta laughed. 'He wants me to put in a good word for him with Katherine,' she replied.

Molly's eyes widened. 'But, my dear, Mrs MacDougall is sure that any day now Captain Duncan will ask ... that is ...' And she looked self-conscious and began fussing with the cloth she was sewing.

'Then Aaron loves in vain,' Bregetta said softly.

Molly looked at her sharply. 'Then he should turn his love to where it will do more good!' she snapped.

Bregetta smiled. 'Is it so simple?'

'Yes, if you put your mind to it.'

'Like Madeleine, you mean?'

Molly snorted, and changed the subject.

Maurice visited once. A harassed-looking
Maurice, who apologised for not coming before.
'My father is driving me like a demon,' he com-
plained. 'I haven't a moment to myself.'

'Never mind, you're here now.' And Bregetta
smiled, genuinely glad to see him.

Maurice took her arm, and they strolled up into
Molly's garden. 'You're looking a little pale,' he
murmured in her ear. 'Were you missing me?'

If only he knew! But her laugh was soft, and he
squeezed her fingers.

'Give me time,' he said earnestly. 'I can win
father around. I know it.'

'Of course you can, Maurice,' she agreed, but
she hardly heard him.

Jim visited occasionally. He still disliked the job
as shepherd, but he stuck at it. Bregetta sym-
pathised but was glad when he left. At least *he* was
safe.

The following Sunday at church it rained, and
Bregetta and Molly sheltered at the MacDougalls'
until it stopped, before heading home. Teddy and
Neil were in the smithy with Mr MacDougall, and
the women chatted and drank tea and ate cake.
Katherine showed Bregetta a new dress she had
made, and they looked through an old copy of a
catalogue for a Sydney store, laughing at some of
the 'new' fashions and gasping over the prices. It
passed the time.

'No, come in, come in.' James MacDougall's
loud, insistent voice sounded from outside the door.
Mrs MacDougall went over and opened it, and
smiled.

'Captain Duncan! Do come in and have some tea with us. Corporal White, too. How nice.'

Bregetta felt herself go numb. Katherine conversely became more animated, smoothing her skirts, patting her hair. A scrape at the doorstep, and the two men ducked in. The room seemed to shrink, especially when Teddy and Neil also entered. Bregetta had the strangest feeling she had not enough air to breathe.

They were all talking, asking questions and answering them. Katherine smiled at something Aaron said, but her eyes were on Alistair. He was frowning at Mr MacDougall, and then he nodded seriously. 'Aye, you're right there,' he said. 'The ground was becoming like granite. We needed the rain, and more of it.'

'Does the river often flood?' Molly asked, her eyes wide. She had heard horrific stories of flooding, and was not keen to sample it.

Neil smiled. 'Not often. Once every ten years or so. But you'd need buckets more than this, Molly.'

'Can you swim, Mrs Field?' Katherine asked her.

Molly shook her head emphatically.

Alistair Duncan gave her a cool smile. 'Never too old to learn, Mrs Field,' he said, and met her angry look with impunity. There was no love lost between them.

Mrs MacDougall and the two girls began to hand out more tea. 'I really shouldn't stay,' Alistair said, 'I should be writing out my report——'

'Your report can wait, surely?' Corporal White dared. 'Anyone would think you didn't want to drink tea with these nice ladies.' His face went slightly pink under the level dark gaze he received,

but he didn't waver, and at last Alistair's stern face
broke into a smile.

'Wait until you get a promotion,' he threatened.
'You'll realise then that for every extra pound the
paperwork increases tenfold!'

'Are you applying for promotion?' Katherine
asked with interest.

Aaron nodded. 'I hope to. If I'm good enough.'

Alistair smiled. 'You're a fine soldier,' he said,
'and you know it. There's no reason why you
shouldn't get ahead. And you've relatives with the
clout to help you.'

'Oh?' Mrs MacDougall was suddenly all ears.

'My uncle,' Aaron answered uncomfortably, and
went on to explain that his uncle had influence in
the right places. But he had been uncertain whether
or not Aaron would stick at soldiering, and so
Aaron had joined as an ordinary soldier to show
him he was in earnest.

Bregetta watched the MacDougalls with interest:
Mr and Mrs MacDougall were enthralled—she
could almost see the pendulum begin swinging in
Aaron's favour; Katherine, serious, with no sign of
avarice in her face; and Susan, slightly bored. Her
eyes moved on and were held by dark ones, full of
mockery. Of himself or her? She didn't know. He
had glanced away almost at once, but she was
shaken.

The rain eased. The guests rose to leave, though
Aaron White was still in deep conversation with his
hostess, who had suddenly developed a keen interest
in the machinations of promotion in the army.

One of the farmers had brought in a horse to be
shod, and James MacDougall bent to it with interest
while Teddy and Neil tried to pretend they were just

as knowledgeable. Molly sighed and stamped her foot, giving Teddy's arm a little tug.

Bregetta walked to the edge of the veranda and viewed the muddy street with a grimace. Strand was grey and dripping, but the air was fresh, as though the rain had washed everything clean again, and the trees smelt sharply of eucalyptus. Taking a deep breath, Bregetta lifted up her skirts and stepped out into the street. Almost at once her shoe slipped in the wet. Her hand went out to catch a veranda post, and caught instead a warm, hard hand which fastened on her own and held her when she might have fallen.

Carefully she found her footing, before turning reluctantly to look back at Alistair. He was looking down at his hand, clasped about hers, as though the sight fascinated him. Her fingers trembled slightly, and he looked into her face with a smile that was bitter.

'I'd stick with Maurice Gordon,' he said at last in a voice like a lash. 'Aaron will probably be a great man one day, but it'll take him time. And it's his uncle who's rich, not him.'

Shock whitened her face, and her gasp was audible. She tried to remove her hand, but he held it fast in his, then with a sudden movement he stooped and swept her up into his arms. She was tempted to struggle, but dignity, and perhaps the shock of his words, held her still as he carried her over the waterlogged street to Neil's cart.

He set her down on the seat and caught her hand as she raised it. Whether she would actually have struck him, Bregetta didn't know, but he was obviously taking no chances. He leaned close, his breath on her cheek, and she saw the tiredness in his face, as though he was working as hard as ten men, and the anger left her. He saw it, for the mockery in his own face changed to something else, and he laughed softly.

'Why is it, whenever I come near you, that I do what I have promised myself I will never do again?'

'I don't know what you mean,' she whispered.

'Oh, but you do. It's the same for you.'

She couldn't deny it. Instead she said, 'Are you going to marry her?'

He didn't pretend to misunderstand her. 'I might,' he said, and glanced again at their hands, clasped together. After a moment, almost reluctantly, he released her. 'I need a wife. I've been a bachelor too long.'

'I thought you weren't going to get involved with another woman,' she retorted bitterly.

He shrugged, and half smiled. 'Sometimes a man needs a woman. And if he's fond of her then so much the better.'

'But that's appalling!' she cried. 'Katherine deserves better than that!'

He raised his eyebrows at her. 'Then why haven't you told her?'

Bregetta searched his eyes a moment, but they were as black and empty as ever. Not even a spark of anything she could recognise. She looked away, towards the barracks where the convicts would be spending their day of rest locked up together. 'The same reason you haven't told Maurice, I suppose.'

Behind him, the others were coming out of the smithy. Bregetta saw Molly's sharp look at his back, and knew the little woman would lose no time in hurrying over. She met his eyes again, and noted, incongruously, those long dark lashes she had once loved so much.

'I wish you happiness,' she said.

He bowed his head, and his smile was secretive as he turned away. Then Molly was there, eyeing him suspiciously, and Alistair bid her farewell with such politeness that it was an insult. It began to rain again before they reached home, but Bregetta revelled in it. It suited her mood exactly.

CHAPTER TEN

BREGETTA looked up at the blue sky, resting for a moment on her hoe. The bush about her lay still and quiet. The rain had gone and the warm weather returned. There had been no floods, to Molly's relief. Neither had they seen Captain Duncan again, also to Molly's relief. She had questioned Bregetta about him at length, but received nothing much in reply except Bregetta's most innocent stare. But she knew! Something was going on. Why doesn't he leave her alone? she asked herself over and over. Why can't she fall for Maurice, or even Corporal White, who seemed to have prospects, and whom Mrs MacDougall was now openly pursuing for Susan? It made her sick to think of the opportunities that girl was allowing to slip through her fingers.

But Bregetta seemed unconcerned by Molly's efforts, and the days went by much as they had since she had arrived in Strand.

Teddy was walking towards her from the cottage. He waved at her, and as he drew closer said, 'I've food to take up to the quarry. I need someone to carry the milk, and Neil's down in the lower paddock. Do you mind?'

Bregetta shook her head. 'No, of course not.'

They went back to the cottage together. Molly was baking today, and the warm smells of maize-bread and other goodies drifted out on the air. She looked up at them, flushed and untidy, a floury smear on her nose. Teddy kissed her cheek. 'You look a picture,' he said. She slapped the hand that sought to squeeze her plump waist.

'We're going to the quarry,' Bregetta told her, laughing. 'I'm to carry the pail of milk.'

'So I believe,' Molly muttered. 'You take care of that girl, Teddy. You know I don't like the thought of them convicts up there.'

The convicts had established a camp at the quarry, and lived and slept and ate there. A band of soldiers kept guard and made sure they worked hard. The only ones who saw those at the farm were those who took the food up through the bush to the hill where the quarry was situated.

'They're no trouble,' Teddy retorted now. 'They're chained down so heavy they're lucky to draw breath, let alone come looking for trouble.'

'We're feeding them too well. All that milk. They'll be getting too strong.'

'Neil only gives them what we have to spare, love. We don't go short. Now do we?'

But Molly only muttered something uncomplimentary to Neil.

Bregetta trudged through the bush behind Teddy, swishing flies away from her face and feeling the sun burning her back beneath the gown. She had been up to the camp once or twice before, and disliked the way the convicts looked at her—desperate, grim men, the humanity beaten out of most of them. The soldiers weren't much better—they stared too, when she wasn't watching, and made coarse jokes out of her earshot.

Bregetta shifted the pail to the other hand and mopped her brow beneath the brim of her hat. Teddy pushed aside a branch and let her through, muttering something about the warm weather never ending.

As they drew nearer, the ground levelled out a bit. There was an acrid smell of smoke, and through the trees they heard the crash of a mallet on rock. Then they came out of the dense trees into the clearing. Voices shouted, and before them lay the camp.

A couple of roughly built huts, big enough to hold all the convicts at night. A fire smouldering, with a pot hanging over it. Convicts in their grey and yellow uniforms were labouring under the hot sun, breaking rock. A couple of soldiers stood guard, slouching lazily against the trees, or stretched out on a large boulder. Bregetta wondered what they would do if Alistair were here, and knew instinctively they wouldn't be so negligent.

The men looked up at Bregetta, and new life seemed to come into them. The soldier in charge straightened up, and the convicts paused in their labour. Someone whistled, but one of the guards shouted a reprimand and there was silence.

Bregetta kept her eyes on Teddy's back and brushed determinedly at the flies. The man in charge came forward and Teddy spoke briefly with him.

'Redmond...troublemaker,' Bregetta heard, and, '...locked up...' She shifted the pail, wondering who they were talking about, when a great commotion came from one of the huts. A shouting and a rattling of chains, and a pounding on the door.

'I want to breathe!' the voice said, the same words over and over again, now shouting, now whispering hoarsely, now in a high note, keening. Bregetta felt the hairs on her neck prickle at the sound. From inside the hut, fists began beating the door so that the whole building shook and vibrated.

The soldiers had rushed over to the hut, and there was more shouting, and then silence. Bregetta met Teddy's eyes. He stooped to take the milk from her lifeless fingers.

'Seems a long time since I saw a lass as pretty as you,' one of the soldiers said.

The words were so incongruous in the circumstances that Bregetta stared at him.

'You're making headway with the road?' Teddy asked drily.

'They're a slow lot, but the "cat" keeps them in line.'

They spoke together for a moment more. Bregetta wiped her brow again with her handkerchief. Then Teddy said goodbye and they started back for the farm.

'What did he say about that man in the hut?' she asked curiously.

Teddy looked grim. 'Evidently he's big trouble. Name of Redmond. He's stirring up the rest of the convicts. Captain Duncan ordered him chained up for a few days. They're sending him back to Sydney on the next boat.'

'Wouldn't he be better in Strand?'

'That's what I said. Seems he's worse there, in the town. Better to keep him as far away as possible.'

'He sounded odd,' she murmured.

'Well,' Teddy grimaced, 'sometimes men go like that. Something just snaps. They told me that after a day or two he gets over it, and he's as normal as you and me. Until the next time.'

Bregetta felt the perspiration trickling down her face again, and sought for her handkerchief. It was gone. For a moment she stopped, puzzled, feeling for it in her sleeve and then down her bodice. But it was definitely gone.

'What is it?' Teddy had turned and was watching her.

'My handkerchief. I had it a moment ago. I've dropped it. I must go back.'

'Bregetta, leave it.'

'No. It's my best one. Madeleine gave it to me. I'll only be a moment. You go ahead to the farm. I'll be with you in a few minutes.'

Then, as he paused, she urged, 'Don't worry! No harm can come to me. I'll fetch it and come straight back.'

'All right,' he said at last. 'I'm supposed to go with Neil into Strand. He'll be waitin', other-wise——'

'You big fuss,' she teased and, with a laugh, turned back the way they had come.

The track to the camp was clear enough. Neil had marked it in the beginning, so there was no fear of her becoming lost in the bush. She walked briskly, her eyes searching the ground, but she thought she already knew where the handkerchief would be. She remembered wiping her face with it at the camp, and very much feared it would be there.

The repetitious thud of the mallet on rock rang through the trees as she drew closer, and Bregetta pushed her way through the bushes. She saw the handkerchief at once, lying white on the ground just inside the clearing where she and Teddy had stood talking. She came forward to fetch it with relief, and it was only then that she looked up.

The soldiers were in a group at the head of the quarry, and they looked anything but relaxed now. There was a horse tethered by one of the trees. Alistair Duncan was there.

He saw her, a momentary wave of cold anger swept across his harsh features. And then he had said something to his men, and was striding quickly across the clearing towards where she stood waiting, the handkerchief clutched foolishly in her hand.

The storm broke quickly. 'What the hell are you doing here alone?'

'I——'

'I can protect you up to a certain point, but if I'm not here and they think you're fair game...' He bit off whatever he had been going to say. 'You're not to come here again, do you hear me?'

'I hear you,' she said, trying to contain her own anger. 'Teddy and I have just brought some food up for your convicts. I came back for my handkerchief.'

He glanced disparagingly at the piece of cloth. 'From your intended, is it?' But he didn't wait for an answer. 'Teddy is a damned fool to let you come back alone. Don't ever do so again. These men are dangerous. Don't let the downcast eyes and the submissive manner fool you. They'd probably think hanging worth it if they could get their hands on a woman like you.'

Bregetta felt cold fear curl in her stomach, but forced her chin to remain proudly lifted. 'Do you mean the convicts or your redcoats?' she mocked.

He eyed her with scorn, and then turned back to his men. 'I'll be back,' he shouted. 'Give them a water-break.'

The convicts threw down their tools gratefully, and Alistair took her arm firmly and led her back into the trees. Bregetta hurried after him, brushing through the twigs and branches, pulling her skirts free from the clinging undergrowth.

'Must you go so fast?' she gasped out.

He turned to glare at her, saying angrily, 'I haven't the time to spare for escorting foolish women to and from convict camps.'

'Oh?' she panted. 'You seem to have plenty of time for escorting Katherine MacDougall.'

'She's not foolish.'

His matter-of-fact statement hurt her so much that she could not answer, and, pushing past him, she hurried even faster ahead than he had done. But her eyes were blurred with tears, and she did not see the snake.

Its long, slender body was half-hidden by a fallen sapling which lay across the track. Only the black scales glinted in the sunlight as the noise of their approach galvanised it into action.

'Snake! Look out!'

Alistair's cry startled her so that she half turned, stumbled, and almost fell. He caught her arm and swung her roughly against him. He was holding her so fast that Bregetta could hardly draw breath. She could feel the hard beating of his heart and his ragged breathing in her hair. Slowly, she turned her head, and looked back towards the track.

The snake was moving on the sapling, gliding up and over it, and away through the soft rustling leaves and twigs. The black scales glittered almost silver in the sunlight. Had she and Teddy stepped over it on their way here? The thought made her shiver violently.

'A black snake,' he said softly above her head. 'Deadly.'

Despite the heat, Bregetta felt chilled. Death was always close for those who lived in the bush, with fire and flood an ever-present threat, but death had never been so close to Bregetta as at this moment. And he had saved her life, the man she loved.

Slowly, Bregetta became aware that his heart was steadying, and, though there was no longer any need to hold her, he had not let her go. She turned her head again and looked up into his dark eyes. They had that strangely vulnerable look that she remembered from before. He smiled ironically.

'It seems I can't seem to be near you without laying my hands on you, Bregetta.'

'You saved my life,' she said huskily. Her heart was pounding now, and with slow deliberation she stood on tiptoe and brushed her lips over his cheek. 'Thank you,' she breathed, and her lips touched his cheek again, waiting. As if he was unable to resist, Alistair turned his face, and his mouth found hers. As their kiss deepened, Bregetta's hands slid over his shoulders and clung around his neck, fingers twining in his dark hair like the snake she had already forgotten. Passion seared her like a fiery brand, and her head spun.

Alistair bent his head with a groan and his mouth nuzzled her throat, while his hands loosened the matronly knot of hair, sending it into wild abandon over her back and shoulders.

'This is what I thought of during those nights without you,' he murmured.

Bregetta felt her breath catch at his words. He dreamed of her, he couldn't resist her. She had braved all her terrors, and his contempt, and he was hers. She began to kiss him again, but he caught her hair up in his fist and held it, pulling her head back almost painfully and looking into her eyes.

'Do you let Maurice Gordon do this?' he asked her harshly. 'Or this?' And he cupped his other hand about her full breast, his touch like fire.

'Alistair,' Bregetta whispered.

'Do you?' he demanded, and he began to un-button the bodice of her gown, stooping to kiss her creamy flesh.

'No,' she gasped. 'Never. There's only you.'

'For some reason,' he whispered, 'you're in my blood, and I'm in yours. There's only one way I know of to make a cure.' He was unfastening his red jacket, and now shrugged it off. Bregetta watched as he laid it down on the ground, making a covering for the warm leaf-strewn earth.

His black eyes met hers, and he held out his hand. Trembling, Bregetta placed her fingers in his, and he gripped them hard. Then he was pulling her to him again, and his mouth was savage on hers. He slipped her gown off her shoulders, and it fell in a puddle at her feet. Perspiration lay shiny on her skin as he peeled off her chemise and her petticoat. Bregetta pulled off his white shirt, smoothing her palms over his warm brown chest and strong-muscled back. She had almost forgotten the beauty of his body—it had been so long.

'There's only you,' she had said, and it was true. With every touch and kiss and sigh it only became clearer to her. He was her man, and there could never be another.

Bregetta lay down in the sun-dappled shadows, her hair like fire about her. He looked down at her for a moment, and his eyes held that same expression of wonder that they had used to, and then he gathered her up in his arms and began to kiss her in earnest.

The fire in them built, tinder catching and flames leaping; his hands touched her body and found her secrets, while she held him as if he was her only refuge in the roar of the fire they had made. At the end he looked down into her face, as though it pleased him to see her made helpless by what he did, and then he was helpless too as she pulled his mouth down to hers, kissing him with abandon, and the world rocked with their passion.

They lay fast together, still lapped by the glow of the embers. Then he had moved away, on to his back, and they lay together in total peace. At last Bregetta turned her head languidly to look at his profile beside her. His eyes were open, he was looking up into the trees, and the moving shadows played across the golden brown of his body. Slowly she put out her hand and smoothed his cheek. He turned at her touch, and his dark eyes searched hers, their expression a mixture of pain and self-contempt.

'I must be mad,' he breathed, 'but I can't seem to help myself. Bregetta, this can't go on. You know it as well as I. We have our own lives to lead.'

'Alistair!' She sat up, her long hair covering her like a cloak. She pushed it back impatiently over her shoulder, and the golden lights of it flickered and danced. He turned away from the movement, as though to watch it gave him pain.

Anger lit her, for a moment overwhelming hurt and caution: she had given him everything she had to give, and he didn't want her.

'So now you're cured,' she said harshly. 'Is that it?'

He sat up too, and began slowly to pull on his shirt. 'Yes,' he said quietly. 'I am.'

Tears stung her eyes. Automatically she began to put on her gown, her hands stiff and clumsy with her fear. She had lost him, lost him, lost him . . . The words reverberated in her head. He was going to destroy her all over again—'Did you think I loved you?' he had said—and she had allowed it to happen. Bregetta shook her head, trying to quell the clamour in her mind. Her fingers shook over the fastenings.

Alistair was dressed, looking almost as smart as usual. As if nothing had happened. Bregetta smoothed her skirts over legs that trembled, rubbing at a smudge of earth on the cloth. There must be something she could say, she thought. There must be something that would sway him, that could touch that cold heart of his.

Bregetta was thinking so hard that she did not hear the intruder until he was almost upon them, so quietly had he come. It was only when he pushed aside the branches directly in front of them that Bregetta looked up, in shocked dismay, and met his eyes.

At first there was only relief in them. 'Bregetta,' Maurice sighed. 'I was so worried! When they told me you had gone back to the quarry alone I thought the worst. I——'

His eyes went past her, for he suddenly noticed Alistair's red coat as the soldier stepped forward.

For a moment Maurice stared, stupidly, and then a crease came between his brows. His gaze came back again to Bregetta, and slowly, slowly, he noted her clothes' disarray, and her wild, unbound hair. She knew her mouth was red from kissing, her white skin showing so clearly every touch upon it. She felt as if the whole scene were being re-enacted before his very eyes, passing from her mind to his.

The bewilderment was gone, and now there was a dreadful pain. 'Bregetta,' he said, 'tell me I am wrong. Tell me I am wrong!'

She shook her head, tears on her cheeks. 'I ... Maurice, you must understand ...'

'Understand?' he cried. 'Why? What is this man to you?'

'He and I ... Oh, Maurice, I have known him since Sydney. You must not think it was to hurt *you*.'

She thought he was going to cry. Behind her came Alistair's voice, harsh with the intolerable situation he found himself in. 'It was my fault. The blame is mine.'

For a moment Maurice looked as if he might strike the other man. And then he shouted brokenly, 'I'll ruin you. See if I don't!' and turned and flung his way back through the bush. Bregetta stared after him, tears streaking her cheeks.

'Poor Maurice,' she breathed. 'Oh, I must go after him!'

'No!' he said savagely, and caught her arm. 'Leave the poor devil alone. I know exactly how he feels.'

For a moment she didn't understand him, and then shock took the breath from her body. 'You talk as though I am like that woman, that soldier's wife, who... Maurice is no dupe!'

'Isn't he?' he retorted. 'He's discovered his beloved has feet of clay. Leave him to come to grips with it in his own way. It might make a man of him.'

'You're cruel,' she whispered. 'You must go after him and explain——'

'Explain what?' he mocked her. Then, looking past her, 'In his place I might have demanded satisfaction. But perhaps he didn't think you worth it.'

'Did you do this on purpose?' Bregetta gasped. 'Just to hurt me and spoil the only chance of happiness I had?'

'Don't be a fool,' he said shortly, a dash of cold water on the heat of her words. 'And have him ruin me, as he says he's going to? If I had known this was going to happen I would never have come here today. As it is, I now have no choice.'

She looked at him so blankly that he almost laughed. 'Your friend Maurice has seen us together in what is called, I believe, "a compromising situation". Strand isn't Sydney—it's a small, isolated community. I am supposedly in a position of authority, and you are supposedly a young woman of spotless reputation. Mr Gordon is the power around here. He might have something to say about my going around ruining young girls' reputations.'

He did smile now, an ironic smile, as the expression of disbelief grew on her face. 'No,' she breathed.

'Yes,' he said softly. 'You have no choice, Bregetta. He won't marry you now; even you can't find a way around this. It's got to be me.'

'But you're going to marry Katherine,' she cried. 'Everyone knows that!'

Alistair looked away. 'I'm marrying you, as any honourable man would. We have no choice, Bregetta.'

She opened her mouth to argue, but he gripped her chin in his hand, 'Accept it, and make the best of it.'

The argument died on her lips. He *was* an honourable man, but this was for his good as well as hers. He could leave her to fend for herself, her reputation in tatters, and he could try and bluff his way through Mr Gordon's complaints. But his reputation would be damaged just as badly as hers. It was clearly the best thing for both of them to marry. She felt so tired suddenly that she knew she hadn't the strength to fight him.

He saw capitulation in her face. His grip tightened and he drew her forward and kissed her lips with a cool chasteness that might have amused her in other circumstances. 'Now,' he said, 'we'll break our news before Maurice breaks his.'

They walked slowly now. Bregetta felt drained. She had known, when she had kissed him that first time today, that she was throwing all she had into fate's hands. She had hoped that Alistair might feel something for her, but never this . . . What had he said? That he was cured of whatever it was about her that was haunting him? And now he was marrying her . . . She felt as if she had trapped him into doing something he did not want to do, and Bregetta was not the sort of girl to be happy with that. 'We have our own lives to lead,' he had said. How could he bear to have his suddenly shackled to hers?

'Alistair——' she turned at the edge of the trees, the cottage visible before them '—I can still go to Maurice. I can tell him it was my fault. He'll listen to me.'

His black eyes were angry. 'What sort of man do you think I am?' he asked softly, and his voice struck her with its fury. 'Look, I like it just as little as you, but there is no choice.'

There seemed nothing more to say after that. She turned and ran jerkily down the slope, past Molly's garden, to the cottage. Molly was inside and looked up at Bregetta with startled blue eyes.

'What on earth did you say to Maurice Gordon?' she cried. 'He just rode off like a bat out of hell.'

'I . . . Don't ask, Molly.'

Molly became aware of her hair about her shoulders, and her white face. 'He didn't try to——?' she began.

Bregetta shook her head sharply. 'No. Nothing like that. I think he's finally come to his senses,' she whispered, and her voice cracked. 'I told you he would, Molly.'

Molly clicked her tongue. 'Shame,' she said sadly. 'I had such hopes!'

And it was Bregetta who comforted her with a hug. 'I know,' she whispered.

'What will he do?' Molly asked her.

'Go to Sydney, I expect,' Bregetta murmured. 'As his father wanted him to.'

'Oh, my dear——'

'No, Molly, it's for the best. It would never have worked. I'm just sorry he had to be hurt so much. . . .'

'What did you say to him?'

Bregetta bit her lip. 'It wasn't so much what I said.'

Molly was frowning, and then her eyes slanted past Bregetta to the door and she caught sight of Alistair Duncan walking slowly towards the cottage.

'What is that man doing here?' she hissed.

Bregetta laughed shakily before the other woman's obvious hostility. 'That's what I wanted to tell you,' she said. 'I'm going to marry *him*.'

Molly looked at her in disbelief, her jaw dropped. 'No!'

Alistair was at the door now, and he heard. He lifted his eyebrows as he stepped over the threshold. 'I see Bregetta has told you our happy news, Mrs Field. Perhaps you'd help her with the arrangements. It'll have to be here in Strand, of course. I can't leave my post.'

'I...' Molly blinked. 'This is very sudden,' she said in a hard voice.

Alistair's mouth twitched into a faint, ironic smile. 'I would have said the opposite.'

'I don't understand,' Molly went on.

'There's nothing to understand,' Bregetta murmured. She was chalky-white now and Molly feared for her. Suddenly anger overcame astonishment and she turned to the soldier standing there so still and assured, as though he were master of them all.

'No,' she said. 'I'll not stand by and see you marry him. If you want to marry then find someone else. But not him.'

Alistair's face was hard and cold as rock, and his black eyes gleamed. 'I'm sorry to have to disappoint you, Mrs Field,' he said softly, 'but the truth of the matter is that Maurice Gordon has just come upon us in a ... a situation which would take some explaining, and has threatened to let the details become public knowledge. I think neither you nor I nor Bregetta would want that, now, would we?'

Molly's face changed from anger to shock, then to dismay. She sighed a deep, heartfelt sigh, and sat down at the table. 'I see,' she said quietly, and Bregetta felt as if she had damaged herself irreparably in that woman's eyes.

'Now,' Alistair leaned forward, his hands resting on the table, completely in charge, 'for all our sakes, Bregetta must marry me. If you think I can't keep her adequately on my captain's pay——'

'Don't be foolish,' Molly muttered. 'I see now why...there is no choice.' And, all unknowing, she had repeated Alistair's own words.

Some of the tension seemed to go out of him, and he looked at Bregetta. 'When do you want to marry me?'

'I don't know. I haven't thought.' She looked back at him blankly, the colour staining her cheeks.

'Discuss it with Mrs Field, then,' he said, as though he were talking with one of his men, giving orders. 'I must get back. I hope to see you on Sunday. I'll make sure that our news gets about.'

And he had gone, leaving Bregetta staring after him in a tangled mixture of bewilderment, elation and dismay.

'That man!' Molly cried venomously. 'Why did you let yourself get into such a...? Bregetta, what is to be done?'

Bregetta looked at Molly, and her eyes were soft with tears. 'I'll marry him,' she said, 'because I love him, and I always have and always will. I think you knew that, Molly.'

Molly's face filled with despair. 'But what of Katherine? She thought...we all thought! And Jim? Will you have him give you away?' with sarcasm. 'What will he think of your marrying Captain Duncan?'

'Perhaps it will work to his advantage,' Bregetta whispered. 'Please, don't be angry. I couldn't face it now,' and her voice broke.

Molly hugged her, stroking the untidy hair from the girl's face. 'I'm not angry,' she said. 'I'm just sad, and afraid for you. I saw what he did to you last time. And now you'll be even more in his power.'

'I won't be hurt like that again,' Bregetta told her. 'I'm harder now.'

Molly just shook her head again. It was not the way she would have chosen, but it was out of her hands.

CHAPTER ELEVEN

THE next few weeks were difficult ones. First Teddy and Neil to be told, and Teddy's amazement to be got around. 'My girl,' he said. 'You've done it this time!' Then the church on Sunday, and people already knowing of the arrangement and perhaps knowing the rest as well. Then Katherine MacDougall coming up to Bregetta, white-faced, and bravely embracing her, offering congratulations. While Mrs MacDougall studiously avoided Bregetta, keeping her dashed hopes to herself.

Alistair Duncan came and took her hand into the crook of his arm, and said all the polite things. But he was frighteningly distant. As if another man entirely stood in his place, and yet looked like him. Bregetta replied to his remarks with the same studied politeness, while inside she was desolate. She could only think that he had loved Katherine, and now his life was ruined.

Mr Gordon had demanded a meeting with him the day after Maurice had seen them. Alistair didn't tell her what he said, but it seemed that Mr Gordon was pleased enough with the explanation he gave, and certainly pleased with the outcome. His son had been saved and the unsuitable woman removed, all in one fell swoop. Alistair Duncan had put himself in a very good light, and would receive only favourable reports from Mr Gordon to his powerful friends in Sydney.

208

And then the news came that Maurice Gordon had gone, and Bregetta remembered the terrible scene as though it were yesterday. She was sorry it had ended in such a way, and he had been so hurt. But in a way it was a relief not to have to pretend any more to something she did not feel. She only wished she could have broken it gently to him, or let the thing peter out of its own accord, as she was sure it would have done in time.

Aaron White was also pleased, and his hearty congratulations to her left her in no doubt of the fact.

Alistair visited the farm once, sat a bare half-hour, drank a cup of tea that Molly grudgingly served him, and left. They had decided on a May wedding. Four weeks to make ready. Bregetta felt she was caught up in a dream, or a nightmare.

Jim visited them at last. He couldn't believe his ears, he said. 'I'll knock his block off,' he kept saying.

'He's doing the right thing,' Bregetta retorted. 'Wouldn't it make more sense to fight him if he had refused to marry me? Everyone must know now that I am as bad as they always thought me. Places like Strand can be ugly for girls like me.'

'And I suppose it doesn't benefit him, getting in good with the local bigwig!' he retorted. Then, 'What about me? Does that mean we'll never be able to see each other again?'

Bregetta shook her head angrily. 'Of course it doesn't! Perhaps, once we're married, he'll decide to forget about your past, Jim.'

Jim looked sceptical, and opened his mouth to say more. The sudden thunder of horses' hoofs stopped him, and a shout of alarm sent him hurrying into the other room. Bregetta stood up, her heart beating in her throat. Teddy's voice was raised in anxious question. Bregetta hurried to the door. A soldier had just dismounted, and others sat on their horses, faces grim and white under the covering of dust. Teddy looked at her, and he was also grim.

'Bregetta,' he said. 'Where's Molly?'

'Out in the barn collecting eggs. Why?'

Not Jim, she thought. They haven't come for Jim...

'That convict's escaped,' he said. 'The trouble-maker Redmond. Killed his guard and took off into the bush with two others. They're searching the whole area for them.'

'Oh, no.'

'They hope to catch them soon, but in the mean-time——'

'In the meantime,' the private interrupted, 'everyone is to be on the alert. Redmond's dangerous. A murderer twice over, or more if the truth be known. They can't last long out in the bush; no white man can. They'll need food and water, and they'll come into the settlement or find a farmhouse.'

'We've guns,' Teddy said. 'We'll be on the look-out for them.'

The soldier nodded, eyed Bregetta as if inclined to dawdle, then reluctantly remounted and led his men away to the road.

Jim came out, and Teddy told him tersely what had happened. 'I'm staying on here,' he said shortly, and glared at Teddy, daring him to argue. 'I'm staying,' he repeated. 'I'm not going to leave you all in danger. I know what these bolters are like—they murder for a few shillings or a pair of boots.'

'You'll as likely get the sack from Mr Gordon,' Teddy reminded him.

Jim shrugged. 'He'll not know. I left one of the lads to cover for me. Besides, they might have caught them by tomorrow, and I can go back.'

'You might be right,' Teddy muttered, but Bregetta thought he looked anxious, and felt the stirrings of fear within herself.

But the next day the convicts were still at large, and the boat came into Strand. Neil and Molly went alone to meet it. Bregetta remembered then what Teddy had told her about the escapee Redmond. They had intended returning him to Sydney on the next boat. He must have known that and what would happen to him once he arrived there. Desperation had sent him into the bush, and desperation kept him there, hidden, despite all their attempts to track him down and recapture him.

But they knew he'd have to show his face sooner or later. The three men would need food and water—and clothes if they were to reach safety without being detected by the military or the police. Teddy had drilled them all in using the guns—there were two shotguns and a hand-pistol. No one was to wander away alone from the cottage, and everyone was to be on the watch-out for anything suspicious. At night they took turns to stay awake and alert. The dog was tied outside the door to give warning.

Already, after one day, Bregetta was starting to feel trapped in the little cottage. A prisoner for her own sake, but a prisoner all the same. She thought she could understand all too well the need to escape.

But not the need to kill. She thought of Alistair, and knew he would be busy. It was his responsibility that this man had escaped—although they had heard that the guard had been careless—and he must see him caught without further bloodshed. And yet she wished he would come and see her, and pretend that he was concerned. For he couldn't love her—no man in love acted as he did—nor did he desire her as he had once done. And if she truly loved him, she would release him from this engagement he must find so intolerable. The thought jagged at her heart like a broken fingernail. She had always had the hope that, in time, he would grow to love her, that love would beget love, but suddenly the platitudes she had fed herself left a sour taste. Let him go, her heart told her. Give him his freedom.

Teddy's shout stopped her agony and brought her outside into the cool, blustery day. She looked at him enquiringly, then shaded her eyes and followed his gaze to watch Neil's cart jolting its way up the track towards them. There was someone else on board besides Neil and Molly.

For a moment she couldn't believe her eyes. The blonde hair tossing in the wind, that slim, slight figure huddled in a big cloak. 'Madeleine!'

Her cry was taken by a gust of wind, but the other girl seemed to hear it for her head came up and she waved her hand.

Teddy made a sound like a curse under his breath, but Bregetta didn't hear. She was hurrying down the track towards them, her smile splitting her face from ear to ear. 'Madeleine.'

'Bregetta.' Madeleine gave her her hand, and Bregetta studied her as she climbed from the cart.

She seemed slighter than ever, fragile beneath the thick cloth of the cloak. Above its darkness her face was drawn and pale, with lines etched at her mouth and between her brows. Lines strange on such a young woman—as though there was no peace within her. The thought startled Bregetta, and she put it aside as she hugged Madeleine and felt how thin she was.

'It's been so long,' Madeleine sighed, and smiled a little wryly. 'You see, I've come as asked. I hope you don't mind. Perhaps you were just being kind. Only...' and now the despair showed up plainly in the blue depths of her eyes '...only I had nowhere else to go.'

Molly began to bustle her towards the cottage. 'Come on, my girl,' she said, 'out of the cold. I've warm tea for you, and some bread and cold mutton if you've a mind to it. You're tired to death.'

But Madeleine was looking beyond her, to the cottage door. Jim stood there, his hair bright, his face blank with astonishment. Then his mouth cracked into a smile, and he came forward to take her in his arms. 'Maddy,' he said, as if he couldn't believe it. 'Maddy, you've come!'

'Yes,' she said quietly, her head resting against his shoulder, and closed her eyes. 'I've come. And believe me, Jim, if there had been anywhere else——'

'This is obviously no time for pride,' Jim retorted. Madeleine looked at him strangely, but said nothing.

They finally heard the full story. Madeleine had removed her cloak, and drunk her tea, and eaten, before Molly would allow her to tell it—for, of course, she had already heard it. Will Tanner was dead. Dead in prison, and whether or not murder had been done they would never know. His enemies and so-called friends had fallen upon his business assets like carrion crows, claiming he had debts unpaid. Madeleine had been unable to prove otherwise, and so they had taken almost all she had. Even Will's influential friend Francis Warrender had not been able, or willing, to help.

'He turned me down,' Madeleine said with a bitter laugh. 'And I lost it all.'

Bregetta squeezed her hand. 'Poor Maddy,' she murmured. 'But you found your way here, to us. You know we're your friends.'

Madeleine looked at her for a moment as if she would cry, and then she closed her eyes. 'I have been a fool,' she said.

Teddy cleared his throat. 'Never mind,' he said gruffly. 'You have a chance now to make a new start.'

Bregetta looked at him in astonishment, and was ready to defend her friend. But Madeleine laughed. 'You never did like me, did you, Teddy?'

He moved uneasily. 'I like you better now than I ever have,' he said.

Molly began to remonstrate with him, but Madeleine just laughed again. Jim stood behind her, his eyes on her bright head. Bregetta saw the soft look of him, and sighed. She hoped Madeleine would be more receptive this time, and that Jim would not be too hurt if she left again for greener fields. But something about Madeleine's tired face and bitter mouth gave her a strange hope for their future.

The autumn winds blew wailing about the cottage all evening. Neil stoked the fire, and they sat close about it until it was time to go to bed. Teddy stood the first watch.

Madeleine was to sleep in the calico-screened alcove near Bregetta, and she watched the other girl brushing out her long fair hair, and then plaiting it ready for sleep. Madeleine's arms were so thin, as though the flesh barely covered the bones. 'I'm sorry,' she said at last, 'about Will. We never got on, I know, but it's a sad end for such a man.'

Madeleine shrugged her shoulders. 'He was a liar and a bully,' she murmured. 'I know that. But in his way he loved me, and cared for me. I was his precious jewel, and he valued me all the more because the rest of his life was a dung heap.' Madeleine had always been one for plain speaking when it suited her, and Bregetta could see the truth of her bald words.

'I can't believe Francis Warrender didn't offer some help.'

Madeleine smiled wryly and set down her brush. 'I offered myself to him. He turned me down.' She noted Bregetta's shocked expression with angry exasperation. 'Don't be such a child, Bregetta! I had no choice. But it failed, and perhaps I'm a little glad I don't have to lie with that old man.'

Bregetta's brows drew together. 'And yet you wanted him to have me.'

'Yes.' Madeleine fiddled with the long, thick plait that lay over her shoulder. Then she said, 'I've always tried to be your friend, Bregetta. I didn't have many true friends. You probably don't understand that, for people have always loved you. They just put up with me.'

Something in her voice was so odd and strained that Bregetta was startled by it. 'Madeleine,' she whispered, 'what is it?'

'Why, nothing,' Madeleine retorted, but her eyes avoided the other girl's. 'I was just telling you something that has always been clear to me.'

'I feel that there is something you haven't told me.'

Madeleine looked at her now, and her eyes were glittering. Her mouth twisted, and for one second Bregetta thought she saw hatred there, but then it was gone and Madeleine was smiling wryly again. 'There's nothing wrong,' she said. Then, 'No!' as Bregetta moved to speak again. 'I'm just glad to be here.'

Frowning, Bregetta turned away. Madeleine was tired. When she had had a good night's sleep everything would be all right. Bregetta closed her eyes, listening to the wind wailing outside, rattling the shutters on the window above the bed and surging through the trees like surf on the beach. And after a while she slept the deep sleep of one with a relatively clear conscience, while beside her Madeleine tossed and turned until exhaustion brought her sleep too.

The next morning Madeleine's strangeness was forgotten in the excitement of Neil's discovery. One of the sheep in the pen had been slaughtered under cover of darkness and most of the meat carried off. They had heard nothing—not even the dog had given the intruder away.

'The wind,' Teddy said. 'Covered any sounds and scents. And the clouds made it black as pitch out here.'

'Someone had better ride into Strand and let them know,' Molly murmured. She looked tired and worried, her hair falling about her untidily. Bregetta slipped an arm about her waist.

'I'll go up to the camp instead,' Neil said. 'It's quicker.'

When he had gone Bregetta wandered back to the cottage. As she entered Madeleine and Jim looked up, startled, as though she had interrupted some secret conversation. She turned to the fire, pretending to stir the embers. Jim cleared his throat. 'At least we know they're still around the quarry,' he said. 'We can make a more intensive search.'

'Some of the bush further back from that hill is so thick that no horse and rider can get through it,' Bregetta said. 'They're close to us, Jim. We're the only farmhouse in this area. And one of them is a killer.'

Madeleine laughed softly. 'I'm sure all of us and three guns are more than a match for three tired and hungry men.'

But Bregetta remembered the noise Redmond that made in the hut, and shuddered. He had sounded . . . demented. Not in his right mind. And people not in their right minds, and desperate to boot, were very dangerous.

Neil came back from the camp, and, after their inevitable cups of Molly's tea, it was decided that Jim would go to see Mr Gordon about returning to help his family until the convicts were caught. He would probably be gone overnight, and left with great reluctance, and at Teddy's insistence. It was past noon when they heard the sounds of horses approaching. Teddy was out in the yard, Molly was sewing, and Madeleine, who looked as tired as she had yesterday, was resting on her bed. Bregetta went out to see what was happening. A half-dozen soldiers drew their mounts to a halt. They looked tired and rather bedraggled, for it had begun to drizzle, but their belts and saddles were bristling with guns.

Alistair Duncan dismounted stiffly. Bregetta thought he looked older, the strain showing in his face. She felt her heart catch inside her with the need to comfort him, but she didn't move.

'The man's like a fox,' he was saying to Teddy without the preamble of a greeting. 'We've been following his trail all night, and then he's gone and doubled back and given us the slip. He must have been meaning to come back here all along.' Obviously he too thought of Redmond as the leader.

'I was on guard,' Teddy said gruffly. 'I didn't hear a thing. The dog didn't give so much as a whimper.'

'Aye, so your brother's told me,' Alistair muttered. He sighed, and ran his fingers in an agitated way through his dark hair. 'I'll leave you one man...no, two. I can spare no more.' His eyes slid, by design or accident, to Bregetta. She felt their touch like a jolt. Absurd as it seemed, she had the feeling that he was trying to protect her.

But he had turned away again, and was pointing out some of the sheds around the farm. 'Are your outbuildings locked and bolted?' he asked. 'Nothing they can use as a weapon?'

'No. We've thought of that.'

'Good man.' He glanced at Bregetta again, and she came forward. 'I've sent for reinforcements from the Windsor garrison. But that'll take a few

days. I'm hoping we'll have caught them by then.'
Bregetta stopped beside him, and as though against
his will he turned to face her.

'Take care,' she murmured.

He hesitated, and then a gleam she had not seen
for a long time came into his tired dark eyes. He
caught her to him and gave her a hard kiss on the
mouth. Breathless, Bregetta stared up into his face;
his lean cheeks were faintly flushed. The soldiers
gave a ragged cheer, glad for something to pierce
their gloom. Then Alistair turned and remounted
his horse.

'You'll take no drink?' Teddy asked as gruffly,
but Bregetta could hear the concern in his tone.

Alistair Duncan smiled wryly. 'I've not the time,'
he said. 'Maybe I'll come back here again before
dark. If time allows. To see that everything's in
order.'

And then he had gone, taking all but two of his
men. Teddy put his arm around Bregetta as the
soldiers rode fast down to the road. 'He'll be all
right,' he said gently. 'Men like our Captain Duncan
are too smart to get hurt by thugs like Redmond.'

Bregetta smiled. 'What do you think of him,
Teddy? The truth, now.'

He didn't pretend to misunderstand her. 'In the
beginning I thought him like all redcoats I've
known, and not to be trusted. But I put up with
him for your sake, girl. Then I hated him for what
he'd done. And now... I think he's a clever man,
and a man not much used to confiding in others.
A man on his own. But a man worth the having,
Bregetta.'

She sighed, and brushed his cheek with her lips.
'Thank you,' she said, and made her way back to

the cottage. Madeleine was standing in the doorway, her eyes on Bregetta. Madeleine stepped back, into the shadows, but Bregetta felt as if in that moment she had seen deep inside her heart and stripped her secrets bare.

'Jim told me you are marrying that man,' she said matter-of-factly. 'I thought that everything must be all right between you. I wondered, yesterday, why you didn't say anything to me about . . . Well, I know now. It isn't all right, is it?'

Bregetta shook her head numbly.

Madeleine smiled strangely. 'I had hoped it wouldn't need to be done,' she said. 'When I told you that if I had had anywhere else to go but here I would have gone, I wasn't lying. But that would be like running, wouldn't it, when the thing I was running from was always with me? There's no escape.' She laughed suddenly at Bregetta's face. 'You think I've gone mad. But you'll see; everything will be all right.'

'But what can you do?' Bregetta asked her in bewilderment.

Madeleine smiled again, and her face looked strained and old. 'You'll see,' was all she said.

The rest of the day was wet and miserable. The three women remained in the cottage, and it seemed cramped and crowded. As darkness drew in Molly set about making the evening meal, and the men trooped in. Their clothes were damp, and had to be taken off and dried, as best they could be, by the fire. The smell of wet cloth permeated the atmosphere. At least the soldiers were outside, camped in the barn with their own warming fire and pot of water for tea. Bregetta felt safer, knowing they were there.

Molly was just dishing up the meal when they heard the horse coming up the track. One of the soldiers shouted. Neil went to the door then slipped outside, closing the door on the gusts of wet rain. After a moment he returned, smiling at their anxious, wide-eyed faces. And behind him in the doorway stood Alistair Duncan.

Bregetta started.

If possible he looked even more weary than he had at noon. His clothes were sodden, and his boots squelched as he stepped inside. Molly came fussing forward, drawing him into the warm, crowded room. 'No, you'll not go out again!' she retorted as he began his excuse. 'Teddy will take some of my stew out to your two men. You can eat in here. I've made plenty.'

'You'd best say yes,' Teddy said wryly. 'When she's in this mood she'll not take no for an answer.'

Alistair laughed as though he couldn't help himself. Bregetta stood up and went to close the door. Outside it was cold, and the wind flung more rain into her face, making her shudder. And he had ridden in that all day. 'Take off your coat,' she said softly, 'and I'll dry it for you.'

It was an echo of other words, spoken long ago. He smiled at her ironically, and she knew he remembered. 'Thank you,' he said, and removed his jacket. He handed it to her carefully, and his fingers brushed hers.

She moved to turn away but he caught her hand hard in his. The others were talking, and Molly was clattering bowls. He said quietly, 'I need to talk to you.'

Bregetta glanced at him sharply. What now? To tell her again it was over? The fear in her eyes communicated itself to him, and he frowned.

'What is it?' he asked. Then, 'If you're afraid I'll take you back to the garrison with me. It might look odd, but you'd be safe.'

Bregetta felt a warm glow inside her, and yet he had hurt her before... 'I can't leave my friends,' she said quietly.

His fingers crushed hers. 'I wish we were wed,' he said harshly, as though the words were forced from him. 'I need to know you're safe.'

Bregetta stood, stunned by this revelation. Then Teddy pushed past them, with two bowls of stew for the soldiers in the barn, and the moment was broken.

Alistair sat down in his shirt-sleeves. Madeleine took a bowl and set it down in front of him. He noticed her for the first time, and surprise lit his eyes like tinder. 'Mrs Tanner,' he said.

'Yes,' and Madeleine's face was closed and grim. 'My husband died in George Street gaol—I don't suppose that will make you grieve, Captain. I have come to be with my friends. You still remember me, then?'

He looked down. 'I'm not likely to forget you,' he said stiffly.

Madeleine smiled and sat down. The thought passed through Bregetta's mind that their manner towards each other had not been that of the casual acquaintances she had thought them, and then it was gone as Molly said, 'Eat, eat! It'll get cold. What a night!' and they obeyed.

Outside, the wind splattered rain on to the roof and against the walls of the cottage. Teddy returned, saying that one of the trees a little way up the rise had lost a branch in the wind. He crouched by the fire, eating his stew with great wads of bread. The room was warm with flames and the bodies of its occupants. Alistair's jacket steamed, and Bregetta got up to turn it so that it would dry properly. She brushed his arm as she passed in the overcrowded room, and he looked at her with eyes that gleamed dark as the night. She felt burned by his glance, and suddenly it was as if the cold, polite man had never been, and Alistair, her love, had come back to her.

'I'll make us all some nice hot tea,' Molly announced, collecting up the dishes.

Bregetta saw the twitch of his lips, and felt her own mouth smiling as she moved to help Molly. Molly handed out the mugs of tea. The dog outside began to bark. Neil frowned, and stood up. 'What's——?' he began.

Behind them the door creaked and opened, and Jim stepped in.

Alistair turned and looked at him, and Bregetta saw him stiffen as he slowly rose to his feet. Jim stared at him, white-faced and determined. Bregetta felt her stomach drop away. 'Good evening, Captain Duncan,' he said.

Alistair swore under his breath. 'You bloody young fool,' he swore. 'Why didn't you stay over at Gordon's, or wherever you were? You know now I'll have to arrest you.'

Jim scowled. 'Do you expect me to hide like a rabbit in a burrow while the only family I have are in danger?'

'I expect you to show some good sense,' he snapped. Then, with a frown, 'Didn't my men stop you? What the hell are they doing out there?'

But, as he moved towards the door, one of his men burst in. His face was white and frightened. 'We heard what sounded like a gunshot up at the quarry,' he said. 'Private Leonard's gone up. I thought I'd best come back and tell you...'

'Good man,' Alistair muttered. Then, savagely, 'The bastards are trying to free the rest of their mates.'

Jim had picked up the pistol. 'I'll go up with you,' he stated.

Alistair looked at him impatiently. 'Mr Field and his brother may come with me if they're willing. You'll stay here and keep an eye on the women.' Then, to the private, 'Get down to the garrison for some more men. I'll ride after Leonard. And hurry!'

The man, his face a white blur, vanished into the darkness. Alistair grabbed up his jacket, buttoning it quickly. Bregetta felt stunned, watching him. He was leaving and she might never see him again. Teddy and Neil were busy loading guns. Madeleine huddled in a corner as though drained. Molly was wringing her hands over her tea. 'They haven't even drunk it,' she wailed.

Bregetta made a movement as if to cross the room to his side, but at the same time he looked up. His eyes were as dark as the open doorway behind him, and in them she read something of regret. 'Jim,' he said quietly, 'take good care of your sister.' And then he was gone, Teddy and Neil with him, their voices outside and fading.

Molly pulled the door to, and barred it. She turned into the room with a sigh. Jim put his arm about her, and his brown eyes were excited in his pale face. 'Cheer up, girls. *I'll* look after you.'

Bregetta stared at him. 'Why did you come back tonight?' she whispered. 'He'll arrest you.'

Jim shrugged, the excitement fading. He looked suddenly exhausted. 'I wanted to face him. I wanted to explain. I know he's a hard man, but he's fair. I thought, if anyone would give me a proper hearing, he would.'

'He goes by the rules,' Bregetta said softly. 'He doesn't take bribes, Jim. He's as straight and honest as they come.' And that, she thought to herself, is partly why I love him. I could never love a man like Will Tanner.

'I'll have to take my chances, then,' Jim said. 'But I'm not hiding any longer.' He was looking at Madeleine as he said it.

She smiled faintly, and looked at her hands. 'I wouldn't blame you for preferring a hangman's rope to me,' she said quietly. 'I'm not a very admirable woman. I've been selfish...I married Will for nothing more than greed, and when I had all I wanted I found it...lacking. And, for that, I sacrificed a man who loved me.'

Bregetta felt the tears on her cheeks. Madeleine looked so small, so fragile—as if a gust of wind would blow her away. Jim must have thought so too, for he came over and put his arms about her.

'I needed time too,' he said gently. 'I had to grow up. If I survive the court and whatever follows, will you be there for me, Maddy?'

'If you still want me to be, Jim, after this.'

Bregetta frowned. 'How could he not want you?'

Madeleine smiled a self-mocking smile. 'Oh, you'll see.'

'Maddy——'

Outside, the dog set up a frantic barking. Jim moved to the door, the pistol back in his hands. Molly's hand, white-knuckled, gripped the table-edge. 'Please God, let them be all right,' she breathed.

Then someone was pounding on the door. 'Open up!' An angry voice. More violent blows upon the door. Behind Bregetta a rain of thudding bangs on the shutters—they split but held together.

Bregetta screamed and heard Molly echo her cry. Then Jim had fired at the window and there was silence. Suddenly the pounding on the door resumed. Jim spun back. 'Get away or I'll fire,' he said savagely.

Laughter. 'Fire away,' a voice shouted. More laughter. The sound chilled Bregetta to the bone.

'It was a trick,' Madeleine whispered. 'To get the others up to the quarry and leave us without their protection.'

Suddenly there was a rattle above. Molly looked up, the cords of her neck standing out with strain. 'One of them's on the roof,' she gasped. 'He'll come through——'

Jim aimed the pistol and fired again. The blast deafened them, and the smell of gunpowder stung their nostrils. There was a groaning cry from above, and then a rattle and rumble as something large and heavy rolled over and over, and then off the roof on to the ground below. They heard the noise of it landing: a dull, dead sound. For a moment silence reigned.

'How many of them are there?' Bregetta breathed. Her throat felt raw with terror. She forced herself to swallow. Molly was clutching her peeling-knife, and the sight was so strange that Bregetta felt laughter creeping into her chest.

The dog was still barking, but it must have slipped its rope, for now the sound moved about the house as though the animal was pursuing some intruder and keeping just out of reach. All the blood-curdling stories Bregetta had ever heard about bushrangers attacking lonely homesteads came back to her. Alistair, she cried silently. Help us.

Then, slowly, the smell of smoke drifted to her senses, and she spun about. At the same moment a burning brand was thrust through the splintered shutters. It caught on Molly's gay little curtains, and the flames leapt hungrily towards the ceiling. Jim swore. Bregetta grabbed up the washing-up bucket and threw the water over the flames. Molly was trying to smother the brand with an empty sack. For a moment confusion reigned as they tried to put out the flames. Only Madeleine was still, crouching in her corner, her hands over her ears, her face a mask of terror.

Bregetta was coughing from the smoke. Somewhere there was a smashing and splintering of wood. But at the same time the pounding came again on the door, so violent the whole frame shook and trembled. Jim turned around, not knowing from which direction the most danger came. He pointed his gun at the door and, as the rattling began again, fired through the wood. A scream more animal than human split the night; then silence again.

Outside, the dog's barking went on and on—it seemed to be coming from behind the cottage now. Molly began to say a prayer under her breath. Madeleine was still huddled in the corner, as though trying to block out reality. Bregetta faced the door, her hands blackened from her efforts to put out the fire. They waited, and she could hear her heart thudding in her ears.

A breeze wafted through the cottage, lifting her hair. It felt cool and sweet, smelling of rain and damp bushland. For a moment she didn't realise that it did not come from the broken window beside her, but from somewhere else . . . behind her. From the other room. She began to turn . . .

Molly screamed. Bregetta saw Jim's eyes open so wide that she could see the white all around; the barrel of his pistol came up. She had a glimpse behind her of something dark, something solid. She smelt earth and leaves and unwashed humanity, and then an arm fastened about her throat. It was like iron, that arm. It pulled her back against a hard chest. She felt the damp cold of his shirt through her clothes. She could not even scream.

Behind her a voice, empty of all compassion, said, 'Put down your gun, laddie, or I'll break her neck.'

CHAPTER TWELVE

SOMEHOW they all knew that the man was beyond caring what happened to him afterwards. Jim put down the gun. Molly's knife clattered across the table and down on to the floor. It was Madeleine who, with a shriek like a banshee's, flung herself up at the convict. He knocked her aside effortlessly. She fell to the floor and lay still, in a small, crumpled heap. Jim's face was ashen.

The convict—somehow Bregetta knew it was Redmond—moved forward. Bregetta saw his hand—large, with ingrained dirt about the nails—snatch up the pistol. 'You've finished for my mates,' he said matter-of-factly. 'But it'd take more than all of you put together to finish for me.'

Bregetta felt his chest shake and knew he was laughing. It was like a nightmare.

'What do you want?' Molly whispered. Bregetta had never seen her so terrified. Jim, too, standing stock-still, was as white as wheat-flour. Bregetta hardly recognised him, only saw that his cheekbones stood out in a way that reminded her suddenly of her mother.

'I want you to get me a horse.'

'They've taken the horses up to the quarry,' Jim said.

'Then you'll have to find one, won't you? Or two.'

The arm that held her tightened some more; the hand with the pistol brushed her cheek. She made

a sound of disgust. Jim's eyes flickered to hers.
'You can have your horse, food...whatever. But
leave her here.' Molly's hand was clutching her
throat, as though she was having difficulty in
breathing.

Bregetta felt Redmond's chest move again in
laughter.

'It's been a long time,' he said, 'since I had a
woman.'

Suddenly the dog was barking again. Redmond's
pistol came up to her head and the cold round circle
of the muzzle pressed to her skull. 'Not a sound,'
he said. 'Anyone.'

A horse whinnied. Redmond stepped back
against the wall, so that Bregetta's body was his
shield from attack from both the broken shutters
and the door. She smelt his sweat, mingling with
the sour damp smell of his clothes. They waited.

'Jim?' It was Alistair's voice beyond the closed
door. 'Jim, for heaven's sake, answer me!'

Redmond nodded at him. 'I'm here,' said Jim.

'Is everything all right? Jim?'

'Ask him,' Redmond's voice was a whisper, 'is
he alone?'

Jim asked. There was a pause, and then, 'Of
course I'm bloody alone! What do you expect, the
whole 50th Regiment? Let me in.'

After a moment Bregetta felt Redmond nod
again, and then Jim moved to open the door.
Outside, the darkness was absolute. And then she
saw his red coat, and the blur of his face, and he
was stepping over the body that lay on the
threshold, and inside the room. Suddenly everything seemed very sharp to her, and very clear. She
saw the shock that hardened his features like a

mask, and heard his breath hiss out. Behind him, Jim rebarred the door.

'Ah, Captain, come in, come in,' said Redmond genially. Only Bregetta could smell the sweat of fear on him, and see the faint tremor of the hand that held the pistol.

Alistair's black eyes had gone blank. They stared straight into Bregetta's. And then, deliberately, he shifted them up to meet Redmond's above her. She saw him relaxing his body by sheer effort of will. His hands, clenched at his sides, slowly loosened.

'Don't be a fool,' he said in his deep, harsh voice. 'You can't get away. Let her go now.'

Redmond said nothing.

'He means to take her with him,' Molly squeaked.

'No!'

It was said before he could stop it. A terrible, flat denial that sent tremors to the soles of Bregetta's feet. The cry of an animal about to lose its mate. Alistair took a breath and in a moment was himself again. 'What is it you want?' he asked more softly.

'I need horses. And more guns. Clothes too, and food.'

Alistair appeared to consider it. 'All right,' he said at last. 'All that if you leave the woman. I won't stop you.'

Redmond moved impatiently. 'Why do I doubt you?' he said quietly. His other arm tightened about Bregetta's throat, and she cried out in pain. 'Besides,' he went on, 'I want the woman. She's pretty. She has hair like fire.' The barrel of the pistol smoothed a truant lock, then moved down, touching her breast. He was watching the other man's face. He laughed.

'This is your woman,' he said, and it was a statement.

Alistair's black eyes flickered to hers, and then away again. His mouth tightened. 'Let her go,' he said, 'and I'll speak for you. I'll see you get heard fairly in Sydney.'

Redmond laughed out loud this time. 'Maybe you would,' he said at last. 'But even if I cheated death there'd still be Norfolk Island. That's hell on earth, you know that. I'll take my chances with your horse.'

Outside the dog was whining. Redmond stiffened. 'Where are the other men?' he asked sharply.

Alistair kept his eyes on the convict's face. 'They're up at the quarry,' he said quietly. 'Tidying up. You made a mess up there, Redmond. But we've caught the two you let out. I came back because somehow... it didn't seem right. And, as you guessed, she is my woman.'

'You shouldn't have left her,' Redmond retorted, and pulled Bregetta back harder against his body. She hardly noticed. She was thinking of the dog, whining: the sound it made when Neil came home. She could see it in her mind's eye, tail wagging desperately as Neil bent to pat the ragged head.

'I had a woman of my own once,' Redmond said. 'I left her in England.'

His voice sounded dreamy. Bregetta remembered Redmond pounding on the door of the hut up at the quarry in an uncontrollable rage, and remembered how she had thought him out of his mind. She knew now it was the truth. And she knew that Alistair knew it too.

'You killed her,' Alistair said quietly. 'That was why you were sent out here. Let this woman go. My horse is outside. Take it.'

Redmond hesitated and they waited. But when he shook his head Bregetta knew that he had never meant to agree. He was playing some cat-and-mouse game with them, drawing out the agony, revenging himself on them for some nameless crime. Molly made a little sound and reached out one hand for the table. Her face was ashen and shiny with sweat, and she swayed. Jim moved to catch her.

'Stay where you are!' Redmond's hand jerked on the gun.

'She's fainting,' Jim said. Molly was indeed slipping down towards the hearth. Her skirts were dangerously near the coals. With an angry sound Jim grabbed the woman as she fell, and pulled her back away from the hearth towards the door. It was then that Bregetta saw something out of the corner of her eye.

A hand on the floor, moving slowly. A small white hand with a large ring on the third finger. Madeleine. She had forgotten all about Madeleine. So had Redmond. But, while they had all been talking, Madeleine had been edging ever so slowly from her prone position by the wall, and reaching out for the knife that Molly had dropped what seemed hours ago, but could only be minutes. Bregetta could just see it, lying near Redmond's boot and her own skirts. Her eyes went back to Molly, lying there, afraid that she could somehow give Madeleine away by watching her, although Redmond could not possibly see the direction of her gaze.

She shifted a little in his grip, moving to shield Madeleine further from his gaze. His arm tightened again. But Madeleine's hand crept closer, slowly, slowly. Alistair was talking again. It meant nothing. Talking about the garrison. The soldiers would come after him, he said, if he took her. But if Redmond left her here, unharmed, he would see that Redmond had one hour's start...two! Redmond laughed again. He was enjoying himself, and seemed in no hurry to be leaving.

'But I want to take her with me,' he said quietly. 'You want to come, don't you?' And he gave Bregetta a shake. 'Don't you?' he repeated between his teeth, and his arm tightened viciously.

Bregetta gasped. She saw Alistair's hands clench again at his sides, and, looking up at his eyes, saw him nod faintly.

'Yes,' she breathed.

His arm softened, and he caressed her cheek with the barrel of the pistol. She saw the butt slip in his palm; it was wet with sweat.

Bregetta flickered her eyes down. Madeleine's fingers were closed on the knife-hilt. And then she moved like lightning, though it all seemed to Bregetta very slow. The knife-blade swung back and then up at an angle, deep into the flesh of Redmond's thigh. He cried out in agony and automatically reached down. Blood spurted from between his fingers. Madeleine threw herself back, out of his reach, and Molly caught her arm—Molly looked very alert, suddenly, for someone who had just fainted. In the same second Bregetta felt Redmond's arm loosen its hold about her throat. Instinctively, she ducked down, escaping his choking grip. She was on the floor, his bulk above her, when she knew suddenly she was not going to get away. His hand came down and gripped her hair, pulling her up so that she screamed with pain. And then there was a deafening roar.

She thought, at first, that it was Redmond's pistol, and that she must be shot. But, when she didn't seem to be in any pain, she lifted her head from her hands, and realised the hold on her hair was gone. She was free. Slowly she turned around. It was Redmond who lay on the ground near her. There was a hole in the side of his head, blackened and gory, and it was bleeding all over Molly's floor. She could only stare at him—it was the first time she had seen him. It struck her as strange that he had held her life in his hands, and yet she had seen no more of him than his hands and his arm, and heard only his breathing and his voice ... He was a big man, as big as Teddy, and he was dirty and unshaven, his clothes stained and torn from living rough; but somehow his face was not the one she had expected. There was no evil there, just weariness in the hollowed cheeks and sunken eyes, and now, in death, peace.

A sound from the window brought her head around. Neil was standing there, his gun resting on the sill, his face white with strain. 'I had to be sure,' he said. 'I couldn't afford to miss.' He looked shocked.

Behind her she heard Alistair move, and then he had knelt down beside the big body of the dead man. He held his fingers to the grimy throat above the collar. Then he took his hand away and gently closed the man's eyes. 'Poor devil,' he said softly. He looked up, straight at Bregetta. 'I meant what

I said,' he added. 'He could have had his one hour, or two. I'd have given that to him for you.'

'I know,' she whispered.

'But if he'd taken you I would have followed him and killed him.'

Bregetta saw the truth of it in his eyes. Then Molly's arm came around her and she was helping her to her feet, and Bregetta turned into the other woman's shoulder and let the tears claim her.

When she had recovered a little Molly helped her to sip some brandy, and Madeleine chafed her hands. 'Are you all right?' she asked, blue eyes bright with concern; there was a bruise starting on her cheek where Redmond had hit her. Bregetta nodded, and took a deep breath.

'I think so.'

The men had removed Redmond's body, and outside there was much noise and confusion. The other soldiers had arrived at last, both from the quarry and the garrison. But Jim was there, and grinned at her over Madeleine's shoulder. 'Maddy saved your life,' he said softly and proudly.

Madeleine laughed shakily. 'It was the least I could do,' she said.

'You were wonderful,' Jim added.

Bregetta laughed as shakily as Madeleine. 'I'd have to agree,' she said. Her voice still sounded croaky. 'Was anyone else hurt?'

'Only the two convicts Jim shot, and they're dead,' Molly broke in. 'He was a hero himself tonight.'

'If we're talking of heroes,' Jim retorted, 'what about you, Mrs Field? Your fainting fit was the most realistic I've ever seen. You even fooled me, although I knew you were trying to draw attention away from Madeleine.'

Molly preened a little. 'It wasn't difficult in the circumstances.'

Teddy came into the room, making it seem small. His arm went around Molly and he gave her a hug. 'Thank God everyone is safe,' he said. 'When we came back from the quarry and saw the bodies we thought...' He shook his head. 'Captain Duncan knew something was wrong. He didn't want to have to fight it out, with Redmond inside and us outside. So he went in, and hoped he could distract Redmond for long enough for Neil to get a clear shot at him through the window. Neil knew he only had one chance—he was the better shot. When Madeleine got Redmond to let you go, Bregetta, he had to kill him.'

Outside, horses were leaving. Bregetta heard the rumble of a cart. 'Where *is* Captain Duncan?' Molly asked suddenly.

'He had to take Redmond and the other two back to the garrison. He said he'd return as soon as he could.'

Bregetta closed her eyes.

'He's a brave man, that one,' Teddy went on. 'Never a doubt that it was anybody else but him who'd walk into this place, with God knew what going on. He's handled this well. I'll admit, at one time I didn't... But you've got a good man, Bregetta. It'd be hard to find one better.'

Bregetta smiled. 'I know.'

The voices went on above her, but she no longer listened. Weariness and reaction to shock washed over her in great waves and, seated at the table, leaning against Molly's shoulder, she was content.

* * *

It wasn't until morning that Alistair returned. Bregetta had been awake since dawn, waiting. She heard the horse, and stood in the open doorway. Teddy and Neil were already up and had gone down to Strand; the others were still sleeping.

The horse reached the tethering-rail and Alistair dismounted stiffly. Exhaustion showed in every line of him. He patted the horse's neck, then turned slowly and almost unwillingly towards the cottage, walking with his head bowed. He looked up as he drew closer, and when he saw her standing there he stopped.

Bregetta's heart began to beat faster. She put her hand to the door-frame to steady herself. She had changed her gown and brushed her hair, but she knew there were dark circles under her eyes and a weary droop to her mouth. She moved towards him.

For a moment he didn't move, and then, as if he couldn't help himself, his arms opened up to catch her, hard against his body.

'Bregetta,' he whispered.

'I've been waiting for you,' she gasped. 'You've taken so long.'

'I've been up all night dealing with this mess. Are you all right?' And his mouth sought hers in a hard, demanding kiss. When he had finished Bregetta took a shaky breath.

'Oh, Alistair, if you had been shot or...or hurt...'

'Would you have cared so much?' he asked, and something hard and cruel in his black eyes frightened her. Please, she prayed desperately, don't let him change again! Yesterday he had been her love, her beloved Alistair, but it seemed the cold man could as easily return.

'How can you ask that?' she whispered.

He moved impatiently. 'Why all the pretence, Bregetta? I'm marrying you; at least be honest with me. If I was shot, maybe you would be a little sorry, but how long before someone else came along? Someone better suited to your ambition than me?'

She shook her head slowly. 'No,' she said. 'No! There's only you.' She caught his face in her two palms, and looked into those frighteningly distant eyes. 'There's only you, Alistair.'

Something about her voice and her expression caught at him, for he gazed back at her, a crease between his brows, as though struggling to overcome some great hurdle in his mind.

'Captain Duncan!' Molly, behind, startled them. Bregetta dropped her hands and Alistair looked past her and forced a smile.

'Mrs Field.'

'Come in, come in. Don't stand out here in the cold. I've made a breakfast fit for a king.'

He laughed, despite his weariness, and walked up to the cottage door. Molly pushed him in, past her, then turned to look at Bregetta. 'Come in, love,' she said gently. 'I need you to help me.'

Slowly, Bregetta followed Molly into the cottage, her feet dragging. She had been longing, since dawn, for him to come to her. Alistair, her love. And now that he was here he was a stranger. She didn't know if she could bear any more.

Alistair was sitting at the table, frowning at something Jim had said. Madeleine was still asleep in the other room. Molly bustled about, serving her maize porridge and her fresh bread and cold mutton.

Bregetta went to the broken shutters and looked out on the clear cold morning. Smoke crept into the sky, far up on the hill, where the quarry was. There was no wind to blow it away this morning. It was just as if nothing had happened.

'I've decided not to mention you in my report,' Alistair said quietly. Bregetta turned and saw that he was speaking to Jim. Jim's expression was something between hope and disbelief.

'I've told you I'm willing to take my punishment,' he said stiffly.

Molly made a disgusted sound, but Alistair spoke first. 'If it hadn't been for you last night we might be burying these women this morning rather than three convicts who no one will particularly miss. You deserve a pardon, and I'm giving you one.'

Jim ducked his head. 'Thank you,' he muttered. 'You don't know what this means to me. I'll make a new start. You won't regret it.'

'I'd better not,' Alistair snapped, but he was smiling. 'When I get back to Sydney I'll make sure that your record is...misplaced. It shouldn't be too difficult. It happens all the time.'

After a moment Molly said, 'You're a good man, Alistair Duncan.'

Alistair shifted uncomfortably. 'I'm only doing what I think right.'

'I'm sorry I was so unfriendly to you,' Molly went on, 'but you'll understand that I had Bregetta to consider.'

His eyes narrowed. 'I can understand your wanting her to make a grand marriage, Mrs Field.'

Molly coughed, fiddling with her plate. 'Yes, well, there was that. But there was more to it, wasn't there? I mean, the way you treated her before.'

He was frowning, as though trying to come to grips with what she had said. 'The way I treated her? I'm sorry, I'm too tired to——'

Molly clicked her tongue impatiently, and now colour stained her face an angry red. 'I don't know what went on between you two in Sydney. I was never told. And I'm glad that it's mended now. But you broke my girl's heart, and that made you my enemy, Captain Duncan.'

Alistair looked across at Bregetta as if he thought his wits were addled. 'Broke her heart?' he repeated. 'Didn't she tell you? Didn't Mrs Tanner— Madeleine—tell you?' Then, shaking his head slightly as if to clear it, 'No, of course she didn't. Why should she? Well, it doesn't matter...'

Before she knew what she meant to do, Bregetta had stepped forward jerkily. 'Doesn't matter?' she asked harshly. 'That you made jokes about me at the tavern—that I was a "new recruit" to be broken in—and told your soldier friends that you didn't like women who clung and spoke of love?' The hurt and bitterness made her voice hard; Bregetta had not realised the pain in her was so strong until this moment when it bubbled up and over. Like a sore inside her which had been half healed and oozing, spilling its poison, and which erupted now into the open. Tears scalded her eyes but she blinked them angrily back. This was her moment for truth, and she would not be denied it.

'You just wanted me the way a child wants a new toy—to show off to your friends, to gloat over. And when you were tired of me you sent me off. And in a way so hurtful that you knew I would never come back. Were you so afraid of me, Alistair? So afraid of my love? Would it have bound you so

tightly? And yet now you say you will marry me . . .
Why? To save your career, to further your
ambition? To please Mr Gordon? I think . . .' and
her voice was a whisper ' . . . I think that is the only
thing that really matters to you.'

He was staring at her like a man fatally wounded.
Bregetta dashed her eyes angrily, wiping at the hot
tears. The sore inside her was drained, and she felt
exhausted and a little afraid of what she had said.
And yet she could no more have stopped her words
than a boiling kettle could stop the scalding steam
from escaping.

When he finally spoke his voice was hollow.
'Who told you these things?'

'Madeleine,' Bregetta retorted. Her nails were
biting into her palms so hard that they drew blood.
'She heard you at the tavern, and found out other
things. She was always my friend.'

He ran his hand through his hair, and then shook
his head. A laugh burst out of him. He shook his
head again. 'Your friend?' he mocked savagely, and
the eyes he turned on her gleamed with an unholy
amusement. 'So I thought, too. That was why I
went to see her. The first time when your mother
was dying, and then . . . at different times. I saw her
that night when she gave you Jim's letter. She told
me then that you had been using me, keeping me
so occupied—shall we say?—that I let Jim get away.
She said to go and read the letter for myself if I
didn't believe her. And then of course I came back
and found you with the letter in your hand.'

'And you said I had sold myself,' she whispered
harshly.

'But there were other things she told me,' he went
on quietly. 'She said that you only looked on me

as a means to an end. You were after bigger and
better fish than a mere sergeant. She said you
wanted to emulate her, only do it better. She said
you were jealous of her success, and, from the
moment you saw me, you knew I was your way out
of the Rocks, as well as Jim's way out of trouble.
She said . . .' and now he was pale, the black eyes
dulled with remembered pain '. . .she said that you'd
only stay with me as long as it took to find someone
who could give you more. She told me that she was
your confidante, and that she was shocked enough
by what you were doing to want to warn me. She
was sorry for me, she said.'

Bregetta's flesh was leaden. She stared at him,
not wanting to believe and yet . . . believing. No one
else in the room uttered a sound, spellbound by
what was unfolding. It was as if they stood alone,
facing each other again, as they had that last night
in Sydney, only this time all the words that were
never spoken were being said aloud.

'And I believed her,' he went on, and his voice
was raw. 'Because I'd once been badly hurt by
another woman, and I had told myself all women
were the same.'

'Did you think I loved you?' he had said, and
all the other things she had not understood which
had been designed to strike back at one he thought
was intentionally hurting him. It had been self-
defence to save himself from the humiliation and
pain he had already experienced once. And he had
thought she knew it. 'I think you understand more
than you're willing to admit,' he had told her. And
she had understood nothing.

Suddenly she heard Jim move. Alistair was
looking past her, his eyes like flint. He moved as

if to rise to his feet, but Molly put her own hand firmly on his shoulder. Bregetta turned, and saw that in the doorway to the bedroom stood Madeleine. She looked tiny and fragile, her hair tied simply at her nape, her face white and chalky. Bregetta found it almost impossible to believe that this woman, her friend, had said such things, had planned and carried out such a deliberate plot. And yet it must be so.

Molly was staring at the other woman, and her eyes were icy. 'I think Madeleine has something to say,' she said quietly. 'I think we should all listen to it.'

Madeleine's mouth twisted into a smile. 'Perhaps you should,' she said coolly, but Bregetta saw her hands shaking as she knotted the shawl at her breast. 'You said last night, Bregetta, that I saved your life. If that is so, I hope it is enough to make up for what I did, for I think I also ruined your life. No!' as Jim moved to intervene, his face pale. Her eyes met his, then shifted determinedly away, as though she could not bear to read what might soon show there.

'I told you, Bregetta, that if I had had anywhere else to go I would have gone there rather than come to you. It was the truth. I was afraid of being found out, as now I have been. And yet I have not slept easy for many months, and probably never will until I tell my story.'

'But you're my friend,' Bregetta whispered, and tried to move forward. But something stopped her. She looked down in bewilderment, and saw that Alistair had grasped her arm and was holding it fast, his fingers white. She looked up again at Madeleine.

'Am I? I've always envied you, Bregetta. I told you the other night that people put up with me, but they loved you. You laughed. But it's the truth, only you could never see it. I envied you and yet I needed you. Your love was necessary to me; the way you looked up to me was necessary to me. I needed to feel better than you, and to do better than you. Perhaps I did love you, but I also hated you.'

Bregetta's eyes widened, for there was something in Madeleine's voice she had never heard before.

'I was so sick of hearing your praises sung,' she went on. 'So sick of hearing that everything you did was right and good. "Fair of face and heart" someone told me once, and I was furious. Did they expect me to agree, and to emulate you, when you were such a fool? It was I who was clever, I who had given up love for a good marriage and plenty of money. Only that was thought sly and bold...' Madeleine forced her chin up. 'I planned so hard for that marriage and all the things I would do. Only once I had my way everything was not so wonderful. Oh, I could peacock over you, Bregetta! But my husband was a lying scoundrel, and our friends were as cold and calculating as me. I began to regret it. But at least I still held the whip over you. You were so grateful for anything I gave, and I meant to plan your life to the smallest detail so that your gratitude would never end.'

Bregetta's legs were so shaky that she had to lean against the wall. Alistair was watching Madeleine with contempt; Jim was looking down at his hands.

'And then suddenly you found a man. But this wasn't just any man. This was love—the grand passion!' and her voice was savage. 'Trust you to find something that made all of our loves pale before it! I saw at once that you meant to give up everything for this man, all my plans for you tossed aside as if they were nothing! And after I had given up *my* love. Bregetta always does the right thing, Bregetta so good and gentle... I could see it all. You would wed your soldier, and have dozens of little soldiers, and live in squalor and be happy! And spare not a thought for what I could have given you. How I hated you then. And I decided that the only thing I could do was finish it.'

Alistair met her eyes. 'So you lied to her, and to me. Lies that struck home with such calculated viciousness that each of us was too hurt and suspicious, too isolated by them, to mention a word to the other.'

Madeleine smiled with a kind of twisted pride. 'You both believed me without question.'

Bregetta felt her throat aching, as though she was going to cry. 'Oh, Madeleine.'

'No,' Madeleine tightened her jaw, 'it's not pretty. I never said it would be! But it all seemed such a waste. To live your life with a sergeant when I could give you so much more. I knew I could make it up to you a hundredfold. But deep in my heart I was glad to destroy your grand love, because my own life was empty of it. I wanted you to be hurt, Bregetta; I wanted to see you on the other side for a change. I wanted to hear them all say, "Madeleine is so good and kind. So charitable. Madeleine has done everything for that girl."' Her voice trailed off, and she took a deep breath. 'But of course they didn't, and now they never will. I destroyed your happiness, but you didn't turn to me for guidance. You left me entirely. It didn't go as I had planned. I was left in a marriage I detested, alone. And finally, when Will was dead, I was destitute, with only one choice before me. The choice I had dreaded and feared all along: to come crawling to you.'

Madeleine bowed her head as if she could not bear to look at them any more.

Bregetta stared at her, seeking words in the fog of betrayal that was clouding her mind. So many things she had thought truth had been lies. The realities of her life had been turned topsy-turvy, but one thing she knew at last: she had her love back. 'You say you don't know if I can forgive you, Madeleine,' she whispered, 'but you saved my life last night. For that I must forgive you. And for Jim's sake, because I know he loves you. But I don't know if I can ever think of you as my friend again.'

'Maddy.' Jim put out his hand to her. She clung to it, desperately, like a child. After a moment he led her towards the door. She glanced up at Bregetta as she passed, and her blue eyes were full of pain and bitterness.

'I've eggs to fetch,' Molly said, and surreptitiously wiped her cheeks as she left the room.

Bregetta had not left her place by the window, and Alistair still sat at the scrubbed table. He shook his head again in disbelief. 'I thought she was your friend,' he said. 'I believed her, though it tore my heart out of my body. I wanted to leave you, but I could not. You held me so fast. Even when you were gone I could think of nothing else. I found out where you were, and when this job came up it seemed as if fate had stepped in. Even though Madeleine had told me you'd written of another man in your letter. All I thought of was you,

Bregetta, all the way here. I told myself I was going to ask you to come back to me, whatever the cost, but when I saw you again you were so cold, so...distant. As though you had cast me from you completely. I couldn't do it. A man doesn't knowingly cut off his arm!'

'I was afraid of breaking down in front of you,' she said huskily. 'Of giving myself away. I thought it would...amuse you.'

His mouth curved into a wry, weary smile. 'I've been afraid to touch you in case I lost that iron hold I had on myself. Even to look at you in church was to commit a sin, in my mind. But at the dance it all shattered like the thin ice it was. I knew I had to stay away from you after that. I thought you were laughing at me, Bregetta. I thought you were using me. I'm a proud man. I couldn't let that happen.'

'Oh, my love,' she breathed. 'My dearest love. I didn't understand; I didn't know what had gone wrong. And when you taunted me about Maurice I pretended I meant to marry him to try and touch some chord in you...some feeling for me I was certain was still alive. I was so hurt that I wanted to hurt you back.'

'That day you met me up at the quarry—I thought if we...I thought if I had you maybe I'd stop dreaming about you at night, stop remembering. But I was fooling myself. I told you I was cured. But I wasn't. It just made it worse, and I knew in that moment together that you would be with me for the rest of my life. And then Maurice found us together. It was like a godsend to me! I could use that to force you into marriage with me. I didn't stop to ask myself what sort of marriage it would be, with you resenting me for spoiling your chances. I was like a man who would willingly have taken poison to get what he wanted.'

'Alistair!' she cried. 'Didn't you feel I could never be so wicked?'

He pulled her down on to his knee and pressed his face into her hair, his arms wrapped tight about her. 'Yes,' he groaned. 'But I fought that too; I thought it was just what I wanted to see in you, not what you really were. Only, when you were in danger last night, none of it seemed to matter any more. I realised one clear and simple fact: if you died then everything would turn to dust with you.'

Bregetta pressed his head to her breast. 'It was as if you had come back to me last night,' she breathed. 'As if the Alistair I had known and loved had come back. And then, this morning...'

He looked up at her and his face was pale and serious. Then he put his palms either side of her face, as she had done earlier, and looked into her eyes. 'When I saw you that first time, in your mother's house, I thought you were the most perfect woman I had ever seen. So beautiful, and so proud. As though the squalor of the place you were living in and your life could not touch you. I felt as if all I had believed until then, about women, was non-sense. I would have done anything for you; I promised myself I would take you out of that and give you all I had to give.'

'Alistair,' she sighed, 'if only you had told me then. None of this need have happened.'

'My love, I'm a soldier. Tenderness is difficult for me—I had not the words to tell you what you meant to me. That, at the age of one and thirty years, I'd fallen deep in love for the first time in my life.'

Bregetta laughed with joy and leaned forward to kiss his serious mouth. 'Do you think we could have married, and gone on mistrusting each other for the rest of our lives?'

He touched her cheek. 'Perhaps not. This morning, when you said those things, I . . . I had begun to believe in miracles.'

'We have been given another chance,' she told him. 'This time without secrets.'

'No more secrets. Ah, Bregetta, let's not wait till May. I don't want you out of my sight ever again.'

'Will you go back to Sydney?' she asked him softly.

He smiled and shook his head. 'No. Everything I need is here. I'll make a life for us at Strand. But first I need a hot bath, a long sleep, and you, not necessarily in that order.'

Bregetta laughed and kissed his eager lips, and suddenly her happiness was overflowing.

'It's my birthday!' he shouted, above the clamour. 'Many happy returns of the day, my darling.'

Smothered in a fond embrace, and the feather boa about her shoulders, he wrinkled his nose. 'You smell nice,' he said – and wondered why everyone laughed.

THE END

THE FAIRFIELD CHRONICLES

BY SARAH SHEARS

Set in the heart of the Kent countryside and spanning the period from the turn of the century to the end of the Second World War, Sarah Shears introduces us to the inhabitants of Fairfields Village. As we follow the changing fortunes of the villagers we see how their lives and loves become irrevocably entwined over the years and watch the changing patterns of English country life through the eyes of one of our best-loved novelists.

THE VILLAGE
FAMILY FORTUNES
THE YOUNG GENERATION
RETURN TO RUSSETS

Published by Bantam Books

Look out for the two intriguing

MASQUERADE *Historical*

Romances coming next month

PERDITA
Sylvia Andrew

Bought from an Algerian Pasha for his own dark purposes,
Edward, Earl of Ambourne finds the girl, whom he names
Perdita, both beautiful and intriguing. She refuses to speak, so
Edward is unaware of any past, save that she had been taken
by pirates.

To Perdita, her silence becomes a form of revenge, the one
weapon she has to frustrate Edward – until she learns the
name of Edward's enemy, the man whom she is being groomed
to lure to his ruin in full view of London Society. For this man is
her own enemy – and she knows Edward's scheme will not
work, unless she joins forces with him . . .

SET FREE MY HEART
Sarah Westleigh

Unhappily married to Don Roberto del Sedano of Burgos,
Spain, Margot is shamingly relieved to hear of his death in the
uprising against the throne of Castile. But this leaves her at the
mercy of the English knights summoned to Castile's aid, in
particular Sir Thomas d'Evraux, into whose charge she is given.

Taken back to England by Thomas, Margot knows *this* time she
loves and is loved. But convinced she is barren, Margot will not
marry Thomas. Instead she will be his mistress! Is a ruined
reputation to be her fate?

Available in October

An irresistible offer for you

Here at Reader Service we would love you to become a regular reader of Masquerade. And to welcome you, we'd like you to have two books, a cuddly teddy and a MYSTERY GIFT - ABSOLUTELY FREE and without obligation.

Then, every two months you could look forward to receiving 4 more brand-new Masquerade Romances for just £1.99 each, delivered to your door, postage and packing is free. Plus our free newsletter featuring competitions, author news, special offers offering some great prizes, and lots more!

This invitation comes with no strings attached. You can cancel or suspend your subscription at any time, and still keep your free books and gifts.

Its so easy. Send no money now. Simply fill in the coupon below at once and post it to - Reader Service, FREEPOST, PO Box 236, Croydon, Surrey CR9 9EL.

- - - - - NO STAMP REQUIRED - - - - - ✂

Yes! Please rush me my 2 Free Masquerade Romances and 2 Free Gifts! Please also reserve me a Reader Service Subscription. If I decide to subscribe, I can look forward to receiving 4 brand new Masquerade Romances every two months for just £7.96, delivered direct to my door. Post and packing is free, and there's a free Newsletter. If I choose not to subscribe I shall write to you within 10 days - I can keep the books and gifts whatever I decide. I can cancel or suspend my subscription at any time. I am over 18.

Mrs/Miss/Ms/Mr _____ EP05M

Address _____

_____

_____ Postcode _____

Signature _____

mps
MAILING
PREFERENCE
SERVICE